Hannah [illegible] ase

"For I know the plans I have for you,"
declares the LORD,
"plans to prosper you and not to harm you,
plans to give you hope and a future."
Jeremiah 29:11 NIV

Praise from around the World . . .

Novelist Arlene Ussery explores the power
and the mystery of a true relationship with God
in a detail-filled thoughtful presentation
of Biblical characters. . . .
It is very good reading and I highly recommend it.
Jack Conner, Superintendent,
Evangelical Methodist Church,
USA

A gripping book
that reveals how God relates to individuals
through the passages of their lives.
A wonderful combination of fiction
with the careful study and insightful understanding
of social and religious customs
makes a profoundly rich reading experience.
Iva Beranek,
Roman Catholic,
Dublin, IRELAND

Hannah's Promise is a very moving book.
I enjoyed it very much–*both* times I read it.
Carol Trachsel,
Retired from World Gospel Mission,
Kenya, AFRICA

Hannah's Promise

By

Arlene Pinkley Ussery

This is a work of fiction.
Other than what is recorded in Scripture and history,
the characters, incidents, and dialogue are products of the author's imagination
and are not to be construed as real. Any resemblance to actual events or
persons, living or dead, is entirely coincidental.
This novel in no way substitutes for the reader's own encounter with the Bible.

Cover Design by Arlene Pinkley Ussery
Preliminary Layout by Marlon Rompis
Final Layout by Zoë Lucy

Key words : 1. Faith, 2. Infertility, 3. Depression, 4. Self-esteem, 5. Israel

ISBN 1450570151/ EAN-13 978145050152

Printed in United States

With love and gratitude
to George Ussery,
my husband,
my Elkanah

Acknowledgements

To family and friends

who prayed, encouraged, and helped me

in so many ways

CHAPTER

1

Off-Guard

Just before I heard the news, Jerusha, I congratulated myself on arriving at the end of my suffering. Then we awoke two mornings later, and Elkanah pulled me close, kissing me with unusual tenderness. Only later did I wonder about that kiss and its lingering flavor of sadness.

I rolled up our mat as Elkanah recited his prayer, the same one I'd heard him say for the three years of our marriage. The words drifted through my mind. Unimportant then. "The Lord is my strength and my song. . . . Who among the gods is like you, O Lord? . . ." We shared our usual breakfast, our usual talk, our usual good-bye hug before Elkanah left to practice music with some other Levites.

"I'll be home before sundown," Elkanah said. He hesitated, his eyes clinging to mine. "I love you, Hannah!" he said with fervor.

"I love you, too," I replied cheerfully, ignoring the tremor in his voice.

I watched him walk away, silhouetted against the rising red dawn. His manly form, his confident stride stirred pride in my heart. Elkanah, my Elkanah, was the kindest, the best-looking man in Ramah. And he was mine. All mine! I smiled.

With a contented sigh, I gathered my garden stick and seeds and headed for my plot behind our house. Many refused to live outside the city wall.

"Playing with danger, that's what they're doing," they said. "Someday, when the Philistines return, they'll be sorry. Only then it'll be too late."

But many years had passed since the coastal people harassed our territory. And I wasn't afraid. I loved the space and freedom–and a garden right under my watchful eye.

I breathed deeply, relishing the nipping air, the scent of new grass, the soft moist soil under my bare toes. Thankfulness flooded my heart, exploding in song. "There's no one holy like the Lord," I sang as I girded my skirt up to my knees. "There's no Rock like our God." I loved that song. It made me feel secure. Over a year ago Elkanah taught it to me, one of the praise songs he'd composed. Many times we'd sung it together. Most of the time I sang it with joyful confidence in Yaweh, the God of Israel.

Most of the time.

And that particular spring day ranked as one of those special moments when sadness, shame, and fear faded into oblivion. I dropped cucumber seeds, beige and flat, into their perfect bed of darkness. As I blanketed them, my fingers stroked the loose softness I'd worked so hard to produce.

Elkanah had laughed at my zealous care. "Why take such pains? Good seeds grow anywhere, Hannah."

"Wait and see, Elkanah. Mine will be the finest garden in all of Ramah." Somehow the memory shadowed my joy. I blinked it away.

From my palm, I sprinkled tiny black radish seeds and covered them from the eyes of hungry sparrows chirp-hopping nearby. Another song, one from my childhood, sprang to mind, bringing with it recollections of the uninhibited faith of my youth—a natural, simple, trusting faith. Easier then, I thought, because I'd not yet engaged in a strong argument with God.

As I dug holes for my onions, more recent visions rose before me, dark days and nights after my marriage to Elkanah, times when I couldn't understand God's ways, why God refused to answer my earnest prayers. As I slipped the onion bulbs one after another into the shadow of the earth, I felt grateful that in the past year, I'd finally struggled up out of my pit of darkness to a place of light where I could once again cling to God's love. But as I patted my way down the rows, I sighed. For in spite of all my progress, I still endured periods when the light of faith dwindled to a faint, feeble flicker. With one last caress of blessing, I rose and brushed the soil from my knees. Surveying my garden, I envisioned the crop to come.

Then I frowned, my satisfaction shifting to impatience. The noonday sun warmed my back, but under my feet, the earth remained cool. I wished for warmer weather. The sky stretched wide, an uninterrupted blue. Who could tell how long it would be before our next rain? But why wait? If I hurried I could carry water from the well and still prepare the evening meal.

Rushing into the courtyard, I grabbed my water jar and headed down the road my Elkanah trod that morning. At the bend I met Diza and Miriah.

"My, aren't you happy!" Diza said, but her voice curdled like sour milk.

"It's a beautiful day!" I smiled at both of them.

Diza shrugged. "Most women in *your* position wouldn't be noticing."

"What do you mean?"

Diza's brows rose, and she glanced at Miriah.

"What's wrong?" I asked. Uneasiness cramped my chest, and my throat tightened. I'd never known why, as soon as I became engaged to Elkanah, Diza, whom I'd considered my friend, turned against me. Today, something about her demeanor seemed different—fierce. Her body straight, hard. Like a warrior rather than a mean hen. The gloating look of victory in her eyes filled my stomach with vinegar. I held my breath.

"You *really* don't know?" Again Diza turned to Miriah, an incredulous smirk on her face. "Can you believe it, Miriah? Elkanah never told her!"

Miriah elbowed Diza. "Be quiet!" Her face flushed, and she refused to look me in the eyes.

Diza arched her brows. I hated how she relished her power to hurt me, yet I had to know what they knew. I clenched my teeth.

"I *really* don't think you want to know," Diza said, pausing only slightly before bursting out with her announcement. "Elkanah's taking another wife!" Her smile outgrew her face. "Do you *still* think it's a beautiful day?"

My heart stopped. Warmth drained from my cheeks. My brain locked, and my knees trembled.

Miriah frowned. "You shouldn't have told her!" Hurriedly she lifted the jar from my shoulder and set it on the ground. Wrapping her arm around my waist, she guided me to the low rock wall in front of the nearest house. "Here, Hannah. Sit down."

I sank lifelessly onto the wall.

Diza swaggered over and stood in front of me, her hands on her hips, a smile in her eyes. "Well, aren't you going to say anything?"

"It's not true!" My throat felt parched, making my voice hoarse, husky. "Why are you making this up?" My hands shook.

"I'm not making it up. Did you forget my brother married Elkanah's sister? Everyone in the family's been discussing it for weeks! Well, obviously, everyone but *you.* I really am surprised Elkanah never told you."

"Be quiet, Diza!" Miriah's soft voice broke in.

"Why should Hannah be so shocked? Any intelligent person would've figured this out long before now. A woman who can't produce children should *expect* her husband to get another wife. Neither you nor I would be so stupid."

Miriah turned from Diza's glare.

"Is it true, Miriah?" I pled for her to deny Diza's tale. "Is it?" As I reached out to her, Miriah wordlessly wrapped me in her arms, and my head dropped onto her chest.

What was said after that, I don't remember. The sounds and sights of the outside world faded as my anguish mounted. I only remember Miriah's softness, the smell of olive oil on her skin, the vibrating muffled sound of her voice as her chest rose and fell while she and Diza argued. Then me running, or rather stumbling home with Miriah trailing me, calling out about my jar.

It felt impossible to survive. Just when my life finally stabilized, now this. This! Surely not even the Lord God Almighty could make anything good from this! Weariness engulfed me, and I wondered how much more I could take.

None of it made sense to me. I knew Diza was right about most husbands. But not Elkanah. It couldn't be! He never condemned me as other men might, but only comforted me in my fears, encouraging me when my distress over my barrenness overwhelmed me.

Sitting in the darkness of our room that outwardly glorious day, I went back in time, replaying my misery, remembering how we'd come to this place.

For the first four months of my marriage I'd kept private my fears about my inability to conceive. I guess I expected to become pregnant the first month, like my mother and her mother. But after four painful months I decided to talk to Mama.

"Oh, Hannah, you're just too impatient. Give yourself a few more months before you begin to worry. Of course, it wouldn't hurt to try eating mandrakes. My mother claimed they work wonders. Our great ancestors, Leah and Rachel, believed they helped them conceive." Mama smiled and shrugged. "It certainly won't hurt to try. Here, help me finish grinding this wheat, and I'll show you some good places to hunt."

Soon I knew every mandrake patch within three miles. Day after day I climbed the hills around Ramah hunting the short-stemmed herb, searching for the large deep green leaves spread beneath long stems dangling bright yellow orbs. Day after day I bit into the pulpiness of the small apple shaped fruit, hoping it would help me to conceive a child. Month after month I remained disappointed.

I prayed, too. Elkanah and I together. Each of us alone. But nothing happened.

It seemed to me everyone in Ramah kept watching me, waiting for my body to swell with life. Women are very good at counting days. They notice if a bride delivers too soon, but they also stay alert to signs of barrenness. How I hated that word! Strange how I seldom noticed it before, but soon that evil word echoed in my brain day and night. Never had I even dreamed of being barren! Women in our family stood out, publicly admired, for their fertility records. My mother bore six children, and I expected to do just as well.

Hadn't I always received what I wanted in life? The only daughter after five sons, my family cherished me in a way few daughters experienced. Long before my birth, Mama adjusted to caring for a large family with the help of a hired girl, so I grew up with more freedom than if I were one of the older children. My brothers doted on me, carrying me with them like a pet. And Papa believed a man's wealth should be seen, not only in the number of his sons and flocks, but also in the attire of his women. Then when I prayed for Elkanah to become my husband, I got what I desired. So why should I even imagine I wouldn't bear all the children I wanted? After having grown up being the envy of all the girls in Ramah, I found it unbearably difficult to handle the shame of infertility.

Each month I confessed my inadequacy to Elkanah. "I'm sorry Elkanah. Another month, and I'm still not a good wife to you."

"Hannah," he said, as he took me tenderly into his arms. "Stop belittling yourself. You make it sound as if your only value comes from producing children. What about our relationship? Do you think I don't love you for yourself? I'm sure you'll conceive in God's time. But even if we never have children, I promise, Hannah, I'll never stop loving you."

Since I wanted to cling to his hope, and since I couldn't deny his love, I let him kiss away my tears. Then we would sit in our little courtyard in the light of the stars and sing songs of faith. And I would hope again that the next month, we would sing songs of joy.

So how could this happen? How could Elkanah, whom I trusted; Elkanah, whom I loved; Elkanah, who loved me . . . how could he take another wife? How could he—after his promise, after knowing what I endured dealing with my childlessness? The questions wound in circles leading nowhere, coming to no conclusion, and the ache in my chest grew. How long I lay there crying, I don't know. Life ended for me, and nothing mattered. And God . . . He seemed so far away. The memory of my innocent happiness that morning mocked my grief, and I wondered, Jerusha, if I would ever feel the joy of life again.

" . . . Hannah
. . . the LORD had closed her womb."
1 Samuel 1:5b

CHAPTER

2
Reaching Out

The wind rustled the large pink blooms on the almond tree, fanning their sweet fragrance to the two women seated below. But neither noticed. The swish-swish of carding wool slowed as the younger woman glanced up. The older one, Hannah, leaned back against the wall, her hands lying limp atop the embroidery in her lap, a far away look in her eyes. As she turned toward Jerusha, a gentle smile spread across her face.

"More than fifty years ago," she said, her voice as gentle and sweet as the breeze. "But the memory—it seems as fresh as yesterday."

Jerusha smiled back and returned to her carding. For more than a year, Jerusha had been married to Joel, Hannah's grandson, but the relationship between the two women had really begun only three weeks ago, blossoming in a way that surprised them both.

They first met at Joel's and Jerusha's wedding.

"Look! She's here."

Excited whispers buzzed through the courtyard, and Hannah scurried to join the others in observing the young bride as she entered their home with her family.

"No wonder Joel grabbed her!" someone said.

They all laughed. The cousins commented on her beauty—her luxurious long tresses, the firm roundness of her flushed cheeks, the tenderness of her lips, but especially her large eyes, softly brown but variegated, like fur of field rabbits.

Wide, watchful eyes, Hannah observed. They reminded Hannah of a puppy her brother Dan rescued once many years ago.

"You have to be careful with dogs," she'd overheard their father warn her brother, "especially when you don't know where they're from."

Dan had insisted that he would train him to be a great sheep dog. And he had. Still it took time for the dog to develop trust.

Eager for love, yet afraid, Hannah thought. *And the girl's eyes, in spite of their striking beauty, they lack the normal twinkle characteristic of the young. As if the wonder of childhood died too soon.* But Hannah's attention had quickly shifted to the festivities, greeting old friends and making new ones.

Jerusha on the other hand, barely noticed anyone at the wedding, anyone but Joel, of course—and his famous father with the great massive beard and uncut hair. Everyone else faded into a blur of noisy excitement, an overwhelming whirl of laughter and smiles. Even after the wedding week ended and the guests left, Jerusha felt a bit stunned by the bustle in Joel's household. And Joel wasn't surprised.

"I tried to warn you," he said.

Jerusha supposed he must be right. But, to tell the truth, she couldn't remember much of anything he told her before their marriage. After all, she'd only seen him four times during their engagement year, and then she'd been so excited and nervous she could only pretend to listen while she observed the stranger soon to become her husband.

"For this one year, you're mine alone," Joel proudly reminded her the morning after the end of the weeklong wedding celebration.

But during that first year of marriage, even while being treated like an honored guest, Jerusha had plenty of time to watch Joel's family. That's when she first noticed Hannah. Amid the chatter, Hannah's quiet joy intrigued her. The older woman listened more than she talked, using her eyes, hands, and posture to eloquently communicate her concern for others. They flocked to her–children and adults–full of stories, laughter, and tears. Hannah wasn't as scary as some of the others, and Jerusha longed to get to know her. But month followed month, and Jerusha did nothing but watch.

"Our special year together is over," Joel complained on the night of their year anniversary. "Tomorrow they'll give you your household tasks."

In spite of desperately missing Joel, Jerusha liked her assignments. Milling the grain in the morning. Carding wool and twisting it into thread during the afternoon. Then helping to prepare the evening meal. She'd been surprised at the lightness of her load.

"They do it on purpose," Joel told her as they sat in the courtyard one evening enjoying the starlit sky. "They still want us to have plenty of time together," and he smiled as he drew her close and kissed her forehead. At least Jerusha didn't have the earliest shift at the mill, or cleanup after dinner. Joel was glad of that.

Each morning after breakfast, Jerusha and Keren, one of Joel's younger cousins, settled down to a session of grinding. Working with Keren relieved Jerusha of all pressure, because Keren loved to talk, and she never noticed if no one answered. Later when Jerusha sat carding, that's when she felt lonely. Not that the others were unkind or exclusive, but

Jerusha felt awkward joining their groups. Even when she sat with them, she had nothing to say. So sometimes she sat alone.

Hannah noticed her and remembered her concern at Jerusha's arrival. "Now don't forget to include Jerusha," she reminded one after the other. And they complied. Hannah also did her part, sprinkling each day with a few comments and many smiles for Jerusha, hoping to help her feel at home.

The kindness of many of the women in the family stimulated Jerusha's hunger for friendship, but she remained unable to respond. *Maybe if I can make just one friend, it'll be easier*, Jerusha thought. So she chose Hannah. But even after making her decision, she struggled for two more weeks.

Tonight, she told herself firmly as she set the small clay lamp on the shelf in the room Joel had made for them during their engagement year. *Tonight, as soon as we settle, I'll get Joel to help me.* Her heart pounded as she lay down on the mat beside her husband. She drew her cold toes under the blanket and snuggled down, thankful for its warmth now that the nights were cooler.

"Grandmother Hannah seems to be a nice person," she said, hoping Joel would volunteer information.

"Nice enough, I guess." Joel reached for her in the semi-darkness. "But not nice like you!" he whispered in her ear, savoring the sweet softness of her. Joel could hardly believe how much he missed his wife, now that they'd lost their time of privilege and returned to normal life. He drew her nearer.

Jerusha allowed Joel to pull her closer, but she refused to relax. "Tell me about her, Joel," she insisted, determined not to let the moment pass.

Joel sighed. His grandmother had never rated as his favorite topic; they'd never had much in common. Besides, the thought of lying in bed with Jerusha and talking about Hannah hardly ranked as his top priority for the night either. But already he knew better than to say anything to upset his bride, especially at bedtime. "I think you should talk to Grandmother Hannah yourself. She'll love telling you her story. Talk to her tomorrow while you work."

Jerusha watched the soft lamplight dancing about on the ceiling beams while she considered Joel's recommendation. Then she turned toward her husband, her cheek resting on the hardness of his muscular shoulder. "But I don't really know her, and I feel strange just going up to her and saying, 'Tell me about yourself.' How will I do it?"

Looking into her eyes Joel found it hard to concentrate on Jerusha's concern. He buried his face in the fresh fragrance of her hair. "Mmmm. Ask her to tell you about me when I was a boy. That'll get her started." He kissed Jerusha's crown, her forehead, her nose. "Now," he whispered, the soft warmth of his breath in her ear, "put Mother Hannah out of your mind until tomorrow, and think only of me."

And she did.

But the next morning it hadn't been easy for Jerusha to carry out her plan. In spite of willing herself to be soothed by the melody of Keren's voice and their rhythmic swaying over the mill, fear crept up her back. What if Hannah didn't like her? What if Joel's grandmother uncovered the fear, shame, and turmoil Jerusha hid deep inside? Surely, Hannah had never endured problems like hers! How could she understand? Jerusha bit her lip as she dipped her hand into the basket of grain and poured the golden kernels into the hole in the top mill wheel.

Yet as her eyes returned to Hannah, she knew she *would* talk to her. She had to. In spite of her fears, something about Hannah drew her, something too appealing, too tempting to be ignored. She straightened her shoulders. *But be careful,* Jerusha cautioned herself. *Just ask questions, listen to Hannah, and don't reveal anything about your problems.* She hoped Joel was right, that his grandmother would like talking to her and be glad to find someone to listen to her stories.

The sun climbed higher in the sky, releasing its warmth into the morning air. Finally the two young women scooped the last of the flour into the large bowl.

"Did you ever think you would marry into a family that eats so much bread?" Keren asked. But she flitted away before Jerusha thought of an answer.

Dusting the flour from her skirt, Jerusha stopped to gather carding blocks and a bundle of wool before making her way to Hannah's corner.

As she approached, Hannah's heart thrilled. *Finally she's come,* Hannah thought. But she only said, "Welcome, child," and smiled warmly. *Don't go too fast,* she cautioned herself, *or you'll chase her away.* "Make yourself comfortable."

"Thank you." Jerusha sank gracefully to the ground.

Hannah smiled, remembering those days when she, too, had left the benches for the old. "How are you doing with your new chores?"

"Fine, thank you."

"Is that grandson of mine treating you well?"

"Oh, yes!"

Hannah smiled at the enthusiastic response and took another stitch in her embroidery, forcing herself to wait.

"I . . . " Jerusha gave herself an emphatic shove. "I was wondering. Would you mind telling me about Joel as a boy?" Her heart knocked on her breastbone.

Hannah laughed. "What grandmother could refuse to

talk about her grandson?" She rested her hands on the work in her lap, looking up at the bare branches speckled here and there with the first tiny pink buds. "I'll never forget the day Samuel told me I'd be a grandmother! The joy I felt—no one could describe it!" Her eyes sparkled. "You can never know, Jerusha, how many days in my life, before Samuel's birth, I believed I'd never experience the joy of being a grandmother—or a mother for that matter."

Hannah's comment revived the memory of a conversation Jerusha had overheard at her wedding. An older woman, a wedding guest, mentioned something about Hannah's "barrenness." But it failed to impress Jerusha then, since, by the time they met, Hannah had many children and grandchildren. But now the recollection stirred up hope and curiosity. Maybe Hannah's life hadn't been as easy as Jerusha had imagined. Maybe Hannah, too, understood pain.

"Enough of my story," Hannah said as she smoothed the material on her lap. "Let's get back to your Joel."

Jerusha nodded. But, secretly, she hoped they wouldn't stay there *too* long.

Hannah glanced up, and as their eyes met, the smile radiating from Hannah's face melted away Jerusha's timidity. That smile built the foundation of a beautiful bridge between them, one destined to provide easy entry to one another's hearts for time to come.

"Well, Jerusha," Hannah began as she pressed the needle carefully through the weave of the cloth, "back then, Samuel and Noga still lived in Shiloh . . ."

The day passed pleasantly for Hannah and Jerusha. It would be hard to say who enjoyed it more. So naturally, the next morning when Jerusha finished her morning grinding, she again carried her work to Hannah's corner. This time, with only a little trepidation. While they worked, Hannah told tales about Joel, most of which Jerusha repeated to her husband.

"So," Joel said after several nights of hearing Jerusha's retelling of Hannah's stories, "why don't you make friends with some of the other women?"

But Jerusha, who found it difficult to make friends, felt quite satisfied to stick with Hannah. And in the pleasure of sharing with Jerusha, Hannah's concern for her grandson's wife faded.

One morning not long afterward, after a suggestion from Joel, Keren's older sister, Shana, approached the older women. "Can't you assign Jerusha to go marketing once in while? She's been here more than a year and still doesn't know where we buy our supplies." So it was decided that each Monday Jerusha would trade places with one of young women assigned to market.

Jerusha hardly knew whether to be excited or anxious about the change.

"Don't worry," Joel insisted the morning of her first trip. "You'll find it great fun, I'm sure. It'll be good for you to get to know some of the younger women."

Soon the four of them were off.

"It's a lot faster to go to market by that way," Shana said, pointing to their right.

Jerusha recognized the entrance joining the newer section of Ramah with the older part. In fact, she'd once asked Joel to tell her the history of the new wall, but somehow he'd never answered.

Shana continued. "We take the outer exit and walk around the new wall to the main entrance. That way we get to enjoy the countryside."

"Look. Over there," the tall cousin said proudly. "That road leads up to the high place. That's where Grandfather Samuel built his prophet's school."

Jerusha didn't tell them she'd already been to Naioth with Joel. But he hadn't taken her by the road. They'd crept up the back of the hill, crawling up the rocky west side without the help of a path. "Let's see if I can show you the whole place without anyone knowing we're here," Joel whispered as they reached the top. The hardest part had been suppressing giggles when Joel made hilarious expressions with his eyes and mouth as he communicated soundlessly. Now as she looked at the road winding up the hill, she felt sure it couldn't be near as much fun to go that way, but she only smiled and nodded.

"See? Over there. The main entrance," Shana said.

Jerusha followed the pointing finger, remembering the first time she'd seen that gate. She'd been so anxious she had to restrain herself from chewing on her fingernails. It was just one day before her wedding. Her family had approached Ramah from the other direction. As they pressed through the gate with the crowd, a gatekeeper forced them into the room between the double walls and began questioning them. Her apprehension grew as her father and brother became defensive. Just as she felt certain something terrible would happen, an older boy ran up.

"It's okay." He tapped the gatekeeper's arm, greeting him with a breathless smile. "This is Joel's bride and her family," he said.

Immediately the gatekeeper's fierceness melted into a grin, and the interrogation ended with an apology.

The boy, who introduced himself as "one of Joel's many cousins," escorted them through Ramah. Jerusha, however, remembered nothing about the marketplace but a wide blur of color accompanied by a menagerie of sounds and smells. The violent pounding of her heart distracted her. The gatekeeper had seemed less frightening than meeting Joel's family.

"We're here. At the market." Shana said, drawing Jerusha's thoughts into the present. She grasped Jerusha's arm as they jostled their way toward the vegetable lady. *A short round woman with pucker lines around her mouth,* Jerusha told herself. She wanted to remember so she could recognize the right merchants just in case, some day, they sent her to market alone.

"We buy grain here," the cousin with round cheeks said. Jerusha studied the man's thin face, large ears, and bent shoulders.

"*Never* go to that one," Shana whispered pointing to a man with a broad forehead and a crooked nose. "He *always* cheats us."

Behind the back of her hand the tall one murmured, "He *hates* Grandfather Samuel."

After hanging the bags full of grain on their shoulders, the trio herded Jerusha toward the wool section. "Noga wants some dark wool to weave a decorative line into a winter robe for Samuel," said Shana. They all dipped their heads, like ducks in a pond, into the large basket of wool bundles. Jerusha stood away from their flapping elbows, looking around at the marketplace.

"Aren't you Joel's wife?" The vendor, an old woman, eyed Jerusha as the others rummaged.

Jerusha nodded.

"So, you've been married more than a year now."

Again she nodded.

Putting her hands on her hips, she cocked her head, and studied Jerusha's abdomen. "Still not pregnant, I heard."

Jerusha's cheeks burned.

"Too bad." But the vendor's lips curved in a smile. "Like Hannah, I suppose?"

Shana's head popped up, a frown furrowing her forehead. Stepping between Jerusha and the woman, she called back to the others. "Drop that wool! We'll buy elsewhere!"

Jerusha never heard anyone discuss the incident. But Joel did—although he pretended he didn't. And wished he hadn't. It opened too many doors in his mind. He watched Jerusha after that, noting her silence and the sadness of her eyes, but said nothing.

The next morning dawned extra cold, and Hannah moved closer to the outdoor oven. The crispness of the morning air chilled her nose, but the smell of fresh baked bread and the warmth of the oven added coziness to the crisp day. That comfort, combined with the fact that yesterday Samuel arrived home after completing his circuit to the towns of Israel, filled Hannah with extraordinary contentment.

Perhaps that very contentment accentuated what she saw in Jerusha. That morning, Jerusha kept her face down, more silent and withdrawn than usual as they ate breakfast. Hannah felt certain the redness of Jerusha's eyes and nose hadn't come from either the cold or the smoke. Hannah hadn't noticed any problems between the Jerusha and the other women. Nor did she have reason to suspect trouble between Joel and his wife. Then she recalled her observations when Jerusha first arrived. How could she have allowed them to slip from her mind? With concern, she watched as Jerusha took her place at the mill.

"Grandmother." Shana interrupted her thoughts as she handed Hannah a cup of fresh goat milk. "You need to talk to Jerusha. The wool woman upset her. Talking about her not being pregnant."

Diza! Hannah pursed her lips, but she refused to let her irritation distract her from focusing on Jerusha. *So, that's it. Barrenness.* Yet as she sipped the warm milk and watched Jerusha, she became less sure. No, that couldn't explain everything–certainly not what she noticed upon Jerusha's arrival. Hannah sighed. "Give me wisdom, Lord," she prayed as she waited for Jerusha to join her.

Thankfully the other women had busied themselves on the opposite side of the courtyard that morning where they couldn't listen in as they sometimes did. So after Jerusha joined Hannah and settled into her work, Hannah laid her handwork in her lap and looked at Joel's wife, visually tracing her bowed head, the soft curve of her cheek. "You seem sad lately. I'd be glad to listen, if you want to talk."

Tears rose in Jerusha's eyes, but she shook her head. "You wouldn't understand." Jerusha's long slender fingers rubbed lightly across the sharpness of the carding block, rolling the straightened wool around itself into a long thin stick. "No one would understand."

After a moment Hannah nodded. "That's partly true. No one can understand or feel the pain of another completely. But those who love can still share it."

That day Hannah began telling Jerusha *her* story, the story of her greatest pain—pain that motivated her to make the most important promise of her life.

"The name of his [Samuel's] firstborn was Joel..."
1 Samuel 8:2a

CHAPTER

3

Disappointment

I'll begin my story, Jerusha, with a critical day just one year after Elkanah and I married. I'm not sure why this particular month became so important to me. Perhaps the anniversary of our marriage caused me to remember more vividly the hopes I cherished on my wedding day. Maybe the sweet smell of the lilies stimulated the rush of recollections. After all, the memories did pop up just as I placed a freshly picked bunch of lilies of the field in the vase on the table. Seven of them—the same number Mother wove into my wedding crown. The number of completion, she said. I caressed each one, noting the fragile beauty of their six crimson petals as I recalled my mother's words as she set the wedding wreath on my head.

"You're *so* lovely!" Tears glistened in her lashes. "My only daughter! My baby!"

Gently she arranged the hair around my face. As I admired her beauty, I felt glad for the many times I'd heard others say how much I resembled her.

"You're blessed by the Lord, Hannah."

She kissed me and a tear fell onto my cheek, ran off and dropped onto my lap, leaving a small dark spot on my new wedding gown. I remember wiping it with my finger so it would evaporate before Elkanah saw me. Later I wondered if her solitary tear portended the endless procession destined to fall from my own eyes. But my mother continued, and my thoughts eagerly followed her.

"From the day of your birth, I sensed the Lord sent you to bless the world in a very special way. And through the years, I've witnessed how you brought joy to all of us." She swallowed, and kissed me gently on the crown of my head. "May your joy be a blessing to your husband and to the many children you will bear. May God reward your loving spirit with the greatest of all joys, the joy of motherhood."

Again she kissed me, sealing her blessing. She believed Yaweh heard her heart's prayer. I believed, too, without one shadow of a doubt. Surely the Lord, the God of Israel, would gladly give me the blessing He promised to women who honor Him.

So that night, one year from my wedding week, I bent over the delicate stems, inhaling their light fragrance, recalling all the joys of that special time—my wedding. Then I smiled and laid my hand low on my abdomen. Already one day past time, hope grew strong, vibrant. Surely *this* month a little one lay nestled in my womb, a special gift from God. Still, I would wait a few days longer before telling my patient, loving Elkanah the wonderful news.

My dream, however, quickly died. As I finished the last preparations for the evening meal, I discovered once again that I was not pregnant. Pain stabbed my heart. Then, like an avalanche of rock and soil falling from the hillside after a rain, desperation and despair crashed upon me, battering me, isolating me from the light, from the breath of life. With a moan of anguish, I fled the courtyard around to the back of the house then out to the hillside south of Ramah.

I ran, my heart racing, not from exertion but from fear. Would I never be able to conceive? Was I doomed to face the same shame, month after month, year after year? How could I bear this humiliation? How could Elkanah love me, a defective woman? What sin caused God to punish me so?

My abdomen cramped with the discomfort of my time followed by the sharp pinch from running, but I pushed on—not because I wanted to get anywhere. Maybe I hoped to run away from my problem. Or maybe I felt I deserved the pain, a kind of punishment for my crime of childlessness. I don't remember how far I ran or even where I finally collapsed on the ground. Weeping, wailing, I beat the earth with my fists. Angry. . . questioning God . . . hating myself . . . wanting to understand, to blame someone.

I wept out my misery until finally dusk fell around me. Cold shadows crept over the hills. Crickets sang. An owl hooted. A mountain lion screeched. Shaking with fear and cold I sat up, hugging myself. Earlier, standing near the fire while cooking stew and flat bread, heat had collected in my clothing, flushing my skin with warmth. Now my tunic failed to ward off the chill of the early spring night. The blood of my shame drenched my garments, causing them to cling to me, sticky and cold—accusing, mocking my childlessness.

I stared out into the blackness where stars began to appear, aware that the evening breeze carried the smell of my blood to animals lurking in the darkness. Just enough light remained to reveal what looked like silhouettes on the hillside. Shuddering, I told myself I saw only bushes and trees, rock and mounds of earth. But I didn't believe it.

If I hadn't been so afraid, I don't know if I could have gone home. How could I face Elkanah? I'd hoped—hoped and prayed—that *this* month I could finally tell him we would have a child. Yet even in my desperate state of mind, I knew I couldn't wait any longer; I knew I had to go home.

Stumbling back across the rolling hills, I was glad I'd learned from my brothers how to find my way by the stars. Just before the last hill, I saw Elkanah appear on the western rise, his lamp throwing a wavering glow on his chest and face. "Hannah!" he called into the night, his voice anxious and hoarse. "Hannah! Hannah!" the echo bounced from the surrounding hills.

How can I explain the emotions I felt? Perhaps it's impossible. I was glad to see Elkanah cared, but ashamed of the pain I caused him. Yet those feelings seemed small compared to the overwhelming anguish that drove me to run away in the first place. I couldn't allow Elkanah any more torture; I wasn't worth his worry. "Here, Elkanah," I called emotionlessly. "I'm coming."

My voice halted the form momentarily, and then man and light began bouncing toward me over the rough terrain. Elkanah paused a short space before reaching me. His breath came fast; his chest heaved.

"Don't touch me," I said without feeling. "I'm unclean." Now he knew. What else would make me unclean but the regular time of monthly bleeding? I remember his raspy breathing as I watched him in flickering lamp light. Shadows flitted across his face, revealing pain, questions, then finally relief. Ignoring my admonition, Elkanah stepped to my side and wrapped his left arm around my shoulder. I felt the rise and fall of his chest, the frantic thumping of his heart, as he pressed me to him while holding his right hand away from us, taking care not to spill the oil from the lamp. "Don't you ever scare me like this again!" he whispered, the familiar fragrance of his breath warm on the coldness of my forehead. I bowed my head and walked beside him toward home.

No one could have treated me with more love and tenderness than Elkanah. But instead of bringing me comfort, his goodness intensified my shame. How could he love a wife who frightened him as I had? A woman unable to bear children. A wife God frowned upon.

In the days and nights following I spent much time thinking of my unworthiness. I could hardly function. Days turned into weeks and my sadness and feelings of self-hatred grew.

"I'm not good enough for you!" I told Elkanah each evening. "You should send me home and get another wife!"

"Hannah!" he said each night in a sad and weary voice. "You know how much I love you. I'll always love you!" "Remember Sarah and Rebekah and Rachel–all our ancestral mothers? They, too, were impatient to bear children. Don't worry, Hannah. I know the Lord has something beautiful planned for you, too. Just trust Him and wait."

But how could I? Already I'd prayed to Yaweh for a year, begging for a child. Yet when I trusted Him, He did nothing. Nothing at all.

And the things I heard from others in Ramah didn't strengthen my wavering faith.

My parents raised their children with the stories of the God of Israel, making sure we grew up treasuring our heritage as God's special people. "It's even more important for us, as Levites, to know about Yaweh," my father said, "since He chose our tribe out of all the tribes of Israel to care for His Tabernacle." But most of the stories of power and victory dated back two, three, four hundred years. And the people I knew in Ramah didn't seem very impressed by the ancient tales of glory. In fact, even as a young girl, I faced ridicule more than a few times for taking the teachings of my father too seriously. I couldn't count how many times acquaintances chided me.

"But Hannah, how do you even know those stories are true?"

"People exaggerate over time."

"Perhaps the stories are only wishful thinking, designed to encourage us in hard times."

"Do you know *anyone* who saw the Lord do a miracle? A *real* one? I mean, *today,* in *our* time?"

Their questions lacked hostility, but I got the idea my friends took the ancient stories much less seriously than I—all of them, that is, except for Elkanah. I remember my surprise that day, years before Elkanah and I had become promised to each other. That year when we made the pilgrimage to the Passover celebration at Shiloh, I was no more than five or six. As usual, a group from Ramah traveled together, and I walked ahead of the adults with my brothers and our friends. The part of the discussion I remember that afternoon centered on heroes, heroes of Israel.

"My favorite is Samson," Haskel said.

"Did he live at the time of Moses?" another asked.

Haskel laughed. "No, silly. He's a much more recent hero. He attacked the Philistines single-handedly. He was massive, strong." He flexed his arms. "And he hated the Philistines! I'd love to be just like him."

"And *kill* those rotten Philistines?"

"Yeah!"

A chorus of agreement followed as the boys bared their arms to display the grandeur of their muscles.

"Not me." Elkanah's voice rang with confidence above the din. "I'd want to be like Joshua."

"Joshua?" Haskel scowled. "Joshua never did anything spectacular."

"He trusted God." Elkanah said. "Ten of the twelve spies were scared to death. But Joshua and Caleb believed God would give Israel the victory. Joshua led our people in battles to take this land . . ." He waved his arm at the surrounding hills. "This land . . . the land God promised His people." I noticed how Elkanah pulled his shoulders back with pride. "Even when it was costly and unpopular, Joshua encouraged the Israelites to stand for God."

Haskel wrinkled his nose and shook his head. "I still go for Samson," he said.

Most of them agreed with Haskel. But not me. From that day on I took a new interest in Joshua . . . and Elkanah. It comforted me to know my brother's friend also took the teachings about the Lord our God seriously.

But in the second year of our marriage when I went though those difficult days, down into the depths of despair, Elkanah's steady unwavering faith in the Sovereign Lord irritated me, becoming a source of frustration. How could he be so sure? How could he *know* the Lord really heard our prayers? Especially when nothing happened. Surely if he were a woman, if *he* suffered from barrenness, he wouldn't be so confident.

In the first year of my marriage, I often overheard talk about Canaanite fertility gods—women standing near me whispering to each other at the well, the market.

"There *are* ways of dealing with barrenness," one would say to the other.

"Worked for me," the other would answer.

I knew they awaited only a flicker of interest, and they would give me the exact details I needed. But their talk repulsed me, pained me. I couldn't imagine how God's people could consider appealing to pagan idols! But as I moved into that second year of barrenness, my pain caused me to question many things I'd accepted all my life.

"There was a man named Elkanah
who lived in Ramah in the hill country of Ephraim. . . .
he loved her [Hannah, his wife] very much,
even though the LORD had given her no children."
1 Samuel 1:1 & 5 NLT

CHAPTER

4

Darkness

In that second year of my marriage, that year of despair, many times I accused God Almighty of being unfair, even cruel. After all, what had I done to deserve this fate? I obeyed my parents, showed respect to my elders, was kind to the less fortunate. Early in my childhood my grandmother warned me that one day I would reap what I sowed, good or bad. I believed her and watched my actions carefully. Every day of my life I tried to sow some kindness, but what good had it done?

In those days of my grief, I preferred to be alone rather than with the other women of Ramah. Yet the more I tried to withdraw, the nosier the women grew. Diza snooped. Miriah hovered. Elkanah's mother, Hamutal, watched with silent closed lips. She made me nervous. I was glad there hadn't been space for Elkanah to build a room onto their home. I wanted her to like me. But even when Elkanah and I first married, before my barrenness became obvious, she acted cold and reserved. Perhaps I shouldn't be so judgmental. Who knows the thoughts in her mind? Maybe she, like my own mother, felt possessive of her child. Maybe she thought no one could be deserving enough for her only son. However it appeared from her perspective, to me, her eyes looked critical and cold. Other gazes besides Hamutal's stirred up uneasiness in me. Her daughters, except for Serah, seemed much like their mother.

And Timara, who lived next door, nearly drove me crazy, peeking in on me at odd times, never making any noise or giving a greeting, creeping up to observe before announcing her presence. One day she walked right up to the door of my room while I sat on the floor crying, hugging my pillow, weeping and rocking back and forth, back and forth. Wailing. Barren for sixteen months of disappointment. I kept count of them all. How long she watched me, I don't know. But she heard my laments and discovered the cause of my anguish. When I looked up, she glanced behind her then crept over and leaned in so close I could smell the sourness of her clothing, the garlic on her breath.

"Wait," she whispered. "I can help you."

She disappeared into the brightness outside, and I sat frozen in surprise, wondering what she could mean. I didn't wait long. Soon she slipped through the door, this time pulling it closed behind her, shutting out most of the light. I should have guessed, but grief numbed my mind. Kneeling beside me, she reached inside the fold of her wide striped belt and pulled out a small object, not much longer than her palm. I squinted, trying to see in the dimness. There on her open hand lay an image, a small female carving with full breasts, wide hips, and a swollen abdomen, quite obviously pregnant. Ashtoreth! The Canaanite goddess of fertility! I drew back in horror!

"Timara!" I gasped. "Take it away! Get her out of my house! How can you touch such an evil thing?"

Timara only smiled and raised the image close to her heart. Then silently, slowly, with one finger, she caressed the circles of the idol's breasts, the left, the right, and then the protruding stomach. She looked at me. First into my eyes, then at my flat, empty abdomen. Timara lifted her chin. "Don't be so proud, Hannah. You have nothing to be proud about." Tossing her head, she stood upright and very slowly began rubbing her empty hand across her abdomen revealing a slight but suddenly obvious roundness. She smiled, and lifting the idol to her lips, kissed her stomach lovingly. With a sigh of contentment, she tucked the Ashtoreth safely back into her belt. At the door Timara paused, "When you come begging, Hannah, I won't even laugh." With another smile, she vanished.

Disgust and shame flooded over me. I understood my disgust at the wickedness of Timara's trust in that pagan symbol of sensuality. But my shame? *That* I found more difficult to understand. Had I, and my home, become unclean, somehow participating in her idolatry? Obviously, I didn't ask her to bring her idol into my house, but I still felt at fault–as if I my wavering faith in the Almighty One made her think I could be tempted to such betrayal. I attempted to push the scene from my memory, to forget the whole incident. What a fool to think I could!

Who could count the number of times those moments replayed in my mind during my year of sadness? The vision of the Ashtoreth came uninvited–when alone, when in a group, when I felt happy, when I was distraught. It made no difference. That little image taunted my mind, my heart, with promises of hope. Could it be true? Did the goddess possess the power to give a barren woman children? I found it impossible to avoid seeing Timara nearly every day, and watching her body swell with life didn't help. Nor did the silent knowing look she gave as she laid her hand over her womb with that satisfied smile.

Why hadn't *my* God answered? For more than a year I'd prayed that the Almighty One would give me a child. I waited. I trusted. But nothing happened. The disappointment, the questions, prepared my mind for disillusionment and doubt. Now that Timara introduced another solution, I found it difficult to chase it away. When I tried to talk to Elkanah, he brushed aside my concerns, telling me to stop worrying and trust God. That was not easy for me to do. For the first time in my life, the stories of our God produced more questions than comfort.

My doubts attacked more than my confidence in God. During that year my feelings for Elkanah changed as quickly as the shadows, but they, unlike the shadows, were not predictable at all. I became crazy with grief over my childlessness. Full of anger, demanding that Elkanah give me a child. Clinging to him tightly, first out of the desire to force him to give me a child, then out of fear that he no longer loved me. Between the times of grasping, came times of pushing him away—times of total despair, overwhelming shame and self-hatred.

Even now, when I remember those days, I feel a deep compassion for Elkanah. How difficult I made his life! Each night when he arrived home, his eyes searched mine, hunting for clues as to what he could expect from me that night. Would I be gloomy, silent, and sad? Or withdrawn and sullen? Should he expect tears, or would I talk incessantly about my unworthiness? Would I question him, demanding proof, solid reasons, for his continued trust in God? Or would he find me too emotionally tired to care about anything at all? I'm convinced any other man in Ramah would have lost patience with me, and even to this day I'm not quite sure why Elkanah didn't give up. No, I guess that's not quite true. I'm sure all of it—both Elkanah's love and my pain—were parts of God's design.

But at the time I lived through those dark days, nothing seemed planned. Certainly not that night two weeks before our annual trip to Shiloh. I set dinner out as soon as Elkanah arrived, and things went pretty much as normal until Elkanah mentioned the trip.

"We'll be leaving early," Elkanah said, "so we can arrive well before dark. Ash, Chiram, and your brother, Dan, will be traveling with us." Elkanah dipped his bread into the lentil soup and took a bite, nodding and licking his lips approvingly.

"I . . . I want to stay home," I mumbled.

Elkanah frowned as he finished chewing. "Why?"

I shrugged. "I just don't want to go."

As Elkanah tore off another hunk of bread, he looked at me with concern. "You're not sick are you?"

I shook my head. He didn't even ask if I were pregnant. It would have hurt if he did, but not to ask made it seem as if he'd already given up on me.

"Hannah." He spoke too patiently, as if to a child. "You know I made a vow to the Lord. Before our marriage I vowed I would lead my family in serving God. That vow includes celebrating the Passover at the Tabernacle and giving the Lord an offering there." Again he dipped his bread into the soup and ate.

I sat in silence, my eyes downcast, glad Elkanah's hunger kept him from reciting the long version, the one with the history of his vow. I didn't want to hear again about his ancient ancestor who saw Joshua take a stand for God and how hearing the story changed Elkanah's life.

The fragrance of the soup, the warm glow of the lamplight, my husband's manly form, all implored me to settle with what life expected of me. Peace spread around outside me, but turmoil boiled within. I felt tired of pretending. Obviously, Elkanah believed the discussion ended with his explanation. He continued eating with an enthusiasm complimentary to any wife under ordinary circumstances.

It was foolish to say more, and I knew it. I knew it, but I didn't care. The thoughts I'd kept private for almost a year refused to keep silent any longer.

"I don't want to worship God this year." At that moment I couldn't fathom what I would want by the next year, but I hoped that portion about "this year" would soften my statement enough to get Elkanah to let me do as I wished.

Elkanah stopped eating and stared at me. I clenched my hands firmly on my lap to keep them from shaking. My chest throbbed under my embroidered yoke, but I refused to lower my eyes.

"What are you saying, Hannah?" he asked, his voice low and steady.

I licked my lips and took a deep breath. "This year's been hard for me, Elkanah," I said, fighting to keep back the tears that suddenly wanted to come. "I . . . I can't understand why the God of Israel doesn't hear our prayers. I don't want to pray to a God who won't answer me."

Elkanah sighed. "This year's been hard for *you.* Well, what do you think it's been like for *me?"* His eyes searched mine, bold and unflinching. "Do you think I enjoy watching you cry, trying to find ways of bringing you comfort, wishing time after time for the days before you became obsessed with your barrenness? Do you think you're the only one who hurts, Hannah?" Sadness lined Elkanah's face, making him look old, tired. Did his chin quiver ever so slightly? Memories of Elkanah's tenderness toward me flooded my mind.

Then he leaned toward me. "You think I understand how God works? Why He chooses to withhold children at this time? No, Hannah, I don't understand. But who am I to give orders to the Almighty One? Do I have the right to defy Him when He doesn't give me my desires?" Elkanah leaned back and remained silent, but his eyes challenged mine.

Then they softened. "Come with me, Hannah. Come to the Tabernacle." Not pleading. Not a command. Just the voice of the man who loved me–and loved God, too.

How could I refuse him?

But even though Elkanah was pleased at my going, the trip was difficult. I remained consumed with my sorrow. The little things along the way that usually brought me pleasure only mocked my sadness, their beauty sharpening my grief. Elkanah and my brother, Dan, tried to cheer me with songs and stories. But if I could not have a child, why should I laugh or be happy? Not until after our return did I discover just how much my behavior upset my brother.

"Now this man [Elkanah]
would go up from his city yearly
to worship and to sacrifice
to the LORD of hosts in Shiloh."
1 Samuel 1:3 NASU

CHAPTER

5

Escape

Two mornings following our return from the Tabernacle, after Elkanah left for singing practice, I sat on my mat in the shadows. Around me lay unfolded bedding, breakfast remains, and my unmilled grain. I clasped my legs, resting my chin on my knees, savoring my sorrow.

"Hannah!" The voice in the courtyard startled me. "Aunt Hannah? Where are you?"

I recognized the voice of my oldest brother's son. "I'm in here," I called, rising quickly. "Is everything okay?"

Goel peered into the house squinting, searching for me in the darkness after having been in the bright light. I suddenly became conscious of my messy house, my unkempt hair. But my concern outweighed my humiliation. "Is something wrong?" I asked again.

"No," Goel replied, shaking his headful of curls. For a moment, time retreated, and I saw before me the darling baby of a few short years ago. "Uncle Dan says you must come see him right now! Go to the north pasture beyond the big rock. He said it's *very* important. I must run ahead and tell him when you're on the way."

What could be important enough to provoke Dan to send for me, practically forcing me to come? He'd never done this before. My mind whirled with possibilities–none good. Hurriedly I got myself ready and started off toward the north pasture. Maybe my father and my older brothers had all been killed, making Dan head of the clan. I tried to lick away the dryness of my mouth. Goel ran ahead toward the hills, stopping every now and then to check on me, making sure I followed.

As I came over the last rise, I saw Goel standing beside Dan, pointing back at me. Dan patted his shoulder and waved him off toward the sheep. Obviously Dan wanted to talk to me alone. As I drew closer, trying to suppress my fears, I searched my brother's face for clues. The look I found surprised me. It displayed neither shock nor grief. His gaze fell upon me, solemn and unsmiling. I knew that look. I'd seen it at times in my father's eyes–only a few times for me, many times for my brothers. "You're in big trouble!" it said.

Although I enjoyed good relationships with all my brothers, Dan and I shared something exceptional. Maybe this came from being closest in age. But I always believed the kinship of spirit we shared spoke of something deeper than that. We communicated without words. We discovered joy in the same things, little things usually, like a bird's song, or the working of an ant in the grass. It would be impossible to tell how many songs we made up together over the years as we watched the sheep. Dan taught me to play the shepherd's pipe, and together we produced melodies that floated over the hillside on the warm summer air. As a girl I often believed we shared one heart. As I grew older, Mama insisted I spend more time working at home, but even then the closeness between us remained. When I married Elkanah, Dan's best friend, rather than being taken from my brother by my husband, our friendship continued. It's true we rarely spent time together, but whenever we did, it seemed as if life between our visits hardly existed and certainly failed to drive a wedge in our relationship.

So I couldn't imagine what would make my brother look at me so strangely. "Sit down, Hannah," he said stiffly, motioning to a rock.

As I seated myself, the beauty of spring called out to me–in the thin layer of warmth on the rock, in the smells of damp earth and new grass at my feet, in the caress of the cool morning breeze on my flushed cheeks. But I pushed such thoughts aside and focused on my brother.

His eyes searched my face. Then he bit the left side of his lip, a sure sign he was deep in thought. Slowly, he drew his breath. "Hannah, it's impossible for me to sit back any longer." I noticed he clenched his hands, something both of us did when we felt stress. "Perhaps it's not my place to talk. But Hannah, you're destroying yourself! I can't believe what's happened to you! I should have seen it before. I probably did, but I thought it would go away." Dan's voice trembled slightly.

I looked down at my hands.

"I know you're disappointed about not having a child. But being upset, refusing to eat, to enjoy life, won't help. Look at you! Where are those beautiful round arms and those dancing legs? Where is the pinkness of your cheeks? Where is that delightful, mischievous sparkle in your eyes? And where, Hannah, is your laughter, your contagious smile? It pains me to see you like this!" He stared away into the pure blue sky, and then turned back.

"Yes, I hurt for you, but I also hurt for my friend. Have you seen what you've done to Elkanah? You're destroying him with your sadness! I don't know how he can sing when his heart is breaking. I would never have guessed you could be so cruel."

I flinched. My cheeks burned.

"Yes, my sister, you've been cruel to the kindest man in Ramah. Elkanah never speaks a word against you, although I've given him many opportunities to talk. Even when I ask, he carefully avoids saying anything to put you in a bad light. But he doesn't need to talk. I've seen enough for myself, especially on our trip to Shiloh."

So, that's what prompted this. A long parade of memories marched through my mind, one after another. I blushed.

"Where is your brain, Hannah?" Dan paused for a breath. Surely he heard my heart pounding. "Do you think so highly of yourself that you believe Elkanah can't send you away?" He sighed. "Perhaps we should take some of the blame, spoiling you as we did. But I still can't understand how a woman in your position would be willing to take such a great risk. It's almost as if you are trying to force Elkanah to get rid of you. Are you trying to punish yourself? What do you hope to gain?"

Finally Dan stopped talking, but my ears continued to burn. A lamb bleated on the lower hill, and its mother answered. Warm tears splashed onto my hands. I saw only wiggly blurs melted together—grass green swishing around rock gray and flesh brown. My chin trembled, and I shivered with cold in spite of the sunshine.

We sat in silence. If it hadn't been Dan talking to me, I'm certain I would have reacted in anger. Never had I known my gentle brother to be so stern, but I knew he spoke from a weeping heart, a weeping heart of love, for me and for Elkanah.

The pain in my chest continued to swell, growing larger and larger, forcing a continual flow of tears from my eyes. My bowels ached with grief and shame. The realization that Dan spoke the truth hurt most. I *was* destroying myself! Why hadn't I seen it? I was destroying Elkanah, too. Memories flooded my mind—the hurt expression on Elkanah's face when I shrank from his touch, the sadness in his eyes on mornings when I refused to walk outside to see him off, the awkward silences when I avoided conversation.

"Don't be a fool, Hannah!" Dan's quiet, firm voice broke in. "Elkanah loves you, but he may not put up with this foolishness much longer. I doubt your barrenness would ever turn him against you. But your self-pity, your resentment—*those* may destroy his love. Then what would prevent him from yielding to the pressure to return his barren wife to her father's house?"

My lips drained of blood. Dizziness and weakness swept over me. How could the picture Dan drew for me be so shocking? Hadn't I thought and talked about Elkanah rejecting me for more than a year now? Those thoughts, internal and spoken, I suddenly realized, were only frantic cries for reassurance. Now, for the first time, I imagined how empty my life would be without Elkanah, without his love. Dan was right. My anger had failed to gain me a child, but it robbed me of happiness as Elkanah's wife.

I began to cry in earnest. Crying because finally I saw my foolishness. Crying for fear of what my foolishness might have caused. How different than the sorrow I felt, the sorrow over my childlessness! This grief was born of my own choices and thoughtless actions.

Dan came to me and put his hand lightly on my shoulder. "Don't cry so, Hannah." His voice pled with me. "I hope it's not too late to mend your relationship. I've never seen a man love a woman more than Elkanah loves you. Don't give up hope."

After my tears subsided, Dan took out two pipes. "Now, Hannah, it's time to practice being happy for the good things you have. Think only of the blessings God has given you and play songs of praise."

So that marked the beginning, the very beginning of my year up. At first I fought continually not to let my mind slip back into the habits of sadness and despair. But on the hillside I'd made an important choice. I wanted to keep Elkanah's love. And I got a little closer to believing I wanted to enjoy life, even if I couldn't have children.

For several months I spent at least one afternoon a week on the hillside with Dan. We rarely talked about my sadness directly. Dan, never one to criticize or correct others, gladly encouraged me. Day after day he pointed out the beauties around us: each new variety of wildflower, a newborn lamb, a bubbling spring with dancing dragonflies. Each visit he gently prodded me, insisting I describe every small incident in my life that brought me joy since we talked last: the smell of newly baked bread, the fluffy baby chicks, the beauty of the sunset. Then we played together on his shepherd's pipes and sang songs of praise to God. Each day I spent with him, we composed at least one new song of thanksgiving, usually weaving into it the joys I reported from that week.

Dan always sent me home singing. On the hill, my brother playing for me as I stood beside him and sang. He continued playing, and I singing, as I began my walk homeward. Across the hills the sweet high tones followed me as I walked farther and farther away. Even after the hills hid the shrinking form of my brother, his music drifted after me.

Sometimes I stopped singing so I could savor it again, the faint sweet melodies of hope.

I've always wondered when Elkanah first noticed the change in me. We never discussed it. I guess my embarrassment at my past behavior silenced me. Besides, many times my success seemed too wobbly to brag about. A constant battle continued to rage in my mind between old discouraging thoughts and the new thoughts of hope and joy. The old dark thoughts pushed me away from the Holy One of Israel, shoving me toward despair and frantic self-destruction. I never could figure it out. Why did my dark thoughts profess to have the answers to my pain, an escape from my suffering, and yet insistently propel me toward actions and attitudes that cut me off from love and life?

"You must learn to accept your life just as it is," Dan told me on one of my later visits with him. "You can choose to focus on the things you wish were different and be overwhelmed by sadness and anger. Or you can choose to look at the things in life God gave you to enjoy, and be thankful."

Yet at times I found the bright thoughts just as uncomfortable as the old ones. The things worth rejoicing about seemed so small and insignificant at times, and the problem of my barrenness, so big, so unfair. Often I wondered if I were foolish to believe Dan, foolish to struggle to have hope.

At times Dan surprised me at how much he sounded like my Elkanah. No wonder they became such close friends. But I found it much easier to learn from Dan than from my husband. Like our conversation about my attitude toward God. I think the discussion began one day when I complained to Dan that the Almighty One failed to answer my prayers for a child.

Dan frowned, "You should hear yourself, Hannah."

I stopped petting the young lamb lying on my lap and looked up. "What do you mean?"

Dan turned away from me, raising his eyes up to the billowy white clouds sliding slowly across the azure sky. "Do you remember the time Uncle Sasson and his friend stayed with us for a week? I was eight at the time. He and some friends had just returned from a trip to Egypt and were full of tales of strange and wonderful things. Night after night I sat in the shadows near the fire, enchanted by their stories."

I heard the excitement in Dan's voice even after all the years and felt relieved I didn't have to confess I could only vaguely remember this incident, one that obviously stood out as very important to him.

"But as I listened to Uncle Sasson," Dan continued, "an uneasiness settled over me. As he told story after story, I began to notice his fascination with the pagan gods—the many gods of Egypt as well as the worship of Dagon, the Philistine fish god. He sprinkled his comments about his exposure to the Canaanite worship of Ashtoreth with what I would now label 'lustful laughter.'" Dan paused, and a sickening feeling rushed over me. I held my breath as I resisted memories of Timara and her idol pushing to come forward, thankful when my brother continued.

"Uncle Sasson enumerated the advantages of worshipping the different gods, what benefits the worshipper could expect from each. He spoke as if he stood in a market looking over the merchandise, hunting for the tastiest fruit or the most comfortable sandals. I remember the shock I felt—a man of Israel, a relative, lowering himself to evaluating the Almighty One, the Ever-Living God of Israel, as if Yaweh stood lined up on a shelf along with all the pagan gods.

"It angered me so much I got up and left the courtyard, refusing to stay and listen to any more of his stories. I doubt Uncle Sasson noticed my disappearance, but I greatly missed hearing the rest of his tales. Yet, my decision not to listen marked an important choice for me. That night I established a standard for myself."

Hannah noticed a far away look come into Dan's eyes. "As I moved away from the warmth of the fire that night and wandered toward the hillside, I gazed up at the stars, bright and glistening in a clear moonless sky. Millions of stars. My heart warmed with pride. *My* God made all those stars. My God, Yaweh, Creator, Lord of the Universe, the One True God." Hannah strained to hear Dan, his voice having grown soft with wonder. After a pause he continued, his voice round with feeling.

"Perhaps my God refuses to flaunt His powers in gaudy display, at bargain prices to the highest bidder—making cheap promises to give a son, bring a large harvest, rout out a neighboring enemy. Perhaps He *is* demanding and stern, calling for loyalty and obedience *before* handing out His blessings. But even at eight years of age, I wondered if the *best* god would easily be manipulated by human desires. The great God of Israel is Almighty, all-powerful, all-wise. Based on His boundless wisdom, He makes His own choices; He pursues His own designs. The best choices, the best designs. Plans so grand they often exceed our comprehension. Yes, my sister, He invites His people to have a part, to join Him in His great plan, but He remains the One in charge, not they. That night, I exulted in the character of my God." Dan paused and looked straight into my eyes. "That night, Hannah, I determined I would never bow to a god I could control."

Under his gaze, I carefully gathered his words, tucking them away for later times of contemplation.

Dan continued. "I remember wondering why I felt safe under the power of such a sovereign God. I realized I would have been terrified if other gods possessed the absolute power of the Almighty. Because, unlike the God of Israel, those gods care nothing about their people. But our God yearns to relate to us, so much that He lowers Himself to reach out to us in love. The greatness of His love makes safe the magnitude of His sovereign power."

Dan fingered the shepherd's pipe in his hand. Then his eyes clasped mine. "Hannah, you're angry at the Lord because He doesn't work according to *your* plan. But could you really respect a God who bowed to human whim? I think Hannah, you're not appreciating the awesome character of the Lord."

What could I say in reply? I doubt Dan expected me to say much, but he planted words in my mind and heart. As the days passed, I found myself thinking more and more about the character of the God of Israel. I began to wonder if I'd been wrong in my anger toward the Almighty. Perhaps Dan was right. The Lord God must be the Sovereign One, the One in charge, or He wouldn't be worthy of my worship. And if sovereign, then I must bow to His will—not He, to mine. Perhaps He had a design in all that happened in my life—a design too big for me to understand.

For months I worked on acknowledging God's right to direct every event of my life. *Then* I heard about the plans for Elkanah's second marriage.

". . . one was called Hannah."
1 Samuel 1:2 NIV

CHAPTER

6

Fears

"Hannah?" Elkanah called as he entered the semi-darkness of our home on that dreadful day of discovery.

I sniffed, keeping my face buried in my blue pillow.

"Hannah?" His voice moved closer, pleading with me to be understanding.

I resisted. It was his responsibility to explain why he agreed to take another wife—without even telling me. I refused to make it easy for him.

Elkanah gently grasped my shoulders, lifting me to stand beside him. I turned my face from his. Silently he wrapped me in his arms, wrapped me in the sadness that had surrounded him that morning. A sadness too deep for words. His sorrow touched my heart, deeper than logic or argument could have.

"Oh, Hannah!" Elkanah's voice broke with pain.

We clung together, our bodies trembling, our clothing watered by each other's tears. Finally our weeping subsided.

"Come," Elkanah said as he walked to the shelf and picked up a bowl. "I stopped by the market and bought some roasted grain for tonight. Not fancy. But unless you have something ready for dinner, I'm sure this will do."

So we settled down to our simple meal. Elkanah, as usual, prayed. As we ate, Elkanah began the inevitable story.

"The pressure wouldn't have been so bad, Hannah, if I had brothers. But Father's getting older, and you know how it is. He's afraid we may never have sons."

I grimaced. *Sure,* I thought, *Elkanah speaks as if we share the responsibility equally between us. But I'm no fool. If they don't think I'm to blame, why would they be so sure another wife will solve the problem?* I felt myself growing hard and defensive, but Elkanah continued as if we engaged in a merely intellectual conversation. "If I had brothers, there would always be the hope that one of them could produce grandsons to carry on the life of our father and his clan." Elkanah looked at me as if begging me to understand.

"So your father is the one who insisted on your taking a second wife?"

With his finger Elkanah stirred the grain lying in his palm. "Well, not just my father."

My cheeks flushed. I knew it! I knew his mother with her mean eyes and tight lips instigated this plan. Probably those sisters, too. I hated them for interfering in my life! But I also knew better than to say anything critical to Elkanah about his family.

"Hannah, you can't blame them for wanting me to have sons."

No, I didn't blame them for that. But I didn't like the thought of them discussing me like inferior merchandise. And I certainly didn't like the thought of sharing my husband with another wife.

"When will you marry?" I had to know how much time remained for us, how much time before our life together would be invaded.

"We've set the date for fall, after the harvest."

Six months. Six months before Elkanah took another wife. "Who is she?"

"Her name is Peninnah. She's a Levite from Shiloh. My father's known her father for many years."

"Is she more beautiful than I am?"

"Oh, Hannah! Why are you making this difficult for yourself? You know I love you. I'll always love you! No one can ever take your place in my heart. If there were any way to avoid this, you know I would."

Elkanah always had a way of making his thoughts seem so right and logical, and mine so foolish. But I honestly wasn't so sure the issues lay in nice neat lines, simple and clear. They certainly weren't to me!

My pain made me daring. "But Elkanah, you're the one who always said we should be patient and trust God–that God would give us children according to His timing."

Elkanah sighed. "Do you think I wanted things to happen this way? You have no idea how long I've been under pressure to take a second wife! I constantly stand up for you, Hannah. But time has run out. It's my responsibility to carry on our family line. Neither my desires nor your desires must stand in the way of family duty."

Elkanah stood up. My argument appeared to be answered from his perspective, but certainly not from mine.

Why couldn't I accept life like other people? I watched them. They had problems, difficulties in life, but they didn't seem to struggle with their thoughts as I did. They just got on with their lives. How I wished I could brush the questions away! Then it wouldn't concern me if the answers fit together or not. But, for me, trying to silence the questions only seemed to make matters worse–like swatting at swarming bees in order to calm them.

What use had it been to work so hard to break out of my sadness? Had all my efforts prevented Elkanah from taking another wife? What was going to happen to me now? Would I fall back into my despair? How could I share my husband with another wife? Did I even want to try–or should I give up and convince Elkanah to let me go home to my father's house?

What about God? Where was He in all this? In the past months I thought I'd accepted Him as the Sovereign One with the right to order all the events of my life. I never thought He would plan this! Why? What purpose could there be? I'd struggled to convince myself that the Lord was a God of love, that His love guided all His actions toward me. How could this new complication in my life be a demonstration of His love, of some great plan?

Perhaps I'd been wrong. Perhaps I fooled myself in order to create some comfort and hope. Was I wrong about the God of Israel? How could I know?

I tried talking to my mother. But the second wife issue upset her so much that discussing the subject became impossible. Mama fluctuated between dissolving into tears and making angry accusations about Elkanah and his family. It wore on me, having to comfort my mother when I needed someone to comfort me. I hated feeling trapped into defending Elkanah when I wanted only to vent my disappointment and anger. So Mama certainly wouldn't be much help with my feelings about God.

Dan helped me more than anyone else. "Don't waste energy fighting against the inevitable, Hannah. Who knows why God has kept you from having children? It's a question without an answer. Your barrenness forced Elkanah to take another wife for his family's sake. There's nothing you can do about that. All you can do, Hannah, is to decide what attitude you will have."

As day followed day, my thoughts raced back and forth as rapidly as the spindle on my loom. What attitude would I take? Would I choose to keep my renewed faith in the Almighty, or would I go back to my doubts and questioning accusations? I thought about it. Often it seemed most logical to turn against the Lord, to renounce Him because He didn't save me from suffering and pain.

But something must have happened in my heart during those months of learning to give thanks, learning to have an awesome fear of the Sovereign One, learning to bow myself in submission to His plan for me. It had rooted itself deeply in my heart, I guess. That tiny assurance, so small it hardly deserves that name. A small assurance that the Lord is the true God, the Lord of Love, the One Who knows what is best. Over and over songs of praise and confidence returned to my mind unbidden, singing themselves to me as I prepared meals, cleaned house, worked the garden. Every time it happened. Exactly as it did during my year of recovery. Once I lifted my eyes off myself and my problems, allowing myself to believe in God's love for me, something changed. In place of the turmoil and overwhelming hopelessness, a peaceful calm settled over my heart. Not that it remained indefinitely. No, it required persistence to keep my thoughts focused on faith in God. But music helped, that's for sure.

In those months before the wedding, I spent much time thinking–not just about God and whether I could trust Him. As I cleaned my house, I thought about the days ahead when my bowls, my stove, my home would be shared with another. What would she be like? Would we be friends? As the first wife I would have some prestige, but if she produced children, especially sons, she would gain honor. So much remained unknown, but I tried again and again to imagine what it would be like.

As I look back now, I almost smile at the foolish fantasies I entertained in those days. But I don't smile. The little scenarios I imagined and grieved over could not even touch the edge of the sorrows lying ahead for me. If I'd realized even a little of the reality to come . . . well, Jerusha, I probably wouldn't have had the courage to face it.

". . . one was called Hannah."
1 Samuel 1:2 NIV

CHAPTER

7

Yearnings

The stars above looked down into the courtyard as if happy to see them sitting still in the darkness. Joel and his wife.

She turned to him and smiled. "This feels like our wedding year," she said as her fingers lightly caressed the hairs of his arm.

Joel nodded. He could see how their quiet repose would remind her of the unhurried intimacies of that time. But to him the night felt different. He pulled her closer, endeavoring to eliminate the space between them. "What do you two talk about all day long?" Joel asked.

"Who? Hannah and me?"

"She can't know three weeks of stories about grandson Joel."

Jerusha smiled. "Now she's telling me about herself. *Her* story."

Joel reached out and took her hand in his. Even without the light of the sliver of moon, he would recognize her hand amid all the hands in Ramah, or Israel for that matter. The small bones of her wrist. The long slender fingers. Her hands had lost their roughness during their marriage year, taking on a silky smoothness. He swallowed. It'd been harder than he anticipated. Leaving her. Going back to work. And, according to his mother, his wife spent practically all her time with Hannah. That night weeks ago when he'd encouraged Jerusha to talk to his grandmother, he never dreamed they'd become so attached. His arm tightened around her. "Why don't you make friends with the younger women?"

"I go to the market with them every Monday." Jerusha's chest tightened.

"One day a week?" He laughed. "My brother's bride, Mazel, will make a good friend for you. Not right now, of course, since they've just married. But later, after their year together."

Jerusha bit her lip. Joel loved Abijah. She'd never seen brothers any closer. Naturally, they'd want their wives to be friends. She shivered and folded her arms across her chest. But Mazel? She swallowed. Mazel scared her. Joel's mother, Noga, too. But she'd never tell Joel that. Joel's mother and brother were the most important people in her husband's life. Other than herself, that is. She smiled.

The next morning as she sat at the mill, Jerusha thought about Hannah. Joel hadn't said it, but he didn't sound too happy about their friendship. She felt torn. She wanted to please her husband. She'd never dreamed of having a husband so loving and kind! But for all her life, she'd also craved the love of a mother, love like Hannah willingly gave her. How could she turn it down?

Yet, at times, her growing attachment to the older woman discomforted her, too. Their friendship enticed her to open her heart. But then whenever she started to reach out, she became afraid and retreated. Other times the desire to share herself became urgently painful, but her thoughts and feelings refused to be translated into words. Once, when words formed in her mind, they sounded so ugly, they frightened her. How could she admit them to anyone?

But that morning–the one after her talk with Joel–when Jerusha joined Hannah, she once again heard Hannah claiming many of her emotions: anger, despair, fear, self-condemnation. When Hannah talked about the trauma of changes in their household, Jerusha understood. The memory of the day she moved into her father's house raised a huge lump in her throat. *Who knows,* Jerusha thought as she savored the gentleness of Hannah's kindly face*, if life will ever offer me another chance to safely share the pain I've kept secret for all these years?* In that moment, she decided to speak before she could change her mind. "When I moved into my father's house, I had lots of worries, too."

Jerusha's voice, barely discernible above the rustle of the leaves, surprised Hannah, leaving her uncertain as to whether the girl had spoken, or she'd imagined it. She looked at Jerusha. The girl's fingers moved gracefully twisting the wool. Only the flush of Jerusha's cheeks convinced Hannah she hadn't imagined things. Hannah waited, and when Jerusha looked up from her work, Hannah smiled her encouragement. "Where did you live before?" she asked.

* * * * *

Timur refused to look at the small bundle the midwife left flailing, wailing in the cradle. He clenched his jaw again. His teeth hurt from clenching, but he welcomed the pain. His eyes focused on the motionless form of his lifeless wife lying on the bloodstained mat at his feet. His abdomen tightened at the sight of her pale lovely face, now still and gray. How could she be so beautiful, even with agony written over her features, with her hand still clutching the blanket under her chin, her gold bracelet glistening in the flicker of the lamp, her luxurious hair matted and tangled from writhing in the pain of childbirth?

"Daddy?" A tug accompanied the little boy voice, but Timur remained rigid and unresponsive. The bundle near them continued to twist and scream. "Daddy?"

Nothing changed until, finally, a woman, the sister of the man, entered the door behind them, panting, her forehead damp with perspiration. Elsa hurried to the crying bundle, tucked it efficiently under one arm, and turned on her brother. "Well, Timur, are you going to do it, or do I have to take care of *that*, too?" Irritation edged her voice as she jerked her head in the direction of the body lying on the floor waiting to be prepared for burial.

Two children who trailed after the woman, peeked through the doorway. The younger one, a boy, wrinkled his nose at the strong sweet smell of fresh blood. Behind him, his sister curiously surveyed the crimson-spotted blanket covering most of the woman's legs.

"Get!" Elsa yelled at the two children, but they continued to stare. She grabbed the shoulder of her brother's whimpering son, rolled her eyes despairingly at the unresponsive father, and chased all three children from the room, still clutching the wailing infant firmly above her hip.

That evening following the funeral, after the friends returned home, the family sat on the ground around the fire.

"Never!" Timur's voice cut the cold crispness of the night air with the sharpness of icy spikes. "I won't touch it!" He stared forward, refusing to look at the infant who'd stolen his wife's life. "I told you I don't care *what* you do with it!"

"Don't try to dump her on me!" his sister said as she pushed her open palms repeatedly against the air. "My husband forbids me to take her. He says he has enough trouble feeding our two." Elsa glanced over her shoulder at the girl and boy chewing on bread in the background, their wide eyes reflecting the light of the fire. "Besides, Ham, you *are* the oldest, so it *is* your job."

Across from the fire a large man shifted. Ham was tired from the hurried trip he'd made that day in order to be at his sister-in-law's funeral. He was tired of sitting on the hard ground, but he had no other choice as long as he remained in the house of mourning. He was tired of his sister's bossy bickering and his brother's stubborn silence. He was tired of the constant crying of the motherless infant his sister had carried into the house. But no one cared if he was tired.

Ham sighed. He stroked the massive black beard covering his chest. "Yonita already has a baby to tend."

"But that's an advantage, Ham. It'll be no trouble for her to nurse another. Now what would *I* do? Or Timur?" Elsa forced a laugh. "What a blessing that Yonita produces plenty of milk!"

Ham wondered if his wife would see it that way.

"Timur's keeping the boy," Elsa continued with a cheery chirp, "so that's one child you don't need to worry about."

As if that should delight me, Ham thought.

"If you didn't live so far away, I could take turns helping out, but, of course, the way it is . . ."

As Elsa chattered, Ham realized tomorrow he would return home with a niece added to his own brood. His family accepted the little one as a matter of course. After all, what could they say? Elsa was right. Custom required the eldest son, as leader of his father's clan, to care for the needs of other family members in emergency situations. Isn't that why he'd received that extra portion of his father's inheritance?

The children named her Jerusha. *Married?* Ham shook his head. *One who is loved and cherished in close relationship?* A strange name for a baby no one wanted. But he said nothing.

Years passed, and Jerusha grew into a beautiful child. Very soon she helped Aunt Yonita and cousin Rivka, Ham's only daughter, with chores around the house: gathering firewood, carrying water, sweeping the courtyard, carding the wool, milling the grain. Rivka, who was four years older than Jerusha, supervised and ordered her about. The two older boys generally busied themselves too much with their own interests to be concerned about Jerusha. But from the very beginning, Liban, his Mama's baby, hated sharing his mother. When he felt Jerusha stole too much of his mother's attention—with a firm shove, or, as he grew older, a less obvious twisting pinch on the arm—he told her to keep her distance. Often the flesh remained red and painful, sometimes even leaving twin bruises, but the lonely pain inside hurt much more and never quite went away.

Although Jerusha had no recollection of her beginning, she sensed it. A black gaping hole. An intolerable emptiness. How she longed for a place where she belonged, where she was wanted! Hope for love flared strongest on the few occasions when she saw her father and brother. But every experience ended in bitter disappointment. Her father refused to speak to her, touch her, or even look at her face. In the early years, her brother, Dov, tried to mimic his father, crossing his arms in her presence, pretending Jerusha didn't exist. However, a few times he childishly gave up that denial and honored her with a glare or a curse, even once spitting on the ground at her feet.

One night after returning from such a visit, five-year-old Jerusha, after hurrying through her nightly chores, hid behind her uncle's house to be alone with her grief. Crouching down near a bramble bush that had grown up there unwanted, Jerusha found strange comfort in the prickliness of its spindly branches. Hot tears dropped and ran silently from her knees down her legs. When the sound of voices came around the corner of the house, Jerusha quickly rubbed her forearm across her face to dry her tears and pressed closer to the bush. Leaning into the thorns, she watched the forms of a man and three boys, her uncle Ham and his three sons.

"But why didn't they *keep* her?" Jerusha recognized the boyish voice of Liban, the youngest, whining in complaint.

Uncle Ham sighed. "No one says, Liban. I think she reminds them too much of her mother's death. I feel sorry for her, not being wanted and all."

"I don't!" Liban insisted. "She killed her mother!"

"Liban! She didn't *kill* her. Things like that can happen when a baby's born. But it's not the baby's fault."

"Well," Ethan, the middle son, joined in, "Dov *says* she killed her—that it was all her fault."

"It's true, Father," Jehu, the oldest, agreed. "Dov *really* hates his sister. We don't always like Rivka, especially when she gets bossy." He laughed. "But Dov. . . ."

"That's why I haven't pushed them to take her," their father interrupted. His voice softened as they moved farther from the house. "I've always been afraid for her."

Jerusha strained to hear.

"But they have a step-mom now," said Liban, the youngest, his voice high and pinched with insistence.

"Maybe *she* wouldn't like Jerusha either." Ethan laughed. "You know my friend, Zachariah? Well, he got a new mom and . . . "

The conversation faded, but what Jerusha had heard echoed loudly in her heart. Night after night, she fell asleep remembering. Week after week she grew more and more convinced—the family didn't want her—not even her uncle. With that lonely realization, Jerusha began to dream that one day her father would let her live with him.

Two years later that day came.

* * * * *

"Why did your father decide you should leave your uncle's house?" Hannah asked.

"My father remarried. My stepmother soon bore four children and wanted help. So my father sent for me." Jerusha pulled off another portion of wool.

In the quietness that followed, Hannah wondered what story hid in those few words. What emotions. Hannah wouldn't ask. Someday, when Jerusha felt ready, she might tell. For now, the demonstration of confidence Jerusha gave in this small self-revelation warmed Hannah's heart.

But, for Jerusha, the memories of that distant trauma of moving to her father's household couldn't compare with the more eminent sharpness of Jerusha's secret fears as Joel's wife. Listening to Hannah soothed her, at least for the moment, diverting her attention from her past and present problems, letting her feel nurtured by Hannah's love. Jerusha studied the shadows in the courtyard. Enough time remained to hear more of Hannah's story before she had to help with the evening meal.

"What happened, Grandmother Hannah? What was it like when the new wife came?"

Hannah smiled a sad smile. "It was bad. Very, very bad."

". . . one was Hannah . . ."
1 Samuel 1:2 RSV

CHAPTER

8

Apprehension

Those six months before Elkanah's marriage to Peninnah were full of imagining. I couldn't help it, Jerusha. Even when I tried to keep busy with life, I was always reminded that this would be the last time for this to happen in just this way. Next year I must share my garden, and who would decide where to plant the onions? Soon there would be three places at the table, someone else's clothing to wash, someone else listening in on my conversations with Elkanah. I refused to think about the nights I would lie alone in my bed. Even with that exclusion, I found hundreds of things that would be different by next year.

Little things. Bigger things. It seemed everything would be different.

I was right. They were.

But living in the future is a dangerous thing. Even then I felt the danger, and I fought to enjoy the present. Throughout those six months, the garden I planted grew to be one of my greatest sources of joy and diversion. Day after day I carefully guarded it against the chickens, keeping my fence high and my gate secured. Each morning I gazed upon it with wonder and joy, watching for the tiniest bit of growth, then for the blossoms and the developing crop. Few weeds dared to invade, and those that did quickly met their fate at my determined hand. Even the rains came at just the right times. I knew with certainty I would harvest abundant crops. And I did.

Elkanah boasted about my produce to everyone, especially his family. I felt uneasy. It made me wonder. Was he attempting to convince people his wife could compensate for her childlessness with her garden produce? Was he trying to assure me of his love? Or did he want to cover his own discomfort over the coming changes?

We found it hard to be open with each other. I became just as defensive as he. Every statement, no matter how innocent, could be interpreted as some sort of accusation or condemnation. Why did these agitations multiply just when I wanted so much to make the most of every precious moment, squeezing out the last drops of the pleasure of having Elkanah all to myself?

Each day as I awakened, I watched Elkanah. Some mornings I woke before he did and lay very still beside him, studying his face in the crack of early dawn. His cheekbones rose artfully, yet strong and very male. His shoulders measured over a hand's span more than mine. Dark hair feathered lightly over his chest, his arms, his legs, and his toes. My eyes greedily caressed my man until the hunger for him reached my fingertips. But I knew even the tiniest touch would end my visual study, because Elkanah balanced on the threshold of waking. The most minute movement would prompt him to reach out and draw me to him. Then I would close my eyes and absorb his nearness: the warmth of his body, the smell of him, the movement of his breath coming, going, warm and relaxed, the low throbbing of his heart under my ear.

Other days Elkanah awakened and arose before me, and I watched him from my mat on the floor. Feeling the emptiness beside me. Touching the spot where he lay to discover if his warmth remained. Peeking from beneath my cover, I watched him wash. I watched him bow to Yaweh and heard the familiar prayers. *"Always, always remember this,"* I told myself. *"Never forget!"* I tried to preserve it all, to keep every memory tucked away, safely, forever. I made a collection of them, all the memories of Elkanah when he belonged only to me.

Each day as I got up from my mat, I reminded myself, *"Today you must make happy memories, memories to cherish always."*

But how can one make happy memories of getting ready to bring in another wife?

"Haskel will be bringing in wood today or tomorrow," Elkanah said one morning at breakfast.

"Wood?"

"Yes, wood. We'll need another room, . . . unless you want all of us to sleep together."

It *wasn't* funny. Anger warmed my cheeks and neck, but thankfully I kept my mouth closed.

"We planned to build another room sometime," Elkanah continued, oblivious to my anger, "and now seems to be the time to do it."

Yes, I remembered those plans. They didn't seem anything like what was happening now. We'd discussed those plans for our house soon after our betrothal. A clear cool winter day with the sun shining warm on my back as we walked toward the plot of ground were Elkanah had begun constructing our one-room house.

Like me, Elkanah grew up inside old Ramah in a home handed down from one generation to the next–a household bulging to the seams with uncles, aunts, and cousins of every age. When Elkanah's uncle produced five sons, he warned his younger brothers, including Elkanah's father, that they would need to provide different housing for their sons when they married. So, soon after Elkanah's birth, his father purchased, at an excellent price, this open property outside the wall.

"I know we're starting small, Hannah," Elkanah had said that day long ago as we planned our future home. Elkanah's presence beside me made it hard to concentrate, and anything he suggested would have delighted me. "One room will be enough for the two of us. Later when it becomes crowded, we'll add on a larger room right over here. When our sons marry, there'll be plenty of room to add more and more rooms."

I beamed my agreement. But the "crowd" I envisioned that day in the winter sun included only children, children belonging to Elkanah and me. It certainly never included another wife. It angered me that Elkanah accepted this intrusion as if it were no big thing. Sometimes I hated men. Sometimes I hated being a woman.

Elkanah went right on planning. "Do you think the large room would be better on the north or over here?" He pointed to the south end of our one-roomed house. "Do you want a window here or there?"

I tried to listen, think, imagine, but why should I care? I wrestled with something much more important than a window or a door. My mind was crowded by the woman who frequented my dreams—a very large woman, with no eyes or nose, only a huge mouth, who shoved her way into every corner of my house. Laughter echoed around her. She reached out strong, solid arms to embrace my Elkanah, and puckered her huge full lips into a great kiss. I tried to push her away, but I began shrinking–getting smaller, smaller, weaker until I seemed no more than a tiny, helpless, unheard ant on the floor.

I'm surprised we ever managed to get the room planned. But soon the building began, and under different circumstances I'd have been delighted. The large new room, with plenty of shelves and an indoor kitchen area, captured the earliest rays of the morning sun, flooding the room with brilliance. The other end of the room, which would be used for sleeping, remained darker, cozier. It was perfect. Would I sleep in this new room, or would she? The smell of freshly cut branches, moist mud and rocks, the newness and beauty of it all, enticed me, yet how could I give up the home I'd shared with Elkanah, the very place where day after day, night after night, we'd shared our lives, our love, our laughter, our tears? Some day soon Elkanah would tell me, or ask me, where I would sleep. If the choice fell to me, what would I choose?

Again and again I wished for a friend to talk to, a real friend. But even if I'd found someone I thought I could trust, I doubt it would have helped. Most often my thoughts and feelings seemed beyond the description of words. Saying them to someone would have reduced them to husks.

So the rumblings of my mind remained hidden away deep within–most of the time. Sometimes when I was alone, I would sing. I sang my questions, questions without answers. And more and more I directed my questions to the Almighty One. I can't say I remember any responses, but just talking to the God of Israel soothed my fears and gave me a sweet peace and an unexplainable confidence that somehow—I certainly didn't know how—everything would work out right.

From the women in Ramah, I received plenty of advice. Everyone *was* someone or was related to someone who had gone through the trauma either of being replaced or of becoming a second wife. It was worse than listening to stories of childbirth.

I learned to dread going to the well, to the market, down the street. As the time grew closer for the marriage, my situation seemed to be the most interesting topic of discussion to everyone but me.

"Be tough, Hannah. Don't let her push you around or you'll never have any respect."

"The second wife is the one *I* feel sorry for!"

"If you're kind, Hannah, both of you'll get along just fine. After all, it's not the most terrible thing that could happen! What if he sent you home?"

"Don't ever let her forget that you are the *first* wife!"

On and on it went.

I remember one day in particular. I'd taken some cucumbers and onions to my mother-in-law. Out of respect for Elkanah and for my own self-preservation, I tried to keep my relationship with his family as good as possible. After all, I understood their desire to have grandsons to carry on the life of their clan.

"My, what beautiful vegetables!" Hamutal said as she lined them up on the table.

I smiled. "It's much easier to tend them with my garden just outside my door," I said. (She had to go outside the wall to care for their plot.)

We chatted about my garden, Raya's weaving, and Kitra's new recipe for bean paste.

"Could I walk home with Hannah and see the new room?" Serah asked her mother when I started to leave.

I enjoyed Serah's company. Although she was only ten years old, I felt more at ease with her than her older sisters, perhaps because she reminded me most of my Elkanah.

The sun beamed on our heads, and the breeze blew on our arms and necks, warm and dry. I hoped the weather wouldn't get too hot. I didn't like to carry water for my plants, but I certainly didn't want the garden to dry up before its time.

"I'm sorry about the second wife." Serah broke into my thoughts. "Elkanah didn't want to, but Father insisted."

"I know."

We walked in silent sadness.

"I hope she'll be nice," I added. "Do you know her?"

"Not really. But we did see her the last time we went to Shiloh."

My heart skipped. Finally, I'd found someone I could question. "What's she like?"

Serah didn't smile at my eagerness. "She's not pretty like you. She . . . well, she just sat there while her father told us what a good worker she is: an expert cook, an immaculate housekeeper, a talented weaver." She licked her lips, then glanced at me. "Her father promised she would produce many children, especially sons. But . . ." She shrugged. "How can he know?"

"Hannah! Serah!"

At once I recognized Diza's voice. By then we'd reached my house. I could still call it my house then. Serah and I waited as Diza hurried up the road, herding two children and carrying a baby on her hip. The little one was hers, the two older ones belonged to her husband's first wife.

"Is the room finished?" she asked breathlessly.

"Nearly," I said.

"It better be! It won't be long until you'll be needing it, you know." Diza smiled. "So, aren't you going to show it to us?" Diza pushed the children's heads, one after the other, in the direction of the new room. Serah and I followed.

"Where will Peninnah sleep?" Diza asked as she surveyed the large room, and the two older children scurried around like mice hunting for crumbs.

"Elkanah hasn't said."

Diza raised her brows, then smiled. "The two of you aren't talking these days? Too bad. I'd think you'd be doing everything possible to make Elkanah happy—before Peninnah arrives. How long is it now? Just two months and then the wedding. You're not pregnant yet, are you?" Diza eyed my embarrassingly flat abdomen and then waited pointedly for my reply.

"No." I forced the word out of my mouth.

"Too bad." Diza turned toward Serah, "There *are* ways you know, but Hannah is too *good* to use them. Now she must pay for her pride. Don't *you* be so stupid, Serah. When you grow up, take advantage of the charms of the Canaanites. They really work. See?" She tipped her head toward the child in her arms.

Uneasiness lingered, like a bad smell, even after Diza left. When Serah went home, I retreated to the security of my old room and began cleaning—working my way down the shelves of bowls, jars, neatly folded cloths. But even there, Diza's words followed me. Why had I refused to try the fertility rites? Was it only because I knew Elkanah would be horrified by such a thought? No, even if my husband encouraged it, I would have feared participation in pagan ritual. What caused my fear? Reverence for a God Who could not, or would not, give me a child? Why, when so many of the other Israelites willingly took advantage of both religions—the old Israelite God and the many Canaanite gods—why did I refuse? Especially when others flaunted the success of their gods in my face?

Was I proud, as Diza claimed? Thinking myself better than others? Holding onto the old ways as a form of superiority? I didn't think so. Maybe once, before I suffered the shame of barrenness, maybe then I'd been proud. Not an intentional kind of pride, just a confident self-centeredness, feeling I deserved good things, and no one had the right to deny them to me.

But I'd been humbled, first by my barrenness, and now by the coming of a new wife, a wife everyone hoped would be able to accomplish what I had not. A wife who could give my Elkanah a son—or many sons. Strangely enough, that day I didn't feel repulsed by my humility—by acknowledging my limitations. I began to wonder about the changes I saw in myself, changes resulting from my years of adversity.

Those last two months, I harvested my garden, drying and setting aside food. Each jar I packed with loving care, with prayers for the blessing of the Lord on our family. *All* our family.

Three weeks before the wedding as I set out the food for our evening meal, Elkanah came in and announced the completion of the room. "Tomorrow you may begin moving in," he said. "Go ahead and unpack the new supplies."

I looked away from his smile. Slowly my eyes reached up and caressed the old beams of our first home. Braided onions and garlic hung neatly in a row from the rafters. On the shelf high on the center post sat the lamp Dan had given us for our wedding. In the corner lay the cushions where Elkanah and I reclined when the evening felt too chilly to sit outside and where I laid out our bed each night. The cushions no longer looked as new or as bright as when we were first married. There was a stain I couldn't get out where we spilled grape juice one night when we were being silly. Still, the pillows seemed so much at home arranged neatly in their corner. How would they look in the new big room? How would her things look in here? Would she put her bed on the very spot where mine had been? Where Elkanah and I became one for the first time?

"What's wrong, Hannah?" Elkanah's eyes pled with me silently, begging me not to make our last days together difficult. Elkanah wouldn't understand, and I wasn't at all sure I could explain.

"I . . . would you be offended if I stayed here . . . and let Peninnah have the new room?"

Elkanah looked surprised. "I thought you'd want the new room. It's bigger, better and all. I want you to have the best, Hannah, the very best I can give." He stepped close and wrapped me in his arms, his chin resting gently on the top of my head.

I've never forgotten that moment pressed against him: the roughness of his robe on my cheek, the even rise and fall of his chest, the smell of his skin mixed with wool. Up close, my one eye viewed the brown weave of his garment, the hollow indention on his throat, the familiar hairs peering out from the opening in his tunic—the tunic I made for him myself. Whose work would clothe him when this one wore out?

Would he always love me so? Or would that change, too?

Now at last, I was sure. More sure than most times in life. I wanted this old room to stay the same, to be mine, to remind me of all we had shared—before she came.

"There are too many memories in this room, Elkanah. Don't make me give it away." The lump in my throat grew larger.

"You can have either room you want, Hannah. But if you stay here, people will say I gave Peninnah the best."

"Let them say what they want," I said in the bravery of the moment. "I want to keep this room for just you and me—for you and me and the memories we share." *And for no other woman,* I added in my mind.

Elkanah pressed me close, and I felt his abdomen tighten with emotion. I lifted my face for the kiss I knew would be waiting.

The soup got cold that night, but we didn't care.

". . . Hannah and the other . . ."
1 Samuel 1:2 NIV

CHAPTER
9
The Wedding

It seems strange, but it wasn't the wedding feast that bothered me most. Perhaps I kept too busy then—making sure food remained available, that people enjoyed the time of celebration. Even when I happened to see Peninnah with Elkanah, the sharp pain I expected never appeared. Maybe I'd already grieved so much that by the time of the celebration, I could push my feelings aside—at least with others around.

But nights were different.

I'd asked Elkanah's permission to sleep at my father's house on the nights of the wedding week. He seemed relieved. Elkanah watched carefully each evening to see when my family got ready to go home. When the time came to leave, Elkanah led me into our room where we stored supplies for the celebration.

Tenderly He wrapped his arms around me. "I love you, Hannah." He lifted my face to his. "I will *always* love you. No one will ever take your place in my heart." Gently, he kissed me. His lips soft, sweet, warm. Not passionate or fierce as sometimes. Yet as I walked to my family's home, it seemed the glow of that kiss spread from my lips all through my body, filling me with my husband's love.

My family tried to include me in their conversation on the way—telling funny things that happened that day, news they'd heard about old acquaintances. Mother constantly complimented me on how good the food tasted and how well I'd organized the festivities. Dan just walked beside me, speaking little. But even while my family's love surrounded me, I remained alone—alone in the crisp coolness of the night and the darkness of the clear starlit sky. Yet, I was not alone, because Elkanah's kiss lingered and his words vibrated in my ears, in my heart.

But each night, by the time I got to my father's house and lay warmly wrapped on my mat, the kiss had dissipated. Nothing remained. I tried desperately to recall it, to recreate the beauty of that moment, but instead, other images invaded my mind.

Elkanah and Peninnah alone—lying together under her new gray blanket. Was Elkanah rubbing her back like he did mine? Did he kiss her hair and pull her chin up ever so gently as he laid his mouth on hers? I chased the thoughts from my mind. Burying my face in my pillow, I silently wept out my grief and fell asleep with a prayer for strength on my lips.

Each morning I trudged back to Elkanah's home on the upper side of Ramah. One or two of my nieces or nephews accompanied me when I returned to get things ready before guests arrived. The morning the wedding week was over, however, Dan waited for me in courtyard.

"I'm going with Hannah today," he told the young ones. "The feast is over. You can visit Hannah another time."

We'd hardly left the house when Dan drew a deep breath. "I know it's been hard, Hannah, but I'm really proud of you! I didn't know how you would do." Then he glanced down at me in concern. "You understand how I meant that?"

I nodded.

"You have reason to feel sad about Elkanah's marriage, Hannah. I'm sure the coming days will be difficult, but trust the Lord for courage."

Again I nodded in response.

"Remember the songs," Dan continued. "Remember the things you learned about trusting in God. Don't expect life to be easy." He smiled gently as he looked into my eyes. "Be cheerful, even in the hard times."

Again, if someone else had been talking, I'd have been defensive, probably irritated, but Dan was different. Dan had helped me in my suffering. He, too, knew about suffering. Dan's first son died in infancy, and I'd witnessed how he reached out to the Lord. So I stored his words away, little knowing how much I'd need them later.

Dan bid me good-bye in the yard, and I entered the quietness of my little room and lay my small bundle in the chest. The sound of Elkanah's voice saying his morning prayers drifted to me faintly from the new room. How strange it seemed! Hearing him so far from me. But I determined not to dwell on such things. Today was an important day, my first with Peninnah.

After checking my hair and clothing, I took a deep breath, prayed silently for strength, and walked determinedly to the big room. When I entered, I saw Elkanah with his head bowed and heard his voice rhythmic, low, warm. Peninnah lay on her mat, her head covered with her blanket. Elkanah must leave soon, but she'd put nothing out for him to eat. Quickly I placed bread and some fig cakes on a platter. Then I hurried outside to milk the goat.

I'd just finished when Elkanah came around the house and greeted me.

"Good morning, Hannah," he said, as if absolutely nothing had changed. "Thank you for breakfast." He held out his cup for fresh milk. The sound and smell of the warm milk being poured, comforted me. "Peninnah's tired this morning," Elkanah continued. "She doesn't want to get up yet. I planned to spend some time talking with both of you, but I guess it can wait. I'm sure everything will go well. Don't worry if you don't get everything cleaned up from the feast. Take some time to talk to Peninnah and help her feel at home."

I nodded. Why did I feel shy with my husband?

In the seclusion of the goat pen, Elkanah put his arm around me and kissed my forehead. "I love you, Hannah. Always remember that I love you."

"I love you, too," I whispered as my throat tightened.

"I love you! I love you! I love you!" I wanted to scream after him as I watched his manly form walking down the road. But I said nothing. Instead, I pressed the swelling emotions into a corner of my heart and commanded them to behave.

Lifting my chin, I peeked inside the new room. Peninnah lay in a huddled lump on the mat, still and gray. I reached inside for the broom, backed out the door, and began cleaning the courtyard. After sweeping, I got the water jar and headed for the well.

I met Miriah coming home with her jar, looking happy to see me. I could see she brimmed full of questions she felt embarrassed to ask. So I told her we hadn't had a chance to talk yet. She *said* she was sure everything would be okay, but I got the uneasy feeling she expected things to get worse. Why, I wondered? Had she heard that Peninnah was unfriendly? Had she noticed something during the wedding feast that I'd missed? *Don't worry,* I told myself, *Miriah always fears the worst. That's just her way of looking at life.*

I tried to divert my thoughts, singing quietly Dan's favorite praise song. "Praise to the Name of the Almighty, to the One Lord who holds me up. . ." The song held my fears at bay. Still barking and snarling, but not able to bite me. I'd sprinkled all but a small portion of the yard when I sensed Peninnah's presence in the doorway of the big room.

As I turned and saw her, my song and welcoming smile melted under her dark glare. Matted hair framed her glowering face. "I would think you could have the courtesy to be quiet when you know I am very tired from a big week and long nights." She put significant emphasis on the words "long nights."

I blushed and bowed my head. Surprise, intimidation, embarrassment, and anger all mixed together. "I'm sorry," popped out of my mouth before I could think of anything else. I have often wondered how it might have been if I'd been more secure at that time. But such wondering is useless. When I'm fair with myself, I realize I shouldn't be critical of the person I was. After all, I'd learned a great deal in my few years of marriage, even if I hadn't yet learned everything I needed to know . . . and certainly, even now, at my age, I have more to learn.

So as my heart thumped frantically in my chest, I glanced up to see Peninnah disappearing into the large room. What was I to do? How could I approach such a woman? She seemed so much older, so much more in charge, and yet we were nearly the same age. And *I* was the first wife! How dare she march in and push me around?

But in spite of my indignation, I certainly wasn't ready to raise her fury again by entering her space. Still, I needed to mill the grain if we planned to have any bread for dinner. Fortunately some supplies remained in my room, so I got a bowl of grain and sat down at the mill in the corner of the yard.

I'd finished grinding the wheat and making the dough before Peninnah reappeared at the door. "Where's my food?" she asked. She seemed a little less ferocious than before. Perhaps she'd just been tired, I thought.

"There's bread and some fig cakes," I said trying to hide my nervousness and be friendly and cheerful. "I'll get them for you."

After covering the dough, I left it to rise and followed Peninnah inside. She examined the breads and chose the fig cake, but she appeared less than content. I waited while she ate, forcing myself not to nibble my nails or jiggle my knee. She didn't speak to me.

"I'll be glad to help you get settled." I smiled, hoping she'd accept my friendship. "I already cleaned the courtyard and made the bread, so there's time left before we need to get dinner."

"My, my, aren't you the busy one?" She gave me a bored look, walked over and seated herself on the chest in the corner near her mat. "I can take care of my own things. You're welcome to clean up the wedding mess if you need something else to do." Ignoring me, she began combing her shiny black hair.

Nothing was going as I'd imagined. I'd feared the first day might be awkward, but I'd never met anyone like Peninnah. Her coldness built an effective wall between us. Her attitude confused and angered me. I felt helpless to say or do anything to correct the situation. So for the second time that day, I found myself obediently following the instructions of this disagreeable wife.

I longed to have Elkanah come home, certain that somehow, when he arrived, things would improve. They couldn't get any worse. Could they?

". . .and he had two wives;
the name of the one was Hannah,
and the name of other Peninnah."
1 Samuel 1:2 ASV

CHAPTER

10

Deception

That first evening with all of us together proved a strange one. After sleeping and sitting around primping by herself all day, Peninnah burst into life. The transformation occurred when she spotted Elkanah coming up the road. Peninnah sprang to her feet and, with a flurry of motion, ran to the outdoor stove, snatched up the pot of stew I'd made, and whisked it indoors to the table. As she flitted back out the door, she paused dramatically and pushed a loose hair back from her face, like she was straightening herself after an afternoon of tremendous exertion. Then a small cry of joy escaped her lips, as if she'd only then noticed Elkanah's approach, and she hurried to meet him.

Such an attitude of reverence and awe I never saw demonstrated by any wife in Ramah! Oh, most of us felt quite happy to see our husbands arrive home, but we lacked her technique. She didn't dance about like a childish girl as I had so often done. No, she possessed a dignity about her, like a woman who knew her place and gladly served one so worthy.
Elkanah looked a bit surprised, but he acknowledged her greeting with pleasure.

"Where's Hannah?" I heard him ask.

Where indeed! I still knelt in shock by the fire watching this amazing act unfold before me. Rising, I went to them, feeling a growing sense of uneasiness. This world of mine—which looked the same from the outside—had been completely changed by this woman, and I had not the slightest idea of what to expect next. I felt awkward, an intruder, a blundering child, a wife without a place.

Elkanah tried hard to make both of us feel at easy. Peninnah appeared relaxed enough. She asked the appropriate questions, listening graciously with rapt attention. How could this be the same cold, hostile woman I'd been with all day? I ate in silence, dumbfounded.

"It looks like you two got a lot done," Elkanah commented as he looked around the courtyard. "I really didn't expect everything to be back to normal in one day."

Peninnah smiled sweetly. "That's one of the advantages of having two wives."

Elkanah paused as if taken by surprise, then smiled. "I'm glad you two have had a chance to become acquainted." Elkanah seemed pleased and a bit relieved. He gave me a grateful smile. "You seem a bit quiet tonight, Hannah. I guess you're all talked out."

Peninnah smiled again. "The second advantage of having another wife."

Elkanah laughed.

Peninnah laughed, too.

I remained silent.

How could she accept credit for all the work I did? How could she pretend we were friends when she did everything possible to stand in the way of any friendship? How could I explain to Elkanah that nothing was the way it appeared? If I tried to explain, surely Elkanah would think I was the one causing problems. Hadn't Peninnah been much more gracious and cordial than I?

For the rest of the evening Peninnah kept Elkanah entertained, and I sat watching in confusion. Right before my face she worked to charm my husband away from me, and I was helpless to do anything about it. When the time came to go to bed, Elkanah stood and stretched. My heart beat franticly, and a lump rose in my throat. I hadn't slept with my husband for a week, a long lonely week. Where would he sleep tonight? "It's been a pleasant evening," Elkanah said. "These situations are awkward at first, but I'm glad we're getting along so well. I want to thank both of you for making this transition as pleasant as possible."

With a coy smile and a nod, Peninnah accepted his thanks. I have no idea how I looked, but Elkanah didn't seem to notice anything amiss.

"Have a good sleep, Peninnah," Elkanah said. He reached out and helped her up, then kissed her forehead. Turning toward me, where I still sat in my confusion, he offered me his hand. "It's time for bed, Hannah. You seem tired."

From the other side of Elkanah, Peninnah's eyes shot arrows at me. Her lips flattened tight and hard. Elkanah didn't see, and I didn't care. In spite of my stupefied behavior, Elkanah still chose me! I couldn't wait to get out of Peninnah's room! It felt like I'd been holding my breath for hours. As we entered the courtyard, the coolness of the night bathed my face. Stars glistened in a clear sky. I drew a deep breath, and life returned.

We didn't wait outside to appreciate the evening. Instead, we entered my little room and enjoyed being alone.

Morning came too soon. I watched Elkanah wash and listened to his morning prayers. Comfort and hope settled over me. Perhaps things would be better now, now that Peninnah realized her charms couldn't win her Elkanah all for herself. I listened for just the right part of Elkanah's prayer so I would know what time to get up. I put away the bedding, dressed, and went to prepare breakfast. I'd timed it to perfection.

When I went to the big room, Peninnah had already laid out the bread I'd baked the previous day. Today she was dressed and her hair combed. She wasn't especially pretty, but, like Serah said, she was a fine looking woman–when she wasn't being mean. And she did have beautiful thick black hair.

Her pleasant expression vanished as soon as she saw Elkanah hadn't entered with me. "What took you so long? Don't think you can leave all the work to me just because I'm the second wife! If you don't hurry and milk the goat, you'll make Elkanah wait." She threw the empty goatskin at me.

Catching it, I retreated gladly to the animal pen. *Well, today will be no improvement over yesterday,* I thought. So I determined I'd better draw what comfort I could from the things I loved. I tried to soak in the friendly familiarity of my surroundings. The brown nanny bleated her thanks for the extra scratches and rubs. I loved the smell of her hair, her milk, the sound of her happy bleating, her chomping, and the rhythmic music of the milk squirting into the skin bucket. When the pressure of my hands ceased to bring milk, I lifted my bucket and tickled the nanny under her hairy chin before letting her go.

Elkanah sat eating when I entered, and in just moments he was gone. I was left alone with Peninnah. I had no idea what to expect.

"I'm going to the well for water," she said. "Do what needs done here. Don't wait for me to get back." Then she was gone.

I cleaned and put away the dishes and began food preparations. We'd finished the leftovers from the wedding, so I decided to make barley stew with plenty of vegetables. As I worked, I tried to make sense of Peninnah's behavior.

By the end of that week I drew several conclusions. Peninnah wanted to impress Elkanah. She hated me and delighted in making me feel uncomfortable. She didn't like to work around the house, but she did like to go to the well—although I couldn't understand what took her so long day after day. She rarely came home before noon, and then she ate and retired to her room until time for Elkanah to return. What she did in there, I couldn't say. In spite of the fact that she left me with practically all the work, I liked working alone much better than having to endure her presence.

Yet the way she treated me left me really upset. The worst of it was this: Elkanah had no idea what was happening. Before Peninnah came, I felt free to be myself with Elkanah–frivolous, sad, honest, passionate, stubborn. I'm not claiming my unrestrained behavior was always good, for him or for me, but at least we knew each other. Now, since Peninnah arrived, big chunks of my life remained hidden from Elkanah. He believed things that weren't true, and I couldn't tell him about Peninnah's meanness and deception. Yet my refusal to be honest felt wrong, too.

Day after day I pondered my problem. I wished for someone to talk to. I couldn't tell my mother. She would be furious at Peninnah and would certainly say things that would only make matters worse. My father would march straight to Elkanah and demand that he correct the problem. That would humiliate Elkanah, making him appear to be an incapable husband, and I refused to do anything that would bring him shame. I'd already made things bad enough by being childless. *My* problem brought about this marriage in the first place.

Dan was the best option among my brothers, but I wasn't sure he could help either. He'd probably think I was being emotional about having to share Elkanah—that I either imagined, or exaggerated, what happened. If I could convince him that Peninnah really was two-faced, Dan would talk to Elkanah, and Elkanah would be hurt that I'd gone to my brother first without talking to him about my problem. Elkanah would be the right one to tell, but I was afraid he wouldn't be able to believe the truth.

There seemed to be no solution.

The best thing, I decided, would be to avoid being near Peninnah during the daytime. By now her behavior with Elkanah no longer shocked me. The fact that Elkanah more often chose to sleep with me calmed me most of all.

After that first week, I began to feel like I knew what to expect in my new life. But then Peninnah changed. It started one morning when she didn't get up to set out Elkanah's breakfast. She refused to eat and stayed huddled in her bed.

"Watch over her, Hannah," Elkanah said before he left. "Try to get her to eat something." Concern etched his face. We walked out into the courtyard together. I'd hoped for a little more attention for myself, since Elkanah spent the previous night with Peninnah, but Elkanah couldn't get her off his mind. "Perhaps I should stay home today," he said.

I couldn't bear the thought of him pampering her all day. I wouldn't have been surprised if this sickness were another game to get Elkanah's attention. I determined it must not work! "Oh, I'm sure she'll be fine. After all, I'll be here if she needs any help. You go on. Everything will be all right." I wrapped my arms around him and lifted my face for a kiss. I'd never been so relieved to see Elkanah leave! But many things had changed since Peninnah's arrival.

I hurried into the house to check on Peninnah. "Can't you eat just a little bit of bread?" I asked.

"Get away!"

I reached out and gingerly laid my hand on her forehead. She swatted at me.

"Get away! Are you deaf or are you stupid?"

She didn't have a fever. "I'm going to the well since you don't feel up to it," I said, retreating.

I missed my trips to the well, the one time a woman could count on chatting with another woman. A good time, too, to catch up on the news—or gossip, whatever term you prefer. I just hoped that by now the women had settled on a topic other than Elkanah's wives. As I approached the well, the cluster of women fell silent.

"Good morning!" I said, smiling.

"Good morning." They answered in dutiful chorus.

"Where's Peninnah?" Diza asked.

"She's not feeling well."

"Humph!" Symone muttered under her breath. "Who would, living with you?" I thought I heard her say.

"What's wrong with Peninnah?" Miriah asked.

"She won't eat. But she doesn't have a fever."

"She's nauseated?" Diza asked.

I shrugged. "Maybe. Why?"

Diza grinned. "You really are naive aren't you?"

Symone laughed.

"How long have Elkanah and Peninnah been married?" Diza asked.

Silently I figured it. Two, nearly three weeks. . . . Surely they didn't think she could be pregnant! It *was* possible. But only Peninnah knew the day of her last bleeding. I turned away and filled my jar, reining in my emotions. Coldness clutched my heart but I tried to keep my voice light and carefree. "It's too soon to know that," I said hoping I sounded as if I'd already considered this possibility. "If she's pregnant, Elkanah will be very glad."

Diza laughed. "No doubt about *that!* The question is, how will *you* feel?"

I lifted my jar to my shoulder and faced Diza. "We'd *all* be delighted! Now, I need to get home to check on Peninnah. See you later."

As I turned away, my cheeks burned. Could Peninnah really have conceived so quickly? Funny, I wouldn't have been at all surprised if I'd gotten pregnant during my wedding week, but somehow I hadn't even considered it could happen to Peninnah.

My chest tightened and tears caught in my throat. I was afraid. Afraid that if Peninnah bore a child, Elkanah would love her more than me. Afraid that if she became pregnant, Peninnah would be even more miserable to live with. Afraid that the shame of my barrenness would never be forgotten.

"Elkanah had two wives, Hannah and Peninnah."
1 Samuel 1:2b NLT

CHAPTER

11

The Star

I certainly didn't want to ask Peninnah. Nor would I dare to suggest it to Elkanah. But it wasn't long before the subject came up.

As Elkanah finished eating the next morning a serious, concerned look shrouded his face. He walked over to where Peninnah lay on her mat and knelt beside her.

"Do you know what's causing you to be sick?" he asked.

"Mmmmmm." Peninnah moaned.

I thought it a bit dramatic.

Peninnah reached her hand up to caress Elkanah's hair and murmured sweetly in a low throaty voice, just loud enough for me to hear. "I want to talk to you tonight–tonight when we're alone."

I saw Elkanah nod. His reply cut my heart. "Of course. I'll be glad to spend time with you." Silently I slipped away, a trespasser in my own home.

I was hurt. I was angry. I was jealous. My emotions screamed for me to run away. But Peninnah would delight in such weakness. Elkanah was such a fool! Why couldn't he see through that woman's plot? I strutted off, determined not to wait for Elkanah's good-bye. Gabbing the jar, I headed for the well. As I stomped down the road, with every step my throat grew tighter, and so did my chest. In trying to punish Elkanah, I'd robbed myself of a precious part of my day. Why couldn't I just talk to him—tell him the truth? Why couldn't I trust Elkanah to love me, as I'd trusted him before?

I got to the well ahead of the crowd, and that was fine with me. Old Urit greeted me kindly; I saw pity in her eyes. Pity was better than scorn, but I still didn't want it. I wanted admiration. On the way home, tears puddled in my eyes, but I kept blinking them away. I seemed to be getting quite good at that.

It was a miserable, lonely day. Elkanah's gentle, loving promise to Peninnah echoed in my ears. All day long I felt lonely, just thinking about how lonely I would be—lying there on my mat cold and alone, while she rested in his arms cooing in his ear, telling him she was already pregnant.

Why? Why couldn't *I* give him a child?

Evening came and somehow I survived. *Maybe she's just late, like I was.* But I couldn't believe it. After cleaning up, I slipped into my little room and sat there, all alone. Usually I kept my hands busy with mending, carding, or embroidery. That night I just sat on my mat, my arms wrapped around my legs and my chin on my knees. I did nothing, nothing but feel sorry for myself and my lot in life.

For a long time I sat there, my chest hard with cramped anger. I hated life. My life, all life. That stupid baby, too. But especially *my* life. What good was my life? In the last years I suffered one disappointment after another, and now it continued getting worse. How could I survive it? Did I even want to? God must hate me to let all these bad things happen! I wished that, if He hated me so much, He'd just end my life.

My anger swelled in its destructiveness. It felt good, giving me a feeling of power. Cold, hard power. A hateful power, power that wanted to destroy, to hurt myself, to punish others.

Then, I saw the star. The tiny twinkling star, peeking in at the open window. Only a little star, but bright, calm, and steady. As I watched the star, I remembered part of a song Dan and I made up perhaps a year before. "The stars sing of the power of Yaweh, the Almighty Lord. But my heart sings of His mighty, mighty love." Sitting in the darkness of my little room, I heard the song of the stars and realized my fears had crowded the song of God's love from my heart. My chin trembled as I watched the star. Tears blurred the tiny light, then spilled, drop after drop, onto my knees and ran in warm trails down my legs. I swallowed and wiped them away.

Calmness and peace hovered over my weeping heart. And I knew—I was not alone. I need never be alone. My God was a God of Love, and—with Elkanah or without him—the Lord's presence would bring me peace.

I lay down, pulled my blanket around me, and fell asleep.

I woke to Elkanah's muffled prayers and the first rays of the morning sun. Memories of the night before flooded in. I didn't know what the day would hold for me, yet I determined not to allow myself to fall back into the trap of fear and hatred. *Today must be a day of love.*

I saw joy written on Elkanah's face that morning. He met me outside the door of Peninnah's room, holding my milk skin, still eating his bread.

"Let's talk out here while you milk," he said, "so we won't disturb Peninnah."

I knew what he would say, but I took the skin and walked with him around the house to the animal pen. After laying a handful of grass down for the brown nanny, I arranged myself and my bucket at her side. Elkanah watched me—his eyes alive with pleasure, his body tense with excitement. But it had nothing to do with me.

"Hannah, Peninnah thinks she might be with child." His voice trembled with emotion, belying the uncertainty of his words.

I looked up at him. Every part of him delighted me, filled me with love for him. More than anything else, I wanted him to be happy, even if it weren't on account of me. I smiled. "That's wonderful, Elkanah. I'm glad," I said. I really meant it.

His face burst into an exuberant grin, and he sighed. "I knew you'd understand! Peninnah said you'd be upset, but I assured her that you'd rejoice with us."

Angry thoughts about Peninnah jumped into my mind, but I determinedly pushed them away. Elkanah talked on and on about how proud he was of me, how I should take good care of Peninnah for him, and how all of us would make a wonderful family. I wasn't sure he was right, but I was glad for his happiness. I hoped what he said would be true.

Elkanah waited for me as I completed the milking, but before he let me fill his cup, he took me into his arms.

"I love you, Hannah!" His words whispered warmly in my ear. "I love you! I love you!" I felt the passion of his words, his body. He lifted my chin, and the kiss from his lips told me again how much he wanted us all to be a happy family, how he wanted me to share in his joy.

As he walked away with a special bounce in his step, I told myself how glad I felt for him. Glad Peninnah could give him a child. But, in spite of what I said, my heart ached because I couldn't be the one to give him the greatest gift.

The day passed. I worked; Peninnah rested. I tried to keep her happy, and things moved along calmly. She gave me looks and made a few statements I chose to ignore, but what could I expect from Peninnah?

That afternoon I busied myself cleaning out the very last of my garden. It was both a sad and a happy time for me. Sad, because this source of pleasure would be gone until the spring. Happy, because I savored the memories of my success. I gathered the winter squash and headed to the house. Rounding the corner, I noticed Peninnah coming out carrying a bowl. When I saw her face, I knew what had happened.

"You snoop!" she cried, her eyes flooded with hatred. "Why are you always spying on me?"

"I'm not spying. I had to bring these to the house." I showed her my skirt filled with squash.

"You *were* spying! You just want to gloat over my misery! You're delighted, aren't you, you infertile beast! You can hardly wait to tell Elkanah I have no son to give him! You believe you'll get him back for yourself? Never! Next month I'll delight him for sure!" She heaved her cold bloody water at me. As I stood frozen in breathless shock, Peninnah burst into tears and ran into her room.

Amazingly, I wasn't angry at her. As I dried myself, I felt only a great sadness for her. Finally, we had feelings in common. I could understand completely: her frustration, her rage, her intense disappointment–the terrible sting of finding the hope of being pregnant had been entirely false. I was also surprised that, instead of being relieved, my heart bled as if crushed by her grief.

That night a dense cloud of sadness settled over our home. Peninnah, full of tears, needed comforting. Elkanah held back his disappointment. He looked very tired. I wondered if he, like I, kept remembering all we went through in those early days when I kept hoping month after month, only to be disappointed. I did all I could to ease the situation, but I knew nothing would help.

We survived. People do, in spite of disappointments. But the relationship between Peninnah and me changed after that. Perhaps my unspoken sympathy fueled her anger. I can understand why she would have been infuriated at being placed in the same category as barren Hannah.

Day after day she accused me of ridiculing her. If Elkanah chose to sleep with me, I could be certain the next day Peninnah would rage at me, accusing me of enticing Elkanah away from her. Why should he waste his time with me, she asked, when obviously I could produce nothing but blood?

I thought it would help Peninnah if she did more of the housework, anything to keep her mind occupied. One night I spoke to Elkanah about it, surprising myself by taking on for Peninnah's sake a subject I could never have approached for my own benefit.

Elkanah and I lay quietly in bed, my head resting on his arm. The moonlight shone in through the window.

"I'm concerned about Peninnah," I said.

Elkanah turned his face toward mine.

"She sits around all day being sad because she's not pregnant. I think she'd feel better if she did something to get her mind off herself."

Elkanah sighed. "I know you've been stuck with more than your share of housework, Hannah, but try to be patient. It's hard on Peninnah losing the child, even though it happened early in her pregnancy. She needs to rest and build up her strength so she'll be stronger next time."

For the first time, I understood Peninnah had convinced Elkanah that she'd conceived. Having seen what I did, I didn't believe it. I couldn't be positive. But I'd been late before, too. She certainly could have faked her sickness if she thought it would get her Elkanah's sympathy and attention—which it did. If Elkanah believed she'd conceived, then he thought she'd accomplished something I'd never been able to do. A surge of anger rose in me. Then I wondered: if I were in her place, might I have done the same?

". . . And Penin'nah . . ."
1 Samuel 1:2 RSV

CHAPTER

12

Struggling

Peninnah's second month arrived. This time I kept careful count, for her cycle held just as much significance for me as my own. Sure enough, exactly twenty-eight days after Peninnah's first episode of illness, the sickness returned. But I'd decided beforehand to wait at least another week before believing she'd conceived. Elkanah also tried to convince Peninnah to delay her excitement, but of course she refused to miss any opportunity to draw attention to herself. (Or, if I'm kind, maybe she was just as eager as I'd been to be with child.)

One morning–by my figures just a week past Peninnah's time–I came inside to check on Peninnah after giving Elkanah a sweet good-bye. I sang inside myself, so I wouldn't disturb Peninnah with my noise. She'd made it quite plain she didn't enjoy my singing, humming, or instruments.

Of course she said nothing about her dislikes on our music nights. I always loved those evenings when Elkanah played for us. Peninnah always joined me in lavishly admiring his talent. I was sincere, and I assume Peninnah was, too. Anyone would be soothed by his music. After a playing several songs, Elkanah always encouraged us to sing along with him. Then he and I would play, he on his harp and me on my shepherd pipe or the flute Elkanah taught me to play in the early days of our marriage. Elkanah tried, in spite of Peninnah's protests, to teach her to play the tambourine, but after repeated disasters and frustrations, Elkanah stopped insisting. Maybe Peninnah experienced as much pain from our music nights as Elkanah and I received pleasure. I noticed she had difficulty both in carrying a tune and feeling the beat, and I truly felt sorry for her. How would I have coped with my life without the blessing of music? So I tried to remember to keep my songs to myself, especially when Peninnah wasn't well.

That morning when I was wrapped up in my silent music, Peninnah sprang from her mat and lurched toward the door, retching all the way. *That* convinced me a baby was coming.

As week followed week, Peninnah's sickness diminished. But with the certainty she was truly pregnant, other problems increased.

I thought I'd have no trouble dealing with Peninnah's pregnancy. After all, hadn't I already dealt with that possibility the previous month? Yet the knowledge that Peninnah carried Elkanah's baby tormented me. Why couldn't *I* be the one to give Elkanah a child? Sometimes a terrible feeling of emptiness overwhelmed me. Many days I sought out a place of solitude–in my room, with our animals, walking on the hills—where I could weep out my grief. It hurt. Not just the emptiness of my body, but also the emptiness of my heart—seeing Elkanah's joy and knowing that, in spite of all he might say, this joy was not mine, only his and Peninnah's. More and more I felt like an outsider, a lonely onlooker.

One morning as Peninnah ate the almond cake I'd just baked and I prepared to make bread, I noticed we were out of water. The pitcher was empty, the jar was empty, and the extra storage jars as well.

"Where's the water?" I asked.

"My, my, aren't you grouchy?" Peninnah tossed her head. "The water's in the well, last I knew. If you want it, get it."

"But that's the only thing you do around here."

"I'm not going to carry heavy jars of water when I'm pregnant with Elkanah's child."

"Lots of women carry water right up until the day of delivery." I was getting tired of doing all the work.

Very deliberately she picked an almond slice off the top of the cake and chewed it slowly before answering. "Elkanah didn't marry me because he needed someone to carry water." Again she paused for a nibble. "You carried water just fine before I came, and you can do it now. What you *can't* do is obvious. That's why I'm here—to produce children for Elkanah."

If it happened once, maybe I could have pushed it aside. But day after day she told me I was valuable to Elkanah only as a servant, and I should be glad of that. I considered telling Elkanah about this new twist of events, but rejected the idea as useless.

That's why I felt so surprised by the conversation between Elkanah and Peninnah a few weeks later. We'd just finished the evening meal. Peninnah asked to be excused from helping with the clean up because she felt tired.

"Besides, Elkanah, didn't you say you and I need to talk?" Peninnah excelled in finding ways to get Elkanah to herself.

Elkanah hesitated. "Will that be all right with you, Hannah?" he asked.

I nodded. What else could I do?

Before following Elkanah to the other side of the room, Peninnah raised her eyebrows triumphantly and smirked at me.

After they settled on the pillows in her private corner, I overheard Elkanah say, "Peninnah, I know you don't always feel well, but I think you need to try to get up and around a bit, maybe help more around the house."

I couldn't believe my ears! I slowed my work pace, taking great care as I handled the bowls and pans, forcing them into silence as my ears strained to hear.

"Has that lazy Hannah complained to you again?" From behind the shelf, I saw her fling an angry glare in my direction. "She's so jealous! Don't listen to her. Besides," Peninnah wore a pitiful pout as she put her hand significantly on her stomach, "she knows nothing of how it feels to carry a child! Why should you care what she says?"

"Hannah hasn't told me anything."

"Well then, who's the know-it-all who condemns me?"

"No one's condemning you, Peninnah," Elkanah sighed and shifted. Tasting a dab of Peninnah's skill at twisting words made him uneasy, too. He pressed his lips together.

Peninnah didn't miss the cue. "Oh my," she cooed as she caressed his cheek. "Were you talking to your mother?"

His shoulders relaxed, and he covered her hand with his own. I couldn't help but admire her wisdom in knowing when to stop pushing Elkanah, how to back off. I didn't always benefit myself by exercising such self-control.

She laughed lightly to further ease the tension. Dramatically, she lowered her eyes and gently rubbed her stomach. "I'm probably too worried—especially after the first one. I'm just taking care of myself, *and* your precious baby. I don't want to do anything to ruin our good fortune!" She took his hand and placed it on her abdomen, sighing contentedly.

The confrontation ended. Peninnah probably thought she'd won because Elkanah said no more about helping around the house, but later I discovered things she didn't know.

That night Elkanah slept in my bed. We snuggled together, enjoying the quiet closeness with only the sounds of the night as music. My head rested on Elkanah's shoulder, and I softly touched the hair on his chest, thinking about his conversation with Peninnah.

"What does Peninnah do when I'm not here?"

Had he read my mind? It seemed impossible that after four, almost five months, Elkanah offered me the chance to be honest. My heart beat faster, and my mouth felt dry. Would he believe me? Should I tell him the truth? If I did, I may not be able to live with Peninnah. But if I didn't, I'd never be able to live with myself.

"She cleans up her own mat. She used to get water from the well, but she's afraid carrying water might make her lose the baby. When you come home, she puts the food on the table."

"That's *all*?"

I nodded.

I felt his shoulder muscle tense. Then he ran his fingers through his hair. In the dim lamplight I saw his jaw stiffen twice. His lips pressed together. It seemed forever before he spoke, and during that time I told myself five hundred times what a fool I'd been.

"Why didn't I know this?" Elkanah asked. "My mother doesn't even live here, and she had to inform me." He turned toward me and wrapped me in his arms. "I'm sorry, Hannah." He sighed again. "I'll do what I can to improve the situation."

"It's not so bad," I said. I spoke the truth. Peninnah's lack of helpfulness didn't seem so bad–if at the end of the day I could sleep in my husband's arms.

For the first time in my life I fell asleep thanking God for my mother-in-law.

". . . and the other Peninnah."
1 Samuel 1:2 NIV

CHAPTER
13
Disloyalty

The next morning Elkanah informed Peninnah that she wouldn't need to carry water, but he expected her to help with other chores. I returned from the well curious as to how much Peninnah would have done. I was surprised to see she'd removed all the weed seeds and stones from the wheat and had nearly finished grinding it. That was only the beginning. For the first time since she married Elkanah, I believed her father's claims concerning her housekeeping abilities.

But changes for the better in her helpfulness failed to equal changes for the worse in her attitude toward me. She accused me of trying to turn Elkanah against her. She claimed my jealousy drove me to revenge. She'd lost her first child because of my haughty attitude, and now I forced her to work, plotting to make her lose this child as well. My evil heart hated anyone who enjoyed benefits I coveted, and I deserved to be punished by God for my wickedness.

I didn't attempt to argue. I felt sure she wouldn't let me say anything, and that if I did speak, she'd refuse to listen. A part of me knew what she said was totally false–except for the part about being jealous. I must confess: that was true. If I could, I would have gladly made her the barren one and me the one growing with child. Even though in my mind I believed her accusations were untrue, only part of her scheme to make me miserable, hearing them over and over made my shoulders tense and my head hurt.

Her hateful words also revived self-condemning thoughts I'd nurtured in my time of sadness. So, even though I no longer permitted self-hatred to over-power me, her words yanked those thoughts back to life, continually inciting them to fight for leadership in my mind.

After enduring her accusations all day, I can hardly describe the relief I felt that night when Elkanah finally arrived, and suddenly Peninnah became peaceful and doting. Although Peninnah had helped to do much of the work, I felt more exhausted than ever.

"How did things go today?" Elkanah asked as he spread fig paste on his bread.

"Fine," Peninnah said with pride. "Right, Hannah? Tell Elkanah what a good worker I was."

"Peninnah is excellent at grinding wheat and making bread. And cleaning, too," I agreed.

Elkanah smiled, thinking all the problems solved. But of course, he didn't know Peninnah's lack of helpfulness posed only a small problem compared to the cruelty I'd endured.

Elkanah's joy ended quickly. Just a short while after our meal, Peninnah decided she didn't feel well and needed to go to bed. The next day Peninnah spent most of her time complaining about her tiredness and claiming I would be glad if she and the child died. That night she moved with great effort and went to bed early, saying all the work she did the previous day had left her tired and weak.

The next morning I wasn't surprised when she refused to get up. How could I know if her sickness were real or not? Convinced she excelled at deception, I found it difficult to trust her about anything, especially when her behavior seemed to be getting her what she may not have gotten another way. Elkanah's assessment of her condition never convinced me either. Obviously he'd become less gullible than at first, but still I'd watched him fall into her traps too often to have any confidence in his objective evaluation. This time Elkanah also seemed unsure as to how to respond, but his desire for a son outweighed any other. So, we soon fell back to the way we functioned before, Peninnah doing as she pleased and me doing all the work.

But, really, it wasn't the same, because Peninnah never forgot accusations against her. Although Elkanah finally outright told her his mother had reported her laziness (not the word he used, of course), Peninnah continued to see me as the accuser. And Peninnah refused to sit back after an offense.

One morning Timara and I walked home from the well together. Ever since she offered me her idol, I felt uneasy around her. Whenever I saw her carrying her darling chubby-cheeked son, I remembered she believed him to be a gift from Ashtoreth. He rode tied close to his mother's heart that day, his wide eyes searching for new things to see. As we left sight of the women at the well, Timara shifted the sling holding her child and spoke up.

"Why do you let Peninnah rule your house? The Hannah I knew as a girl was strong and confident. I would never have believed you could be such a weakling!"

My face flushed. "Whose been talking about me and Peninnah?" I asked. It hadn't been me.

"Who? Who else but Peninnah herself! Now don't get me wrong, Hannah. I know you and I don't agree on everything, but I would stand up for you any day. Besides, I just can't sit back and let that Shiloh girl take advantage of one of us! She's trying to turn the whole town against you!"

"What do you mean?"

"She claims you caused her to lose her child, and as a result, Elkanah punishes you by making you do all the work."

Then I recalled seeing unfriendly looks from some of the women and hearing confusing statements over the past months. "How long has this been going on?" I asked.

"Since the very beginning! Why do you think Peninnah wanted to carry the water? Not because she wanted the exercise! When one talks at the well, every house in Ramah hears the story by evening."

I sighed. It made sense. Yet I hadn't noticed because, coping with the problems standing directly in my face left me little time or energy to focus on things farther away. One thing, however, didn't make sense. Surely my mother-in-law had also heard these rumors. I never felt like she liked me much, so why hadn't she condemned me, even after hearing Peninnah's stories? Instead, she'd confronted Elkanah about Peninnah's laziness. There was too much I couldn't understand.

I sighed again. This time Timara laughed. I laughed, too. It felt good to laugh together even if I didn't have one single idea of how to stop the problem.

"Well," Timara insisted, "what are you going to do?"

I shrugged. "What can I? People will believe what they want."

Timara nodded, "But there *is* a way you could distract their attention from Peninnah and all her lies."

"Yes?"

Timara eyed me carefully, and then slowly and softly she caressed her baby's straight brown hair. He cooed responsively.

"Oh, Timara!" I said in dismay. "You know I can't pray to Ashtoreth! I'll always remain loyal to the Holy One of Israel."

"But you don't have to *stop* worshipping Yaweh. I take part in the feasts and give offerings at Shiloh—when we go. In fact, it was at Shiloh, at the House of the Lord, that I first heard that it's acceptable to worship as many gods as you want. Go with what works, you know."

I frowned. "Who told you that?"

"The priests."

"Priests of the God of Israel?"

"Yes."

"Are you sure?"

"Hannah! I'm not stupid! Priests wear special clothes. They're the ones who take your animals for sacrifice." Timara laughed. "Do you think I'm some kind of pagan? My husband may not be of the tribe of Levi, and we don't attend the Passover celebration every year, but we *are* Israelites. I certainly know a priest of Yaweh when I see one."

I smiled, but heaviness crushed my heart. "Did the old priest Eli tell you it's all right to worship other gods?"

Timara shook her head. "Oh no. I doubt that old-fashioned white-beard would approve. But his sons lead this reform. I believe their names are Hophni and Phinehas." Timara smiled, a twinkle glinting in her eye. "I could tell you some amazing tales of what they do—right in the House of the Lord, under the nose of their old father. But obviously, you'd never believe me."

As we neared home, Timara's little fellow began whining and pulling at his mother's clothes, telling her in no uncertain terms that he wanted to be fed. So we said our good-byes and went our separate ways. All day my thoughts spun in chaotic turmoil—not about Peninnah spreading lies. That failed to amaze me. But concerning what Timara told me about the priests at the Tabernacle. I searched my memory for any recollection of something I may have seen or heard there that would substantiate Timara's claims. But whenever I 'd gone to the Tabernacle, accompanied either with my father or my husband, I'd allowed myself the freedom of being swept up in the beauty of the music, the ceremonies, and the awesomeness of being so close to the Holy Place of God's Presence. I'd cared little about focusing my attention on anything else. Perhaps Elkanah knew more.

That night I could hardly wait to be with Elkanah in my little room. "Elkanah, do you know anything about the two sons of Eli, the high priest in Shiloh?"

Elkanah stopped rubbing oil on the wood of his harp. He looked up, a frown on his face. "Yes, I know them. Hophni and Phinehas. Why do you ask?"

"Timara says they're not as loyal to the God of Israel as their father Eli."

Elkanah nodded. "That's true," he said, polishing the harp with a soft cloth.

"Timara says they tell people who come to the Tabernacle that it is all right to sacrifice to other gods, in addition to Yaweh."

Elkanah sighed. After a few more rubs, he set his instrument against the wall safely out of the way and motioned toward the corner where I'd rolled out my mat in hopes that Elkanah would join me that night. As we prepared for bed, Elkanah said nothing, but I knew he was thinking about what to tell me. Elkanah was careful in choosing his words, not impulsive like me.

Finally, when we lay snuggled together under our cover, Elkanah drew a deep breath and began. "Things are not as they should be at the House of the Lord. I haven't heard either Hophni or Phinehas say exactly those words. But considering what I know about them, I have no reason to doubt that what Timara says is true."

"But Elkanah, how could that be?" My neck got hot, my throat tight. "They're priests of the Most High God!"

Elkanah reached over and put his arm around me. "Shhh, Hannah. No need to talk so loudly. I'm laying right here." His voice smiled. "I understand why you're upset," his voice returned to its serious tone. "I've been disturbed, too, by the growing number of Israelites who no longer take their relationship with God seriously."

"But I'm not talking about something like neglecting the Sabbath or some required offering. I'm talking about worshipping the idols of the Canaanites!"

"I know. I know, Hannah." He sighed. "People everywhere are becoming more and more willing to pray to foreign gods, right here in Ramah, and probably in every village in Israel."

"But Elkanah, I can understand about the *people*. That's bad enough." The incident with Timara popped up in my mind, but I pushed it back down. Elkanah didn't need to know about that. "But I can't understand how the *priests* could become so corrupt! No wonder the people aren't loyal to God if the priests themselves disobey the Lord's commands."

Elkanah nodded. "I've been concerned about this for a long time now, Hannah. A long time. Way before we married I saw problems at the Tabernacle and wondered what I could do to help. That's when I made my vow to the Lord. I promised I would serve every Passover at Shiloh and do everything I could to enhance the worship music year around. That's the reason I'm so diligent in my composition and practicing, why I spend so much time training other Levites, encouraging them to do their part. I also promised to lead my family in the worship of the One True God." Elkanah sighed. "I know it's not much, Hannah, but it's all we can do."

The conversation ended, but I never forgot the peculiar pain I felt that day. Time and again it sprang up, and I recognized it. A strange ache in my chest, like tears trapped inside unable to get out–tears crushing my heart. Uncommon tears. Not tears of grief for myself, but an aching sadness for the God I'd come to love and know, for the God who'd rescued me from the dungeon of darkness and despair, for the God Who longs for people to know Him and respond to His love.

"Now the sons of Eli were scoundrels
who had no respect for the LORD
or for their duties as priests."
1 Samuel 2:12-13 NLT

CHAPTER

14

Discovery

That Passover only Elkanah and I went to Shiloh. Peninnah wept and begged to go with us. She wanted to visit her family, and she'd be fine, she said. But Elkanah refused. I always wondered if she staged the disappointment drama for added attention, or if she truly felt that devastated. Because if she really were that heartbroken, and if she'd exaggerated her weakness as much as I suspected she did, she got full payment for her deception. After several months of Peninnah claiming to be sick and too weak to help around the house, Elkanah declared a whole day of walking to be completely out of the question. That's how I got my husband to myself–without Peninnah anywhere around–for sixteen whole days.

Our trip to Shiloh rated as the best ever–even better than before Peninnah–because this time, my excitement about having Elkanah to myself and relief from Peninnah's harassment, kept me from dwelling on my barrenness. In addition to relishing my time with Elkanah, as always, I enjoyed staying with my Shiloh relatives, both while Elkanah worked at the House of the Lord and in the evenings when he returned. Even our two dinners at the home of Peninnah's family went as well as could be expected. In some ways, from the personal perspective, that trip seemed like heaven to me—especially when I compare it to the years that followed.

But what we witnessed that year at the Tabernacle transformed it into a tragedy.

Three nights after our arrival, Elkanah returned from the House of the Lord, strangely sad and thoughtful. Uncle found it difficult to get Elkanah to enter into conversation at the evening meal as he normally did. I think my uncle and aunt felt as relieved as I did when the meal ended and Elkanah asked if we could be excused to go on a walk.

"What's wrong?" I asked him as soon as we stepped out into the chill of the night.

In the moonlight I saw him clench his jaw. Finally he spoke. "Remember what you asked me a while back about Hophni and Phinehas?"

"Yes." I'd wondered if that could be what upset him.

"Well, I saw something today I wish I'd never seen," Elkanah said, his voice sounding weary. We walked along in silence with only the crunching of rocks beneath our feet and the laughter from a house down the way drifting through the night air.

"Early today a man from up north came into the House of the Lord to offer a sacrifice. The priest had just finished draining the blood from his lamb when I happened to walk by on my way to find another cymbal. 'Wait!' I heard the man cry. The desperation in his voice stopped me. 'What are you doing?' he demanded as he reached out and grasped the slaughtered lamb that one of the servants had taken from the hands of the priest. 'I'm taking this for Hophni and Phinehas,' the servant said roughly as he shook the man's hand from the meat. 'It's their right as servants of the Lord.' The man nodded. 'But first you must put my sacrifice in the pot and boil out the fat as an offering to Yaweh. *Then,*' he continued, 'you can use the fork to remove a portion—just as our custom permits.' The servant scowled. 'The priests like their meat *roasted*, not boiled.' As he started to leave, he turned and called back, '*And*, if you don't like it, I've been instructed to send someone in to take care of you.'"

We didn't talk much about the incident. What could we say? But it hurt my heart. The next morning as I stood praying in the House of the Lord, I felt terrible, realizing that right where I stood, the priests honored themselves above the Almighty, flagrantly disregarding specific instructions as to how sacrifices should be done, in order to accommodate their personal preferences.

One day later in the week as I was leaving the House of Lord, I halted in surprise at the sound of women laughing boisterously. Turning, I saw four women, Tabernacle helpers, swaying with laughter, like they were drunk. "If Hophni and Phinehas have their way," one snorted, "the male and female prostitutes in the Canaanite temples will lose their business!" One began dancing seductively, and another reached over and yanked at the dancer's dress, exposing bare flesh. "Ooooh!" the dancing woman cried, grabbing at her clothing in mocking modesty. The others roared. Then one of their companions noticed me and nodded in my direction. Their clamor died down, but impudence stained their faces. A cold uneasiness gripped me.

"What they said, Elkanah, what did it mean?" I asked him that night.

He took a slow deep breath. "I didn't want to tell you, Hannah," he said, sadness in his voice. "But I guess you have a right to know. It's become common knowledge that Hophni and Phinehas sleep with the women who help at the Tabernacle. Right there, in the House of the Lord."

I gasped, unable to believe what I heard. "But . . . but

that's as bad as what happens at the pagan temples." My chin trembled, and I felt like I would cry. "Why doesn't anyone stop them?"

Elkanah reached out and put his arm around me. "Hophni and Phinehas have authority in the Tabernacle. It's difficult to oppose them. Besides Hannah, you'd be surprised at how many Israelites favor these changes. They claim the old ways are boring compared to what the Cannanites offer. The only way to keep the Israelites loyal to their own religion, they say, is to make the worship of Yaweh as exciting as visiting pagan temples. That includes incorporating sexual acts as part of the worship of Yaweh."

The shock of that revelation remained with me throughout the following year, opening my eyes to things I'd never noticed. Perhaps I'd been too preoccupied with my own difficulties. Even when I'd seen things, like Timara's offer and others in the marketplace, I'd assumed people were more open around me than usual because they knew I was desperate. But that year I began to notice how drastically devotion to Yaweh had dwindled, even in Ramah. People enthusiastically embraced the ungodly traditions of the people around us, in many ways. Lots of the Levites, even some of our own relatives, now refused to serve the required two weeks at the Tabernacle. Hardly anyone seemed to take the laws of God seriously.

But, in spite of my concern for the conditions in Israel, my problems with Peninnah overshadowed everything else. That year Peninnah made Elkanah a father. I thought I'd prepared myself for the inevitable challenges, but theory is much different than fact. Amazingly though, my greatest difficulty arose neither from watching Peninnah with her baby nor from witnessing Elkanah's delight in his son, a child that wasn't mine. My biggest trauma occurred the following Passover at Shiloh and took me completely by surprise.

"The priests on duty at that time
were the two sons of Eli-Hophni and Phinehas. . .
Now the sons of Eli were evil men
who didn't love the Lord.
It was their regular practice to send out a servant
whenever anyone was offering a sacrifice,
and while the flesh
of the sacrificed animal was boiling,
the servant would put a three-pronged fleshhook
into the pot
and demand that whatever it brought up
be given to Eli's sons.
They treated all of the Israelites in this way
when they came to Shiloh to worship.
Sometimes the servant would come
even before the rite of burning the fat on the altar
had been performed,
and he would demand raw meat before it was boiled,
so that it could be used for roasting.
If the man offering the sacrifice replied,
'Take as much as you want,
but the fat must first be burned'
[as the law requires],
then the servant would say,
'No, give it to me now or I'll take it by force.'
So the sin of these young men
was very great in the eyes of the Lord;
for they treated the people's offerings to the Lord
with contempt."
1 Samuel 1:3 and 2:12-17 TLB

"Now Eli, who was very old,
heard about everything his sons were doing to all Israel
and how they slept with the women
who served at the entrance to the Tent of Meeting.
So he said to them,
'Why do you do such things?
I hear from all the people
about these wicked deeds of yours.
No, my sons;
it is not a good report that I hear
spreading among the LORD's people.
If a man sins against another man,
God may mediate for him;
but if a man sins against the LORD,
who will intercede for him?'
His sons, however,
did not listen to their father's rebuke . . ."
1 Samuel 2:22-25 NIV

CHAPTER

15

The Final Blow

That year Elkanah insisted on all of us staying with Peninnah's family, which drastically changed my Shiloh experience. I'd always looked forward to spending time with my mother's sister while Elkanah worked at the House of the Lord. Instead, I found myself stuck with strangers and nothing to do. Not that I didn't offer to help, but Peninnah's mother refused. So I sat all day listening to Peninnah and her sisters-in-law brag about their children. I never felt so sick of hearing anyone thanking God!

"The Lord has blessed us greatly," Peninnah's mother said over and over. "See," her arm rotating in a wide arch across the screaming children running about the courtyard. "The abundant blessing the Lord gives to those He favors."

All the women joined in, nodding and smiling with pride, each adding her gratitude, until one of them would notice me sitting there cringing in a corner, wishing I could be somewhere else, anywhere else but there.

"We shouldn't be talking like this in front of poor Hannah," one would reprimand the others. (I hated how they called me "poor.")

"How rude of us," another would answer.

"But how can we keep from being grateful for God's blessing on our family?" said the next, and so they returned to their favorite topic.

Every night I begged Elkanah to let me stay with my mother's relatives on the other side of Shiloh, but he wanted all his family together at this special time. He allowed me to visit them twice, but more than that would insult Peninnah's family and stir up needless animosity, he said. I didn't really care about animosity—as long as I could get away. Far away! Instead, I sat in torment day after day, just thinking about my barrenness for whole two weeks.

No one criticized me directly. Maybe that would have been better, better than the false sorrow, the syrupy pity, the irritating encouragement to keep having hope. On top of that, Peninnah obviously delighted in my discomfort, bragging in my presence that with Elkanah as her husband, she couldn't keep from becoming pregnant. Who could contradict her? Year after year, she bore Elkanah another child.

After that first year, it always happened. On every trip to Shiloh I ended up crying, hiding in corners by night and day. Elkanah tried to comfort me, but nothing soothed my misery. I became so sick at heart, I couldn't force myself to eat.

"Hannah, why are you weeping? Why don't you eat? Why are you so downhearted?" Elkanah asked the questions year after year. "I love you, Hannah!" he assured me again and again. "Don't I mean more to you than ten sons?"

I tried to swallow my grief. I tried to occupy my mind with other things. I tried to believe what Elkanah said, that my barrenness didn't matter, that only our love for each other really mattered. In my head, I could almost believe him at times, but in my heart, the horrible emptiness remained.

Questions crowded back into my mind. Was there some hidden sin in my life that made me unworthy of God's blessing? Why would God willingly give sons and daughters to so many other women, and not to me? Over the years I started anticipating the misery awaiting me in Shiloh. Finally, as my dread grew, I began losing my appetite weeks, then months, before our trip.

One year, the tenth year of my marriage, the pain reached it climax. Elkanah became concerned for my health, constantly encouraging me to eat more. But eating rated as a loathsome task, something I forced myself to do.

"Here, have some bread, Hannah. How will you have strength for the trip if you don't eat?" Elkanah asked.

Perhaps I didn't want to have the strength to walk toward Shiloh. Maybe I hoped that if I became sick enough, Elkanah would allow me to stay home. I don't know. I only know that the thought of that trip filled me with dread—and Peninnah and all her little ones with delight.

On the day we left, excitement stirred in our courtyard like energy prior to a storm. Before the sun rose we started off, traveling along with others going to Shiloh. The three older children scampered with excitement and hardly seemed tired when we reached our first stop. Wearily, I sank down to rest. We ate a breakfast of dried fruit and bread with freshly churned butter. I'd milked before dawn, and Elkanah slung the goatskin over his shoulder. By the time we stopped, the rich milk had separated into creamy butter and buttermilk. Everyone ate and drank willingly, while being careful not to get overly full. Everyone ate, that is, but me. I picked at a small piece of bread and forced myself to drink a few swallows of the buttermilk, but I felt as if my stomach would throw back anything I ate.

Too soon Elkanah called us to the road. I plodded along with the rest, dreading what awaited me at the end of the journey. The three older children danced around us while Peninnah carried the baby tied to her, and Elkanah took turns carrying the two smaller ones when they grew weary. When the excitement of the journey wore off, Elkanah called to the children, "Come, walk here beside me, and I'll tell you a story."

"A story! A story!" cried Jemima clapping her hands, her tiredness of the moment before now long forgotten.

"I get to pick," declared Elihu, "because I'm the oldest."

Elkanah smiled. "What story do you want?"

"Joseph! Joseph with the pretty coat."

So the story began. Elkanah elaborated on Joseph's long trip to Egypt, making sure the children realized how the difficulty of Joseph's journey greatly surpassed theirs. Elkanah used the story as a source of incentive for the children to be brave and not complain, even when their feet became tired and their heads hot.

"See. Feel my head," Giddel, Peninnah's second, said. "Is mine as hot as Joseph's?"

Elkanah laid his hand on his head. "Oh my, that *is* hot! But remember, Joseph walked through a hot, hot desert, and we have nice hills that will soon be covered with lovely green grass."

"And flowers!" cried Jemima, the third born.

We trudged along. My mind resisted being charmed by Elkanah's stories. Again, for the millionth time, I noticed the importance of children to this celebration. I didn't begrudge the children the attention they received. I just wished I had at least one child who could be a part of Elkanah's dancing clan. We stopped for lunch just after Joseph got thrown in prison because Potiphar's wife lied about him.

"What did Joseph eat in the prison?" Elihu asked after stuffing his mouth with bread.

"Elihu!" Peninnah reprimanded. "Mind your manners!"

After an exaggerated swallow he continued. "Well, did he have fig cakes like ours?" Elihu had fastened his eyes on the fig cakes as soon as his mother placed them on the cloth.

Elkanah laughed. "No, I think not. Most likely he had only old bread and water. Prison's not a nice place, you know."

"Then I don't want to be in prison," Giddel declared. "I like Hannah's fig cakes."

Elkanah smiled at me. "I do, too."

A bit farther down the road Joseph interpreted the Pharaoh's dreams—the one about the seven skinny cows coming out of the Nile River and eating the seven fat cows who came out before them. Then the seven skinny heads of grain that ate the seven fat heads. "But the seven skinny cows and the seven skinny heads of grain still stayed skinny."

"Hannah's skinny," Jemima observed, "But she doesn't eat that much."

Elkanah ignored the comment and went on with the story. But I saw Peninnah smile, and I lowered my eyes. How I wished my flat barrenness would disappear, that I would grow round and alive with life. Tears gathered in my eyes, but I swallowed them away, and tried to focus on Elkanah's story.

Just as we entered Shiloh, Elkanah reached the ending of his tale. It always amazed me how he could make one story last half a day. It did make the trip more pleasant and bearable, not only for the children, but for all of us.

"So, what do we learn from our ancestor Joseph?" he asked.

"Eat all your bread, and be thankful for your cake," Jemima said.

"Don't cry when your feet hurt on long, long trips," said Giddel.

"Be good to your younger brothers," said Elihu solemnly.

"And sisters!" added Jemima.

"Good!" encouraged Elkanah. "You listened well! One other important lesson to remember is this: no matter what happens, always remember that the Lord God of Israel has a good plan for your life. Sometimes we must go through very difficult times, just like Joseph did. But remember, God took the bad things people did to Joseph and used them to do something good in Joseph's life. So we, too, must always trust in God, like Joseph did."

I'm sure the children lost the impact of those words, because by then they'd become intrigued with the distant view of Shiloh on the hill before them, and just like a donkey getting close to home, they walked faster and faster. In spite of my reluctance, I couldn't lag behind.

The week began and progressed as in the past. We worshipped together during the feast, offering our sacrifices to the Lord. Every year Elkanah gave Peninnah and each of her children a portion of meat, but to me he always gave a double portion. Because he loved me, he said. But I always wondered if he hoped the Lord would notice my special gift, have mercy and give me a baby. I appreciated Elkanah's kindness and enjoyed these times of worship, but, even then, I could never quite chase the agony from my heart, because, in spite of everything we did, the Lord never gave me a child.

Very quickly the same old patterns repeated themselves. I wasn't allowed to help around the house with the other women. I felt excluded from their conversations that centered on family and friends I didn't know. Worst of all, I hated the constant bragging about their children. Peninnah and her sisters-in-law compared stories and complimented one another on their new babies.

"With our last little one, we rank as the largest family in Shiloh," Peninnah's mother said with undisguised pride. "Of course that's not counting any of *Peninnah's* children."

"And she's outdone us all," a sister-in-law added in her high nasal voice.

They all nodded and congratulated Peninnah for being so greatly blessed by God.

"Some people accused your father of boasting foolishly when he promised Elkanah you would be a fertile wife," Peninnah's mother said.

"He should've asked for a higher bride price," another added.

They laughed in chorus.

"I can't take all the credit," Peninnah said. "Married to Elkanah, any woman would stay pregnant!" Then she turned to face me. Her eyes widened and she clapped her hand over her mouth as if in horror. "Oh Hannah, I really shouldn't have said it that way, should I? Oh well, you understand what I meant." Her eyes laughed at me.

"Peninnah just gets carried away complimenting her fine husband," her mother said.

I knew Peninnah said exactly what she meant to say. In spite of all I did to chase them away, her words ate away at my heart all day long. The ache of compressed tears built up until I thought another word about babies and children would make me burst.

That night I couldn't eat. I felt Elkanah's eyes on me during the meal; I sensed his concern. But I refused to look up. I knew that even if he did everything in his power, he couldn't alleviate my torment. Nothing could do that. I'd tried for years now, sometimes more successfully than others, to deal with the problem of my barrenness, to find a purpose for my life. But on this day, all my efforts, all my growth, all I'd learned, seemed totally in vain.

"Listen everyone!" Peninnah called out joyfully at the end of the meal. "Listen!" She clapped her hands for attention, and the groups of talking men, women, and even the children quieted. Her cheeks flushed and her eyes sparkled with a lively intensity that produced its own kind of charm. But I didn't trust her. That flare of energy, in my mind, portended some attempt to gain power at my expense. I waited, hardly able to breathe. "I have an important announcement to make! Before you see us again next year, I'll present Elkanah with *another* child." She glowed with delight. "Seven children, seven years in a row!"

The room exploded into a roar of pleasure. Men surrounded Elkanah, thumping his back, shouting their approval. Women clustered around Peninnah, weeping with joy. The children hopped and yelled in imitation of their elders. I sat immobile in stunned silence. A great ache began swelling low in my abdomen, in the sad emptiness of my womb. The sounds of joy pressed in on me, crushing me, making it impossible to breathe.

I had to get out, to get some fresh air. With my last drop of energy, I forced myself to my feet. I paused to steady my swaying body, to wait until the darkness faded. Silently, slowly, I shuffled toward the door. Everyone in the room remained too involved in their celebration to notice one silent woman slipping from the room, everyone but Peninnah. As I past the group of women, her eyes followed me and, against my will, pulled my eyes to hers. The pleasure I saw, Jerusha, was not the joy of motherhood, but the naked glee of a woman who'd dealt a fatal blow to her greatest enemy.

"Peninnah had children,
but Hannah had no children.
This man went up from his city yearly to worship
and sacrifice to the LORD of hosts in Shiloh. . . .
And whenever the time came
for Elkanah to make an offering,
he would give portions to Peninnah his wife
and to all her sons and daughters.
But to Hannah he would give a double portion,
for he loved Hannah,
although the LORD had closed her womb.
And her rival also provoked her severely,
to make her miserable,
because the LORD had closed her womb.
So it was, year by year,
when she went up to the house of the LORD,
that she provoked her;
therefore she wept and did not eat."
1 Samuel 1:2-8 NKJV

CHAPTER

16

Revelation

Hannah paused, reaching for the small clay cup of water at her side. In the silent, Jerusha glanced up. Again she felt amazed at the peacefulness of Hannah's expression. She remembered how, in the early days in their household, that look led her to assume that Joel's grandmother had enjoyed a life of pure bliss, a life without significant suffering. Nothing could be farther from the truth! Jerusha returned her gaze to the thread she twisted. Could she also be wrong in believing that pain deforms a person, robbing them of their freedom to be themselves, making them unable to give and receive love? At times she felt like that. Defective. Broken. Hadn't her mother's death damaged all of them? Not just her, but Father and Dov, too. As Jerusha reached for another bundle of wool, Hannah interrupted her thoughts.

"Those days were bad days for me, Jerusha. Some of the worst of my life. But life gives every person their unique set of difficulties–pains, fears, challenges." She smiled at Jerusha and took another stitch on the embroidery she'd been working on for nearly a month, an arrangement of small field flowers dancing in every direction, free without disorder, vibrant with joy and life.

Over the past weeks Jerusha had watched in amazement as Hannah brought beauty from what had begun in frantic disarray. Was it possible that Jerusha's life, a life begun in chaos, could also develop into something of beauty? Obviously Hannah's life had. Somehow. It seemed strange to Jerusha that in hearing of Hannah's suffering, her own hope and courage grew. If Hannah had come through her pain with the help of the Lord, couldn't she? As Hannah bared her heart, the desire had grown in Jerusha, not only to see the hidden Hannah, but to let Hannah see into the private places of her life as well.

"My fear is almost opposite of yours," Jerusha confessed. Cautiously, she lifted her eyes from her work and met Hannah's. "You feared not having a child, and I . . ." Jerusha lowered her gaze. "I . . . I'm afraid to have one." Jerusha swallowed, fearful that she would not be able to make herself speak again. But Hannah waited, totally still, until Jerusha finally found the words to go on. "Every month . . . every month I pray that . . . I won't be pregnant." Her voice fell low, almost inaudible, and her head bowed in shame. "Isn't that a terrible prayer?"

Hannah rubbed her fingers lightly over the tiny stitches she'd made so painstakingly, but she didn't see them. *Help me say the right thing,* she asked before speaking. "What we pray, Jerusha, often reflects the pain in our lives. I think the Almighty One understands that."

"Do you really think so? I thought no one would understand how I could be so untrue to my husband, so untrue to my calling as a woman and a wife." A tear slid silently down Jerusha's cheek and dropped into the wool on her lap.

"Why are you so afraid of having a child, if I may ask?"

"What if . . . I were to die, . . . like my mother?"

Hannah nodded. "Many women share your fear."

Jerusha shook her head. "It's not death I fear." She bit her lip. "What if I died and my baby grew up like me . . . never having a place to belong? Unwanted. Unloved." Her shoulders shook as tears flowed in earnest.

Hannah reached out and laid her hand softly on Jerusha's shoulder. In silence she waited, waited for the tears to subside, waited until Jerusha spoke. Piece by piece Jerusha unfolded her story of sorrow, and Hannah gladly took her turn to listen.

"After I moved in with my father, things got worse than I imagined, just like with you and Peninnah. But in our house, *I* caused all the problems. At my uncle's, when my aunt gave me jobs to do, my older cousin, Rivka, kept her eye on me, making sure I did as I was instructed. But when I moved to my father's house, they expected me to handle everything perfectly on my own." Jerusha smiled ruefully. "I'm afraid I didn't do a very good job."

"Handling four small children is no easy task, even for a grown woman," Hannah said. "I'm not surprised a seven-year-old would find it difficult."

"From the very beginning I continually got into trouble. Once while I tended the baby, the toddler grabbed a hot coal. While I amused the younger ones, the two older boys ran off and hid from me. On top of that, my stepmother seemed to hate me. She reported all my failures to my father, and appeared to take delight in his anger at me." Jerusha looked up, sadness in her eyes. "The fact that my father freely showed his affection for Dov only made it worse. Unlike me, Dov could do no wrong. . . ."

Jerusha's carding blocks lay inactive as she tightly gripped the long fingers of one hand with the other, remembering days not so very long ago.

* * * * *

Dov stared at Jerusha. The sight of her made him sick. First the sickness had been from sadness and loss, later from hatred. She'd robbed him of the greatest treasures of his life—the loving embrace of his gentle mother and the laughing playfulness of his father. Dov could hardly remember those days now, days before Jerusha, when his mother kissed and held him, and fed him treats. When his father took him on long hikes, carrying him on his shoulders when he got tired. Tickling his tummy. Laughing. And other times, he'd chased him around the courtyard, lumbering and growling like a great bear. Jerusha had ripped his childhood from him, and he would never forgive her for that. Never.

"I hate you," he snarled nearly every day after she'd moved into their house. "I never wanted you to live here!" He tried to make his eyes pierce like the swords he'd heard about, but never seen—the sharp, iron swords of the ferocious Philistines. He wanted to frighten her, to make her life as miserable as she'd made his. "If it weren't for that lazy stepmother belly-aching about too much work, you *never* would have set foot in this house." He hated her, too—his stepmother—almost as much as he hated Jerusha. But his father's wife wasn't as easy to attack as his younger sister. "You're a bad omen, bringing suffering to anyone you touch! Stay away from me! Stay away from my father! Touch her children if you must, but keep your evil influence out of my life!"

So Jerusha kept her distance. Dov's words struck terror in her heart. Cold and deep. Her brother believed she brought disaster. Was it true? She looked back over her life. First her mother, of course. Then at Uncle Ham's. Right after he brought her home, a mere infant, the sheep developed a disease. More than half died. A terrible setback. She'd heard that story many times. A year later Rivka got a sickness that lasted for months. Once, immediately following her return from visiting her father's home, Ethan broke his arm. Then after she moved in with her father, her stepmother's tiredness grew worse instead of better. "And we thought the girl's coming would bring relief," they said. That had been only the beginning of a long trail of problems that Dov often recounted for her. Could he be right? Did her presence draw evil?

Just as Jerusha began to be convinced of Dov's verdict, Aunt Elsa with her husband and children came for a visit.

"I'm glad Jerusha doesn't live with us!" Elsa's boy, now ten, said to his mother on the second day of their visit.

"Why?" Aunt Elsa paused in shelling beans and turned toward her son. Jerusha, who sat working with her, felt her cheeks burn. She lowered her gaze, but listened carefully.

"Because bad things happen wherever she goes."

Jerusha cringed.

"Where'd you come up with that idea?" Aunt Elsa demanded.

"Dov says so," and Elsa's son began reciting the evidence his cousin had given him.

"Well, I hope he didn't get this idea from my foolish brother," Elsa mumbled. "Don't say that again. It's ridiculous!"

"But Dov . . . "

"He knows nothing." She sat up straight, placing her hand on her hip. "You think we didn't have trouble in this family before she was born? Pash! Of course we did! Bad things happen everywhere. You broke your arm, too. There was no Jerusha around to cause that." She bent back over her work. "Go play. And don't repeat foolish things."

After he left, Aunt Elsa glanced over at Jerusha, and her heart ached for the girl. There'd been many times over the years she'd felt guilty for not taking her. Not that she *could* have, but still . . . She reached over and patted Jerusha's shoulder. "Don't believe that nonsense, Jerusha. Boys! They're full of foolishness!" The tenderness in her voice brought tears to Jerusha's eyes, and she turned so her aunt wouldn't see.

Over the years Jerusha treasured Aunt Elsa's words, clinging to them like she'd clung desperately to the wagon that time she almost fell out. But, while Aunt Elsa's words helped her fight a false sense of responsibility, they did nothing to fill the empty hole in her heart. How she yearned to be wanted, important, valuable to someone! Especially her father. She'd finally given up the hope of love, but she still worked to gain his approval. But how could she, when her life seemed to be only a miserable chain of failures? She grew nervous, feeling destined to live day after day with constant rejection and criticism. She resolved to make herself as small and unnoticeable as possible.

But Joel had noticed her.

Jerusha would never forget that morning. What if she hadn't taken the risk and followed the crowd to the tower to listen to Samuel, the prophet judge? She'd almost gone home. She'd been told to come right back. But she'd heard so much about him, and what if this were her only opportunity to see the famous judge? After paying for her vegetables, she decided to wander over just close enough to see Samuel from a distance without getting trapped in the crowd. Then she could escape in plenty of time to prepare the evening meal.

Excitement fluttered in her chest as she stood on tiptoe. There he was, just as she'd heard him described, with his long hair pulled back in thick braids and his renowned beard: dark but marked with gray, curly, hanging way down past his waist.

"Never forget what the Lord did for you at Mizpah." Samuel's voice boomed with authority in spite of the distance between them. A shiver ran up her spine. "Victory came because of your repentance, children of Israel. Now, stay loyal to the Lord! Keep your hearts pure, and serve Him wholeheartedly. Or you can be *sure*. . . " Silence rang throughout the marketplace. ". . . you can be *sure*," he repeated. ". . . trouble *will* return!"

Samuel's words gripped Jerusha's heart, riveting her in place while everything round her faded. Fortunately, a man with a donkey squeezed by, breaking her concentration. Jerusha glanced up at the sun. With one last longing look at the great prophet, she turned to go.

That's when she saw him watching her. She dropped her gaze as warmth spread over her face. But this time, not from shame. For his eyes spoke anything but condemnation. Could it be? Had that handsome young man, silently—without word or movement—complimented her? How many times had she been told not to make eye contact with men? But she couldn't help herself. For just one moment, she looked at him again, and returned his smile. Then she hurried away. Her heart ran free, jumping, shouting with joy. She hoped desperately that her brother hadn't seen her. She'd noticed him at the market looking at sandals while she was choosing the onions.

Only moments after she arrived home Dov confronted her, backing her up against the garden wall. "I saw you—flirting with that man!" he hissed, his chest held high as he scowled down at her. "Don't you know who he is? The oldest son of Samuel! That's who!" The rotten smell of his breath hit with each burst of air on her face. "What makes you think you're good enough for his attention? You should know your place! You can be very certain I'll tell Father about this!"

Jerusha's chest tightened, and she tried to swallow the fear in her throat as she hurried into the house and began chopping the onions. She was glad for an excuse to let the tears flow. She hadn't meant to be evil, but she *had* looked. Twice. She couldn't deny the thrill of delight that fluttered through her heart at Joel's approving gaze, or the warmth that gathered in her cheeks. All day she waited in misery for what she would face that night.

But neither Dov nor Jerusha anticipated the turn of events. Neither guessed how quick and decisive Joel could be once he made up his mind. Joel had paid a boy to give him all the vital information—her name, her father's name, where her father worked, and where they lived. Then Joel insisted that his father meet with Timur that very afternoon and propose a marriage agreement.

Nor could either Dov or Jerusha ever guess the real reason behind Timur's quick consent. The sight of Jerusha growing into womanhood was like being repeatedly gored by a bull. Day after day—in the movements of her face, the smooth sway of her hips, in that characteristic tilt of her head, the sound of her voice and her very rare laughter—Jerusha reflected clearly a mother she never knew. Longing and anguish boiled into anger so great Timur frightened himself. So when Samuel offered a generous bride price, Timur grabbed the opportunity to push Jerusha far away where she could never again revive the memories of his past, where he wouldn't be tempted to crush her to extinguish his pain and desire.

His wife, Timur knew, would oppose his decision just as she had all the previous proposals made for Jerusha's engagement. She saw no reason to reclaim the responsibilities she'd dropped into Jerusha's lap. But had she known of Timur's turmoil, she would have immediately sent the girl away. As it was, Timur felt sure the bride price amounted to enough to quiet his wife for a while. And by then, Jerusha would be gone.

Their father's reaction to Dov's report of Jerusha's indecent conduct surprised both Dov and Jerusha. Totally ignoring Dov's accusation, Timur informed his family that the next day, Jerusha would be betrothed to Samuel's son, Joel.

"I refuse to listen to arguments from *anyone*," Timur said before they recovered from their shock. "How could I turn down such an extravagant bride price–much more than Jerusha's worth? Now Dov will have money for his betrothal, and we'll have plenty for ourselves as well. In fact . . . " A smile replaced the sternness on Timur's face. ". . . tomorrow, after the engagement is finalized, each of you may select a nice gift for yourselves at the market."

A dazed Jerusha watched the excitement of her family as they discussed what they would do with their unexpected wealth. Dov would get his sandals. And more. Not one of them, not even the little ones, seemed concerned about the girl who would exit their family. Many emotions flooded Jerusha's mind, leaving her bewildered: shame at being treated like an animal sold for a profit, anger at their lack of concern for her, relief at the prospect of escaping her unhappy home, fear of the unknown lying ahead. But behind all those feelings shone a ray of hope in the memory of Joel's approving smile.

All through the engagement year Jerusha clutched that hope. In the times when her stepmother became demanding, Jerusha recalled that expression. What would he be like, her husband? His face seemed kind enough. Would she be able to please him? When her father and brother ridiculed her, she promised herself again and again that if Joel turned out to be as good and kind as he appeared, she would do everything she could to please him.

But life hadn't been that simple. She'd never anticipated her fear of becoming pregnant.

* * * * *

Jerusha rubbed her hands and sighed, refusing to look at Hannah. "I don't belong here." Tears flooded her eyes. "I don't deserve to be treated so well, by you, by Joel, by the others. If they knew what I'm really like, none of them would want me. None of them! But especially Joel. Look at me! In spite the promise I made to myself, I don't want to do the one thing Joel desires most. I don't want to give him a child." Jerusha watched Hannah, searching for signs of shock and disapproval, but she found only love and compassion in her eyes and softness around her lips. "I deserve to be sent back to my father!" Her chin trembled.

Hannah allowed the tears to flow unhindered. Then gently, she drew Jerusha's head onto her knee and stroked the wavy tresses. Finally the sobs subsided. "Jerusha," Hannah's voice caressed her, soft and warm. "I'm confident God wants to heal the pain in your life, although I can't tell you exactly how. What I do know it this. In the darkest times of my life, the Lord said things I'd never have listened to before."

"The sons of Samuel were Joel the firstborn . . ."
1 Chronicles 6:28 NASU

CHAPTER

17

The Promise

That night, Jerusha–the one when I fled Peninnah's father's house–I fled without a plan. The cool night air slapped life into me after the stuffiness of the crowded room. I had to get away, far away, as fast as I could. In spite of my weakness, I began tripping through the winding streets, up and down the hilly roads creeping between the clusters of houses with their lamps aglow and the sounds of laughter and music on either side–celebrations of the Passover Eve. I felt even more excluded, more alone. My heart pounded frantically. My temples throbbed with pain. But tears refused to come; they only grew bigger and bigger inside me.

Just as my legs began to tremble and my lungs felt ready to burst with my frantic breathing, up ahead of me I saw the House of the Lord. I'd never come to it from that round about direction before, but I would have recognized it anywhere. Suddenly the realization overtook me: in all of Shiloh, the Tabernacle provided the only sanctuary for my grief. I slowed to a walk. As I approached, I noticed the old priest, Eli, sitting on lone vigil at the doorpost, his head nodding in sleep. I crept past him into the deserted outer courtyard where women were permitted to worship.

But once I got there, I had no idea what to say, what to pray. Hadn't I already said everything? As I hid my face in my hands, the feelings I'd run away from caught up with me. My body began to tremble. Hot tears spilled onto my palms, ran down my arms to my elbows. The terrible ache in my empty womb tightened, again and again and again.

Why God? I asked. Why do you let me suffer so? Do You know what You're doing? If you have a purpose for my life, what is it? . . . What kind of God are You anyway? Do You even know what it's like to suffer?"

As the words echoed in my mind, silence crept over me like a fog, or maybe like a great bird spreading its wings over me, covering me with a comforting calm. My breathing became soft and gentle, my heart steady. But the question I'd asked God, continued to vibrate in my heart. "Does God know what it's like to suffer?"

Why should the question haunt me, I wondered, when the answer seemed so obvious? How could the Almighty One possibly suffer? Wasn't He powerful enough to stop anyone who dared to oppose Him, anyone who defied His will? Couldn't He always have whatever He wanted? Then I remembered. Timara! She dared to oppose Yaweh. Timara fell in love with another god. Although she claimed she still worshipped the God of Israel, her passion obviously lay elsewhere. How would it feel to be thrown aside in favor of someone else, someone who would perform as desired?

I sucked my breath in sharply. I knew how that felt! Hadn't I been replaced by Peninnah–not kicked out completely, but laid aside, sometimes at least. Yet, in spite the similarities, the two situations seemed different. Yaweh's situation, worse than mine! I was convinced Elkanah's love for me remained strong, in spite of my barrenness, in spite of Peninnah. Timara, on the other hand, appeared to have abandoned her love for the One True God, retaining only the outward form, and that only when convenient.

I paused in wonder. The Almighty God of Israel *did* know what it was to suffer—to suffer like me! I no longer felt alone. Instead, I felt sad, but not sad for myself. I felt sad because Timara, and so many of God's people, had forsaken the Lord to chase after idols—worthless idols, totally unworthy of their love.

What will it be like twenty, thirty years from now? I wondered. *Will there be anyone left who's truly devoted to Yaweh, Yaweh alone?* If I knew of anything I could do to help turn the tide of wickedness, surely I would do it. Elkanah endeavored to make an impact by serving the Lord with his music and providing offerings. But what could a woman do? Producing children rated as woman's greatest accomplishment, and I couldn't even do that. I sighed.

Here we were, God and me, both of us facing desperate situations with seemingly no way out. But it appeared much easier to solve Yaweh's problem than mine. If the Lord possessed even one truly loyal leader—one who loved Him completely, one who delighted in obeying and serving Him—wouldn't the people respect such a man? Wouldn't they listen to the words of the Lord through him and turn away from their wickedness?

Where would such a man come from? He would need to have been raised up to love the Lord from early childhood, even from infancy. As a young boy, he would need to learn to love God. He would need a mother who loved the Lord more than anything else, a mother who would demonstrate by her life her complete devotion to the Lord—even if it meant giving up her son to the service of the Almighty.

If I had a son, I thought, *I would gladly give him to the Lord! How I wish I weren't barren so I could bear a son to serve the Lord for all the days of his life!*

Then I knew! I knew the prayer I had come to pray, a prayer I'd never said before.

Slowly, reverently, I took a deep solemn breath and pressed my trembling hands against my heart. "O Lord Almighty," I prayed. My lips moved, but no sound escaped. My whole body began to tremble with emotion and a lump rose in my throat, my previous calm swept away by the awesome seriousness of what I planned to do. "If You will only look upon your servant's misery and remember me, and not forget your servant, but give her a son, then . . . " Again I took a deep, slow breath. ". . . then I will give him to the Lord for all the days of his life. And no razor will ever be used on his head."

Once I said those words, I knew—this was what I wanted. Yes, I wanted this more than anything! Even more than I had wanted a child of my own, or a child to give to Elkanah.

Then I heard a shuffling followed by the low voice of Eli the priest. "How long will you keep on getting drunk?" His voice sounded stern and sad, but not unkind. When I opened my eyes, blinking away my tears, I saw Eli's pained expression reflecting the same disappointment and grief I'd felt moments before as I remembered the sins of God's people. So, Eli, too, mourned for God. "Get rid of your wine," he pleaded.

The poor man believed that I had resorted to the pagan custom of using wine to induce higher spiritual awareness. As I thought of how I appeared to him, I understood why he misunderstood.

"It's not what you think, my lord," I said. "I'm a woman who is deeply troubled. I haven't been drinking wine or beer. I was pouring out my soul to the Lord. Don't think of me as a wicked woman. I've been praying here out of my great anguish and grief."

The pain in Eli's old face faded away, relief and gladness took their place. He nodded. "Go in peace," he said, "and may the God of Israel grant you what you asked of Him."

"May your servant find favor in your eyes," I replied with a nod of respect. Then I walked out of the courtyard into the street and headed back by the normal route to the home of Peninnah's parents. A strange energy vibrated throughout my whole body. My mind felt light, floating, free of its burden. Finally—after all these years—I'd discovered the solution waiting for me! But what I'd done shocked me. I'd just given away my husband's son! I'd pledged an unborn child to a life of separation to God! How could I be so presumptuous? How would I ever explain? Although the questions arose, they didn't bother me right then. Calm peacefulness surrounded me like a wall of protection. I felt free and alive all over, as if I'd been released from a dark depressing dungeon. The muscles of my body felt relaxed, yet eager, vibrant with life. Soon I arrived at the house. As I entered the yard and smelled the fragrance of food—which just an hour before had made me ill—I suddenly realized I felt hungry, ravenously hungry.

As I reentered the main room, conversation dwindled. Silent eyes greeted me with many varied expressions—curiosity, surprise, relief. My eyes brushed past them all, searching only for Peninnah.

"Peninnah, I'm *so* hungry! Please get me something to eat . . . but nothing with grapes." With a sweeping smile at the sea of eyes around me, I sat down, and waited.

I'm sure Peninnah must have been in shock, but my joy absorbed me so much that I didn't realize I'd just given her my first command. How she managed her feelings about the change in me, I'll never know. I never asked. It wasn't long before she stood before me with a plateful of delicious food. I ate it with pleasure, every little bite.

I rose from my place and faced the women who'd sat in stunned silence around me. "Thank you for the delicious food," I said, smiling at them. "I'm very tired. I'll see you in the morning."

Everything remained quiet—until I left the room.

"Now Eli the priest was sitting on a chair
by the doorpost of the LORD's temple.
In bitterness of soul Hannah wept much
and prayed to the LORD.
And she made a vow, saying, 'O LORD Almighty,
if you will only look upon your servant's misery
and remember me,
and not forget your servant but give her a son,
then I will give him to the LORD
for all the days of his life,
and no razor will ever be used on his head.'
As she kept on praying to the LORD,
Eli observed her mouth.
Hannah was praying in her heart,
and her lips were moving
but her voice was not heard.
Eli thought she was drunk and said to her,
'How long will you keep on getting drunk?
Get rid of your wine.'
'Not so, my lord,' Hannah replied,
'I am a woman who is deeply troubled.
I have not been drinking wine or beer;
I was pouring out my soul to the LORD.
Do not take your servant for a wicked woman;
I have been praying here
out of my great anguish and grief.'
Eli answered, 'Go in peace,
and may the God of Israel
grant you what you have asked of him.'
She said, "May your servant find favor in your eyes.'
Then she went her way and ate something,
and her face was no longer downcast."
1 Samuel 1:9-18 NIV

CHAPTER

18

The Answer

The next morning I wondered if he'd recognize me—the old priest, Eli. He sat as before on his chair by the doorpost keeping watch over all who entered the Tabernacle just as he had the night before. This time, however, I was part of a crowd—not only our family, but Peninnah's family who came to send us off. Eli squinted, as if peering at me, but neither of us said anything.

I followed the others into the women's court–Peninnah, Peninnah's mother and sisters-in-law, and the big cluster of children. With careful precision I walked to the same spot where I'd prayed the previous night. My spirit danced, alive with pure joy. There silently poured out my love to the Lord, an offering of faith and devotion.

The men returned all too quickly from the inner court, and we followed them out of the Tabernacle, back past old Eli, and on down the street to the edge of Shiloh where we said our good-byes. Others returning to Ramah gathered with us there, and soon we began our journey homeward.

In just two weeks, the world had changed as much as I had. The countryside burst with new life. Right after we arrived in Shiloh the early rains fell, and now new fresh grass covered the rolling hills where only brown dryness lay when we arrived. How quickly new life sprouts up! How beautiful! Wildflowers—brilliant dots of life—bobbing their delicate heads, waving with delight as we passed. Red, blue, yellow, and, over there, orange. By the time we stopped for a rest, Jemima clutched, in each hand, a bouquet of flowers—one for her mother and one for me.

"Thank you!" I smiled at her upturned face. I patted the spot on the rock beside me. "Watch, Jemima. I'll show you how to make a chain so you can wear these flowers on your head." Her face bowed over my hands, watching as the subtle stems bent over, around, down, and a halo of color appeared ready to crown the dark little head. Jemima danced with glee until Elkanah demanded that she rest her feet. Obediently she sank back down, pressing close. "I'll pick some more for you," she whispered, "but you have to wait until after my feet rest."

Together Jemima and I gathered flowers from the roadside. Soon she had crowned everyone in the family with a wreath of color; even Elkanah and the boys accommodated her enthusiasm.

The pleasantness of the trip surprised me. Of course I'd wanted to go home other years, but those times I felt as if I were escaping, running away, in hopes that the torture behind wouldn't pursue me. This time I thoroughly enjoyed the trip, the countryside and the children. I noticed Peninnah and Elkanah observing me as if trying to understand the change in me. But the children simply responded with their own joy. Very quickly we spotted Ramah, nestled on a distant hill.

When we arrived home, everything looked different to me. *How did things get so run down?* I wondered. I scanned the neglected garden plot, the courtyard. *This will never do. Tomorrow we'll begin cleaning. But now we must rest.* So after washing dirty faces, hands, and feet, we headed for our sleeping places.

That night Elkanah followed me into my little room. An excited silence, a feeling of anticipation, vibrated in the air. I'm sure Elkanah felt completely puzzled. I, on the other hand, experienced a strange mixture of glorious exhilaration tinged with creeping uneasiness. How would Elkanah respond when I told him what I'd done? Would he be pleased? Would he believe God would give me a son? Would he allow me to keep my vow?

For the first time, as I got ready for bed, I considered that possibility. According to the law of God, a husband could cancel his wife's vow, just as a father could his daughter's. If Elkanah decided I couldn't give away his child, how would God respond? According to the Law of Moses, God viewed the woman's vow as having been kept even when cancelled by her father or husband, so maybe the Lord would still do His part. But if I did have a son, and Elkanah refused to let me give him to the Lord, then who would call the Israelites back to God, away from their idolatry?

I pulled the cover up, startled at the feeling of sadness that thought gave me. Shouldn't I be happy if I bore a son I could keep for myself? I studied my feelings. How could I prefer to give my son to a life of service to God, than to have him for myself? Such a thought seemed incomprehensible, even to me.

"Hannah," Elkanah's voice pulled me away from my contemplation. He paused as if searching for words. "Hannah," he repeated. Even in that one word I could hear his sense of wonder. "What happened to you? You . . . you remind me . . . of the Hannah I married long ago."

I smiled. How true! I did feel like the young Hannah. Hannah full of joy. Hannah full of hope. Hannah free to live life to the full. But a Hannah who was also much wiser now. I turned toward my husband. The light of the lamp flickered yellows and browns over his face, revealing a flood of varied emotions. I drew a deep breath. "It happened the night before we left Shiloh. . . ."

I told him about how I visited the Tabernacle, describing the need for a godly priest who would call the Israelites to turn away from their idols and return to total devotion to the true God. But as I told him about how both God and I understood the pain of being replaced, I felt his body tense. "Hannah," he interrupted, "it's really not the same. You know, you and God."

I waited, uncertain of what he meant.

Hesitantly, he continued. "If you expect me to send Peninnah and my children away, so it will be just me and you again, well, it's totally impossible."

"Oh, Elkanah," I could hardly keep the laughter out of my voice, "it's nothing like that! I just had to tell you that part of the story so you can understand the next."

I proceeded carefully, explaining the kind of man needed to lead Israel back to God. Elkanah agreed that a great leader might help, but he seemed impatient to find out how that related to the change in me.

"Then I got a wonderful idea!" I said. My heart pounded with excitement. "I promised the Lord . . . that if He would give me a son, I would give him to the Lord, to serve Him for all the days of his life."

Silence stretched long as Elkanah thought about what I said. I tried to be patient, realizing Elkanah's ways. But how I wanted to know what he would say! I should have guessed he'd ask questions, that he'd make sure he understood me correctly before forming an opinion.

Elkanah rose up on his elbow and looked down into my eyes. "You made a vow to the Lord?"

I nodded.

"A vow to give your son to the Lord?"

"Yes. If Yaweh gives me a son, then I will give him to the Lord. He'll be a Nazarite all the days of his life."

Elkanah waited. I saw the lump in his throat move as he swallowed.

"You want him to be a spiritual leader in Israel?"

I nodded.

Another long silence.

"Have you carefully considered what this vow will cost you?"

Again I nodded.

"And you're still willing?"

"Yes."

A look of disbelief and wonder spread across Elkanah's face, and he turned his eyes to the ceiling. When his gaze returned to me and he finally spoke, his voice wavered with emotion. "Then I won't stand in the way of you keeping your vow."

I'm surprised at how little emotion that moment produced in me. Obviously Elkanah felt deeply moved. I sensed only a calm satisfaction that I'd done the right thing and a deep thankfulness for such a husband as Elkanah. How many husbands would refuse to give their wives freedom to dispose of *any* of their possessions, let alone a son? I realized Elkanah gave me a great compliment by allowing my judgment to stand, especially when I promised so great a thing. He knew, I knew, it wouldn't be easy to explain such a vow to others. Most people would think both of us crazy. But Elkanah pledged to stand by me. He approved of my vow.

For a long time we lay silently in each other's arms, each of us exploring possibilities that never before entered our minds. Wondering what the future would hold. Finally Elkanah broke the silence. "You're quite a woman, Hannah! Quite a woman!" His lips searched for mine, and after a warm passionate kiss, he whispered, "I love you, Hannah!" I felt the reverberation of his voice around my heart.

"I love you, too!" I answered.

That night the knowledge of the very special vow we shared heightened the joy of our love in a strange, deep way—as if uniting our hearts, not just of our bodies.

The next morning when I awoke, plans already stirred in my mind. Today we would prepare the garden. We needed to get it planted as soon as possible. After telling Elkanah good-bye, I called Peninnah and the children together. "There's a lot of work to be done," I explained. "Did you see how the flowers on the hills grew while we were in Shiloh?" The children's heads bobbed in unison. "That means it's time for us to get our garden ready. If we all work hard, we might even plant the seeds tomorrow."

So the work began. I assigned gardening jobs to everyone but Peninnah and the two babies. They stayed in the courtyard where Peninnah managed the food. I wasn't sure how she would respond to being given an assignment, but I think she still felt too confused by the change in me to raise any objection. By the time Elkanah arrived home, we'd finished preparing the soil and mending the fence. The next day we could plant the garden. Even I felt amazed. The children ran to greet Elkanah, clinging to him, and drawing him by force to the back, pointing out their grand achievements.

After the garden, we cleaned the courtyard, *really* cleaned it; then we moved inside, scrubbing everything. I'm not quite sure when I finally realized I'd taken the leadership role of the first wife. What shocked me most was that I never consciously made a decision to do so. It just happened. Surprising enough, Peninnah didn't put up a big fuss—not even a little one. I'm not claiming she became friendly, but she didn't have as much time to think up mean things to say. I'm sure it helped that I kept her children busy and happy. For the first time, all of us really worked together.

We kept so busy cleaning I had little time or energy to think of anything else. One morning as Peninnah and I washed lamp smoke from the ceiling in my room, I noticed tenderness as my arm brushed against my breast. I frowned, pausing in my work. Puzzled. Could I be pregnant? How long had it been? Sure enough, when I counted back, I discovered my time was already seven days overdue.

How can I explain what I felt? Joy? Yes, great joy. Excitement? Pleasure? Yes, all of those. But they were somehow different than I expected. Usually I experienced strong emotions all over the outside of me, making my skin tickle with delight and my muscles jump and move with pleasure, making it impossible for me to be still or silent. But not this time. The joy, excitement, and pleasure centered much deeper inside me, in the very core of my being. Their warm intensity so strongly overpowered the outer parts of me, it immobilized me, leaving me mute and motionless with a great sense of worship and awe. I felt a lightness inside as if my spirit rose up to bow before the Almighty God in heaven.

"Hannah?" Peninnah's voice drew me back to the present. "Are you okay?"

I smiled and nodded, unable to speak because of the depth of my joy. I felt glad for the routine, repetitious job. Glad we'd allowed the children a special play day with their cousins. Glad for time just to absorb what had happened. At that time, I couldn't think. Thoughts came later. That day I simmered in joy.

I didn't need to tell Elkanah. From the moment our eyes met, I realized that, unlike me, he'd been very aware of the passing of time. As I've thought of it over the years, I've wondered how Elkanah dealt with it all. I'm sure my lack of self-awareness confused him. I remember our conversation that night before I figured out I was pregnant.

"Did you see all we got done today?" I asked as I straightened the blanket on my mat.

Elkanah nodded as he searched my face.

I smiled, unaware then of what he was trying to see.

"Tomorrow Peninnah and I will wash this ceiling," I said, motioning around the room.

"Hannah, you've been working hard for a long time. Why don't you take it easy?"

I laughed, completely missing his concern. "Look at the ceiling, Elkanah. See how smoky it is? Besides, Peninnah's going to help me."

Elkanah glanced up without interest. After turning to me with another studying look, he gave up and came to bed.

Then the next day I understood.

Through the meal and into the evening, the two of us shared our silent delight. After all our years of disappointment, it seemed unbelievable. Around us, life revolved as usual, although I noticed Peninnah taking peeks at us without making eye contact. I wondered if she already knew, whether she kept tract of my cycle as I did hers.

That night of discovery passed peacefully, unlike the days to follow. I'd failed to anticipate the attitude that others would have toward what I'd done. If someone had asked me, I'm certain I would have assured them that, even though my vow was unusual, the people of Israel would recognize the importance of my commitment. There was much I didn't know.

". . . and she was no longer sad.
The entire family got up early the next morning
and went to worship the LORD once more.
Then they returned home to Ramah.
When Elkanah slept with Hannah,
the LORD remembered her request. . ."
1 Samuel 1:18-19 NLT

CHAPTER

19
Arguments

Poor Peninnah. I'm sure nothing turned out as she'd anticipated, nothing but the very first few moments of that night in Shiloh when she announced her pregnancy. I know what she expected. She thought I would be crushed, easy to antagonize and control.

Like I said before, the change in my behavior was not something I contemplated or designed. Maybe our relationship would have been different from the beginning if I'd known how to respond to her behavior rather than being swept along by it. But even if someone had told me what to do, I doubt I could have done it. I've come to believe, Jerusha, that much of our behavior results from our self-perception. So when my perception of myself changed, my behavior automatically changed.

Of course Peninnah didn't understand this. How could she know Hannah no longer viewed herself as a defective woman fighting for respect? How was she supposed to understand that after making a vow in the secret silence of the night, I walked away, a woman dedicated to the service of God, a woman with an awesome commission? I'd accepted a very important task—preparing a man to bring Israel back to the worship of the Lord God of Israel. No time now for pettiness. My life focused on important things extending far beyond myself.

Although I'm sure Peninnah didn't understand the change, I'm certain she saw it plainly, clearly—perhaps better than I did. With so much to do, I found little time to study myself. I've wondered (now that I have the time to wonder) how Peninnah interpreted what she saw. Why, after seven years of dominating me, did she cooperate and follow my administration of the household? I can't believe she felt intimidated or threatened.

After much thinking, I've settled on two answers. I suspect my self-respect influenced her greatly, as I said before. She seemed to value me as I valued myself. But, even more than that, I believe the Holy One of Israel touched her heart. Many people will think I'm strange, perhaps crazy for saying this. So? I'm used to such accusations by now. Besides I've come to believe that nothing in my life falls beyond the scope of God's influence. Could it be that bringing resolution to the historic conflict between Peninnah and me was essential, necessary for providing the proper atmosphere for the baby the Lord allowed me to conceive? Anyway, after experiencing the miracle of conception, another miracle didn't shock me.

"Hannah's going to have a son," Elkanah told Peninnah the next evening as the children played "traveling to Shiloh" in the courtyard. For one moment, Peninnah sat in pensive silence before asking, "A son? How do you know it will be a son?" Not a speck of mockery, or disbelief. It surprised me.

"While in Shiloh, Hannah made a vow to the Lord God. She promised, that if He would give her a son, she would give him to the Lord to serve Him all the days of his life."

Peninnah's gaze momentarily met mine, then dropped abruptly. What thoughts whirled through her mind? Was she impressed that the Lord answered my prayer? Or shocked at the price I was willing to pay to have a son? Did she think about the fact that we would be pregnant together, but she would keep her child, and I would give mine away? Whatever she thought, she said nothing at all—at least that I heard.

It amazed me that after having been the focus of so much attention in Ramah, the announcement of my pregnancy roused so little interest. "That happens when a man gets a second wife," they commented. But they didn't know about my vow, at least not at first.

Not so with our families. Especially Elkanah's. They rejoiced exuberantly at my pregnancy until they heard about the promise I'd made. Then shocked silence.

"You're not going to let her keep such a promise are you, Elkanah?" his mother finally asked, alarm lightly flavoring her voice.

Elkanah nodded. "Why not?"

"Why not?" His mother's face flushed deep pink. "Why not?" Her voice lifted sharply, and she clamped her lips tightly before continuing. "After all these years of waiting, how could you let her give away her firstborn son? Protect her from her foolishness, Elkanah. The Lord will understand. One day she'll thank you for it, you can be sure!"

"But Mother, why is it foolish to want to give a child into the service of the Lord?"

Elkanah's father reached over and put his hand on his son's arm. "You know your mother and I have never opposed service to the Lord. We've always taken our responsibility as Levites seriously, Elkanah. Remember how we encouraged you and all our male relatives to be faithful in serving at the Tabernacle? Did we condemn the vow you made to Yaweh before you reached manhood?" He looked over at his wife.

"But your mother's right. Hannah's promise is very different than yours."

His mother nodded. "Think, Elkanah, why would Hannah make such a big promise? Isn't it the action of a desperate woman?"

Diza's brother, Elkanah's brother-in-law, joined in. "I agree. Just promising that your son will serve the Lord might be reasonable. After all, that's more than most Levites do these days. Most are too busy with their own lives to set aside time each year for the Lord's service."

Another brother-in-law joined in. "How would you like to grow up knowing that you had no choice in your life, that because of a vow your mother made, you were destined to serve the Lord for life?"

"Yes," the last agreed. "And what if your son doesn't love the Lord? What good is his service then? He could be another Hophni or Phinehas, using his position to get personal advantages for himself."

Blood drained from my cheeks. That could not happen! Could it? But I refused to allow my mind to wander.

"I'm not sure it's unreasonable to be born into a commitment," Elkanah's father answered his sons-in-law. "After all, if we take the Law of Moses seriously, none of us Levites has any choice about whether we'll serve God. God Himself gave us our assignments, passed down from father to son." He looked at Elkanah. "But Hannah should have limited her commitment to a simple vow of service like the one you made. Why should she go beyond that? He could serve at the Tabernacle two weeks a year and raise his family to love the Lord. That's certainly good enough."

But later as we walked home, I felt certain such a vow wouldn't have been enough. I admired Elkanah, and I believed in the importance of his vow. Yet his dedication, his loving commitment to serving the Lord, had failed to stay the tide of idolatry sweeping over Israel. I wondered, but didn't ask, if he would change his mind and make me modify my vow.

What a stressful week! Everyone voicing an opinion, trying to get Elkanah to relent before it was too late. No one spoke to me about it. I'd already sealed my fate. I must keep my vow or face the wrath of God. The only escape lay in Elkanah, and his time ran short. If a husband or father waited too long to revoke the vow of his wife or daughter, then God held him liable for breaking the vow. So for the rest of that week, every night someone showed up at the house trying to convince Elkanah of the foolishness of what I'd done.

When it became obvious that, for some reason beyond their comprehension, they couldn't get Elkanah to cancel the vow completely, they still tried to persuade him to modify it.

"Elkanah, don't you think a Nazarite vow is too extreme?" his father asked. "Think about how that will affect the life of your son! He'll always stick out as being different than his friends."

"Can you imagine how kids will make fun of him with his long hair?" a brother-in-law added.

"Every meal he eats he'll be reminded of the vow his mother made for him. He'll always need to be conscious of what's in his food," said Diza's brother (by far the most enthusiastic eater in the family). "Just think how important grapes are in our diet! Most deserts are sweetened with raisins. And we flavor our water with grape paste to cover the cistern flavor. Can you imagine how difficult it'll be for him? What he'll have to give up!"

Although I said nothing, I knew they spoke truth. Ever since I took my vow, I'd come under Nazarite restrictions until my son's birth. In just that short time, I'd become very aware of the sacrifices my son would make, day after day, in order to live the separated life-style of a Nazarite. This level of dedication to God went beyond the call of duty. Very few people took God so seriously—or understood why anyone would want to do so. People valued their right to enjoy the important aspects of Israelite life forfeited by a Nazarite.

"How can you endorse a vow that would keep my grandson from attending to me at my funeral?" Elkanah's father asked. "He'll be a special grandson, the first of Hannah's children. Keep him. Let her promise a second or third son, if she must. She might have more, you know."

"Father, the firstborn is the Lord's already, ever since the time of the Passover in Egypt. Hannah chose a good, not a bad thing."

"Well, if she must put her son under the obligations of a Nazarite, then set reasonable time limits." his father insisted. "The law obligates Levites to serve only between ages twenty-five and fifty, and people taking Nazarite vows can limit them to as short a time as they wish. She could promise only one year or two . . . even five or ten. But for life? I can't imagine it!"

The brothers-in-law agreed. A Nazarite vow was too extreme, especially a vow for life. Such restrictions were totally unfair to a child.

As they left, my father-in-law paused at the doorway and shook his head, adding one last statement. "If Hannah thought for the rest of her life, she could never have come up with a promise more extreme than this. Some might disagree and say human sacrifice (which we know is against the law of God) is more severe. But I'm not so sure." He reached out and put his arm around his son's shoulder and said words that have rung in my heart over the years. "Elkanah, if you refuse to stop this, you destine your son to be a living sacrifice to God for all the days of his life."

Elkanah did not revoke my vow.

"And it came about in due time,
after Hannah had conceived. . . "
1 Samuel 1:20a NASB

"Therefore, I urge you, brothers,
in view of God's mercy,
to offer your bodies as living sacrifices,
holy and pleasing to God —
this is your spiritual act of worship."
Romans 12:1-2 NIV

CHAPTER

20

Unexpected

That morning in my fifth month of pregnancy, Jerusha, was what I call a twisted day. Have you ever noticed how some days burst forth in brightness and with the songs of birds, then end in gloom and wails of pain and loss? Another arrives shrouded with intense darkness, despair, and pain, and yet proves to be the door through which we must pass to receive healing and joy.

I've thought a lot about life, Jerusha. How time and again it's not what it appears to be on the surface. In the present we rarely see the significance of the moment. Often we think choices made in an instant will be over and gone, but many times those choices follow us, for good or evil, the rest of our lives, even living on long after our death.

But, I'll stop philosophizing. Perhaps it's my way of postponing this painful part of our story.

That morning I remember savoring the beauty of the early dawn as I walked to the well. A perfect day. The air, cooler with the coming of autumn, left a refreshing chill on my cheeks, arms, and bare toes. I savored the pure quietness of the morning before time wrote anything into the day, one of those treasured thinking times that have always been a part of my life and keep getting more frequent with age.

I played with my imaginings all the way home from the well. Thoughts about whether Peninnah's coming child would be a boy or a girl. In just two months, she'd deliver, and I, in not quite four. How would our little ones get along? How would Peninnah respond to my son? Would our relationship change? She'd begun helping around the house. For the first time, she didn't demand my service during her pregnancy. I wondered that day, as I drew water from the well, what had caused the change. Was it the alteration in my attitude since her previous pregnancies? Or did the fact of my pregnancy make it more difficult for her to use her own condition as an excuse for being pampered? Maybe Peninnah really felt better this time—where the other pregnancies actually caused her to be ill.

For whatever reason, I appreciated Peninnah doing her share of the housework quickly and skillfully. She also took good care of her children. She always had. The harshness, the meanness, she'd so often dealt me, never presented itself in regard to her little ones. Nor did she display that syrupy sweetness she used with Elkanah. Effective, confident, unsentimental, Peninnah never doted, but I never doubted the sincerity or strength of her love for her children. In spite of her competitive spirit, I never perceived she viewed her children merely as trophies of her womanhood, status symbols. While I remained suspicious in other areas of her life, in regard to her children, I never suspected her of acting. Maybe that's one of the reasons I'd accepted an unfair portion of the housework over the years. After the arrival of her firstborn son, Peninnah no longer wasted time, at least from my perspective. True, she bossed me and demanded unnecessary service, but she spent her time meaningfully in mothering.

But that day as I walked homeward, I couldn't help but wonder if competition might arise between us over our children. I'd seen Peninnah change quickly, dramatically many times. This time my concern didn't focus on the relationship between the two of us—I think I'd finally relinquished all hopes of friendship, content just to survive sharing the same husband and the same house. On that twisted day, I remember trying to figure how we would maintain our peace after the babies arrived. But it wouldn't be as I imagined or hoped.

As I came around the bend toward the house, I noticed clusters of women and children gathered at various doorways along the way. They all focused on a group standing on the road just outside our courtyard—Peninnah and her children and four young men I'd never seen. Philistines! I knew from their dress. My chest tightened. Why had they come inland from the coast into our territory? Why were they talking to Peninnah? One of them, the tallest, shook his fist, then another threw something at her.

I tried to swallow, but my breath seemed stuck in my throat.

"Cursed woman!" From the distance, I understood his words clearly, even with his accent. "I said I wanted *meals* for all of us. *Real* food, not dry bread and figs!"

My ears tingled.

"We're hungry! And we're not wimpy Israelites!" said a second youth, shorter than the first, but muscular. "We're flesh eaters, you ugly slut!" Drawing his sword, he thrust it toward Peninnah's rounded abdomen.

I sucked my breath in sharply. My heart beat frantically in wordless fear. My eyes jerked back and forth, from one house to another. Women with wild eyes silently shoving their little ones toward the safety of their houses. Not a man in sight. All the strong, able-bodied men out in the fields harvesting. Past the well. Beyond reach of our voices. No one would hear a call for help. No one but the Lord.

A deserted stick lay in the yard nearby where children played moments ago. I licked my lips and took a deep breath. Silently I set my jar against the wall. Seizing the stick, I moved swiftly down the road, landing lightly, soundlessly on the soft sand, as my brothers had taught me.

By this time the other two youths moved closer, adding their jeers. Peninnah trembled speechless before them, her eyes lowered. "Maybe this one can't cook," the tall, thin one taunted. "But we know what she *can* do," he nodded toward the whimpering little ones clustering near their mother. His wicked laugher roared in the silence. The others joined him. The voice of the smallest rang high and thin, like a child's, not a man's.

Jamming his sword back into his sheath, the tall one stepped toward Peninnah with a sneer and a deep growl. "Well, if we can't get a good meal out of her, let's get what we can!" He grabbed the neck of Peninnah's tunic, and jerked hard. The sound of tearing cloth mixed with Peninnah's screams, followed by the echoing chorus of her children's high cries.

The Philistines laughed in response, and I was glad for all their noise. No one turned at my approach–except for Elihu, Peninnah's oldest who stood several houses closer to me where he'd been playing with his long vanished friends. As I paused at his side, only his round eyes moved, screaming their silent fear. Bending near, I breathed in his ear, "Go!" and pointed behind me. "Get your father!" I mouthed. Immediately he sped off, his bare feet lighting softly on the dusty road. I was glad I'd taught him my brothers' secrets. Then I redirected my attention toward Peninnah.

"Move!" Peninnah screamed, motioning her children away as the tall one reached for her. Her flailing arm hit him in his face. With a bellow, he pulled back, then charged her with his head, like an angry bull, knocking her to the ground, then jumped on top of her.

The air around me vibrated with mixed cries–the little ones, their mother, and cheering Philistines, but inside me all remained still and silent. My chest rose and fell with deep, slow, silent breaths, pumping fuller of rage and strength. Then sound stopped, and I saw everything in slow motion.

Riveting my eyes on the man astride Peninnah, I ran forward, slipping swiftly between the two closest to me, my stick poised behind my head. Arching back, I gathered all my strength. Silently I swung my stick downward in a smooth powerful arc that landed with a firm, crack on his head.

Blood pounded in my temples, and the scene returned to normal speed and volume. He moaned, turning to see who hit him, and I struck him again. This time blood spurted from a gash above his eyebrow.

I whirled around to face the three, my stick singing as it cut the air. I heard myself scream, and felt my eyes flashing with fury. The startled youths stumbled back. How young! How easily frightened by the ire of a woman!

Behind them Timara ran toward us, her hands high above her head. In moments, she brought a stone crashing down on the muscular one who'd thrown the food at Peninnah. His knees buckled; he bent forward, seizing his head. Groaning.

Before Timara and I could renew our attack, the two uninjured youths hurried to their comrades, each gripping one and pulling him up. Behind us we heard pounding feet and the shouts of the men of Ramah. With one frightened glance in that direction, the four fled across the fields toward the road west of Ramah, two of them holding their heads.

I turned to Peninnah and the children, but soon after I knelt down, Elkanah arrived. He grabbed my shoulder. Hard. As he pulled me to my feet, his eyes swept over me. Then his eyes penetrated mine. "Are you hurt?" he demanded. "Did they harm you?" he asked again before I could answer. I shook my head. But his hands moved swiftly and firmly over me, head to foot.

Then he turned to Peninnah, already being attended by Mara, the village midwife and general health advisor of Ramah. His inquiries, curt and sharp. Once Mara assured him that Peninnah was only frightened, he pushed everyone aside and lifted Peninnah from the ground. With Elkanah on one side and me on the other, we assisted her to her mat while the children pressed in around us.

Before tucking her gray blanket around her, Elkanah questioned Peninnah as he prodded her arms, legs, head, and trunk. He refused to be satisfied until he examined each child, then Peninnah and me once again. Only then did he return to the road to join in the general discussion of what had happened and what must be done.

"Those were just boys," Elkanah assured us when he came back in, "not real warriors. Since no one died, this will most likely be the last we see of them. Probably they intended to impress each other with their toughness. But I doubt they'll want to tell their families and friends the story of how two women defeated them. They'll invent some tale of honor to explain their injuries." Elkanah smiled as if he expected us to be amused. But the event still loomed over us, like a dark, stinging cloud of smoke from a wildfire, too close, too frightening, for any of us to laugh, or even smile. Besides, the concern in Elkanah's eyes contradicted his words.

"Will they come back?" Elihu asked, he voice sounded very small and too young for being almost eight years old.

Elkanah patted his shoulder. "I think not, but the men of Ramah decided to post guards just in case. If more Philistines happen to come, the men will be ready."

I knew better than to think that the men of Ramah could take on a band of Philistines.

Jemima's lip trembled, and Elkanah hurried to add, "But we're pretty sure they won't come back, so let's not worry." He smiled at all the little upturned faces, but no one, including Peninnah and me, smiled back.

Harvest forgotten, Elkanah remained home for the rest of the day, playing with the children, watching the hills, checking on Peninnah and me. "Tonight will be a good night for singing," Elkanah said cheerfully as we ate our simple meal. "Singing makes us feel better." While we appreciated Elkanah's attempt at helping us, if he thought he could get our minds off the events of the day, he didn't achieve his goal. I suspect Elkanah couldn't chase them out of his mind either.

That night we sang indoors in the big room, rather than in the openness of the courtyard. I tried to sing, but it was difficult. Maybe I'd yelled too loudly. Maybe fear was stuck in my throat. Besides, every time I looked at Elkanah, I kept seeing the wild look on his face when he arrived from the field—the piercing quality in his eyes, the paleness of his cheeks, the hardness around his mouth. I felt the harshness of his hands, his voice. A stranger. In spite of Elkanah's outer calmness while we sang, I noticed he rocked his knee back and forth every time he looked at Peninnah.

I shared his concern. After the assault, instead of complaining, Peninnah repeatedly assured everyone that she felt fine. I didn't believe her. She rested all day and ate little. That didn't worry me. None of us felt like eating. But ever since the incident, she refused to look anyone in the eyes, not even Elkanah. Then throughout our singing I noticed she rubbed the right side of her abdomen. Unlike her usual self, Peninnah seemed to want no special attention, so I didn't question her. Besides, I feared my comments might alarm the children.

What a task getting the children to sleep that night! I offered to take some of them to my room, but, in spite of the fact that this privilege rated as a rare treat, not one of them wanted to leave their mother. So I moved my mat into Peninnah's room, and Elkanah and I spent hours rubbing backs and singing songs trying to get them all to sleep. As soon as quiet breathing settled over the room, I moved near to Peninnah. She lay curled up on her side, but shifted constantly as if trying to find a position to relieve her discomfort.

"Are you okay, Peninnah?" I whispered.

She sniffed and nodded, her eyes still shut.

"Do you need anything?"

She shook her head.

I looked at Elkanah. He shrugged.

I went back to my mat and lay down. Elkanah took his place beside Peninnah, gently rubbing her hand and saying things I couldn't hear. It felt like I never slept that night, or if so, only for seconds at a time. The events of the attack played themselves again and again through my mind. The restless whimpers of the children and Peninnah's soft moans called to me. Just as I fell into a troubled dream, Elkanah shook my shoulder, whispering, "Hannah! Hannah! Stay with Peninnah. I'm going to get Mara. I think Peninnah's having trouble with the baby."

I pulled myself up and carefully stepped around the children to Peninnah. She pressed her hand against her side. As I put my hand on her abdomen, it hardened. I blinked the sleep from my eyes. It couldn't be! Peninnah was in labor!

Elkanah returned with Mara, and I left my place beside Peninnah to get supplies.

In the soft flickering of the lamplight surrounded by her six little ones, Peninnah gave birth to her seventh child—a boy with thick dark hair and the face of an angel. But no infant cry woke the sleeping siblings. Only Mara, Elkanah and I heard the sad, almost silent weeping of his mother.

"So in the course of time. . ."
1 Samuel 1:20a NIV

CHAPTER
21
Grief

A cloud of sorrow lay heavy upon us for the following weeks. The burial, the days of mourning passed. Then came the time of adjustment, which in some ways seemed the most difficult. I always felt my own pregnancy sharpened Peninnah's grief. *Why did the Lord allow it to happen this way?* I often wondered.

One day a few weeks later, Timara dropped by to check on Peninnah and all of us. On her way out, she paused at the doorway, standing quite close to me. "Now don't get me wrong, Hannah," she whispered. "I'm just as sorry as anyone else about the baby's death." She bent nearer. "But my ears hear keenly, Hannah. More than anyone else in Ramah, I know how unjustly you've suffered at Peninnah's hand–suffered in silence. You'll probably think I'm harsh, but . . . " She paused, tipping her head to the right as she peered at me. "I think she got what she deserved."

"Timara!" I gasped. Her words pierced my heart, intensifying my sorrow. Grasping her shoulders, I demanded that she promise *never* to say that again.

She shook her head, her dark eyes locked with mine. "I promise, Hannah. But I don't see how you could risked the life of your first child to save *her.*"

As the time of mourning passed, others also laid aside their inhibitions and began to make comments in my hearing. One morning at the well old Urit publicly commended me for my bravery. "You should have seen her! I stood in my doorway, peeking out, praying, praying! 'O Lord, help us,' I whispered. 'Help us, 'cause there's no one near enough to stop them.' But then I saw *you* coming." She tucked in the loose end of the scarf that hung around her head. "Now you younger ones," she said as she wagged her crooked finger at us, "you might not remember, but we've suffered many Philistine attacks in *my* lifetime–none of them good. No, no. Not good at all." She sucked her wrinkled lips into her mouth where her teeth used to be and kept on shaking her head. Her eyes held a haunted looked that made my heart quake.

Oma nodded, her face reflecting the same terror. She and Urit were the age my grandfather would have been were he still alive. "But really, Urit," Oma said, "it wasn't *so* bad for us. Remember the stories our *grandfathers* told? In their lifetime. And with their fathers before them? They had it much worse! Attacking. Raiding, for no apparent reason. Constant fear." She laid her hand on Urit's arm. "Remember *those* stories, Urit?"

Urit lowered her eyes and nodded silently.

Oma nodded, too, then continued. "Fierce soldiers with iron swords–not peace lovers like us. The grandfathers' stories–they left all of us shivering with fear. Full of nightmares. I hated them!" She shuddered.

"My grandfather said it was *our* fault," Urit said. "Our leader, Joshua, had warned us not to stop fighting until we got rid of *all* the pagans in the land. If we'd finished the job, grandfather said, no Philistines would have remained to bother us."

"I get so tired of hearing people *pretending* Israel ever possessed the strength to fight the Philistines," Diza said. "We couldn't take on the Philistines if we tried! Not then, not now!"

"Not on our own," I agreed, "but with the power of Yaweh, we would certainly win."

"Humph! Who do we hear talking? The woman of bravery herself! Are you recruiting a band of women to take on the Philistines, Hannah? Not *all* are beardless boys! When the real warriors attack, what good will your sticks and stones be against their iron swords?" Diza laughed. "Come on women of Ramah! Get ready to join with this mighty heroine! The modern Deborah!"

"Diza!" old Urit said. "At least Hannah stood up for Peninnah! Who knows what evil those Philistines would have done? What if Hannah thought only of protecting herself and the child she carries? The rest of us just stood back in fear and watched–except for Timara. Why, Peninnah would probably be dead by now!"

"In spite of what you think, Urit, Hannah did us no favor!" Fire flashed in Diza's eyes. "Without considering the consequences, she drew the blood of a Philistine! If you believe Hannah frightened them off for good, you're crazy! Kicking a wasps' nest only creates more trouble."

I suppressed a sigh as I watched the women taking sides–some labeling me brave, and others foolish. Why had I imagined that, once I became pregnant, my problems with the women would vanish? For all my married life, I ranked as a favorite topic. How did other women avoid the problem of continually being discussed and condemned?

I'd asked that question many times before, but for the first time, I became aware of a possible answer. In every case I could remember, Diza seemed to take the lead in turning others against me. Could she be the instigator of my difficulties? But why would she want to hurt me? As one of my childhood friends, we played together, worked together, talked together. True, many times Diza complained about my "wonderful life." My family enjoyed too much prosperity. They spoiled me. I would make a terrible wife because of their doting ways. But I had always felt sorry for her. After witnessing the negativity and harshness of her family, I could understand why she would wish she, too, had something better. So in our growing up years, I tried to be a good friend to her, to compensate as much as I could. Then why, after all my kindness, should she turn against me as soon as we became young women old enough to be engaged.

But the responsibilities at home quickly pushed thoughts of Diza from my mind. With Peninnah still recovering from the loss of her child, I assumed the extra housework as well as the care of her children—who demanded more attention than usual since the Philistine incident and the death of their little brother. The other times, at the end of Peninnah's isolation following the births of her other children, she returned to the courtyard and eagerly swept her brood from my care. But this time, a gloomy lifelessness surrounded her, frightening and confusing the children.

After several days of breaking up fights and wiping stormy tears, I decided to put the children to work. Usually I saved carding and twisting wool for winter—or other times when I needed to fill quiet moments alone. But I decided these jobs could occupy Jemima and the younger ones if I supervised them. The older boys, supervised by with Dan's older sons, gladly escaped to the hillside to collect brush for kindling. Keeping them busy helped settle the children, but Peninnah remained unchanged.

One evening Elkanah took all six children to visit his parents and return his father's borrowed clamp, leaving

Peninnah and me alone. For a long time now I'd wished for an opportunity for the two of us to be alone. I know it's ridiculous, but I imagined Peninnah would gladly take the opportunity to unload the things going through her mind. First, she would thank me for saving her. I would tell her how sorry I felt about her baby's death. We would hug and weep together, and then, finally, we'd be friends.

As I cleaning up after the evening meal, I reviewed my hopes once again. Peninnah sat in her corner checking the wool strands the children had worked on and repairing places too uneven for the spindle.

"The children did a good job for as young as they are," I said, eager to get a conversation started. After all, her children seemed a safe enough topic.

Peninnah nodded, but said nothing.

I washed the utensils in silence, wishing I knew how to break through Peninnah's isolating wall. It seems strange to say it, but at times I thought her condemnation and ridicule would be more tolerable than this sad silence. That day I realized I'd never really given up hope that someday we'd be friends—or maybe I had given up, but my feelings of sympathy toward her revived that hope.

I tried and tried to think of something to say, but nothing seemed appropriate. No way could I talk about the things occupying my mind or blurt out all the questions jumping around in my brain. Like, what are you thinking about all the time in your silence? Are you grieving over your baby? Or is it more than that? Do you worry about whether the Philistines will return even though Elkanah repeatedly assures us that if they planned to retaliate, they would have already done so? Does the wall they're building around new Ramah bring you any comfort? Do you dream about those four boy-man faces? I do. Time and again I feel the power drawing up in my shoulders. I feel the stick hitting his head. Thud! Thud! The jolting in my wrists. And always, always, I see the blood, that spurt, spurt, spurt, its thickness trickling down the side of his face, purple red turning to bright crimson. And the hate, the cold piercing hate in his young eyes.

Why are you so quiet, Peninnah? Why don't you look at people any more? Or interact with your children as you did before? Do you blame yourself for your baby's death? Are you angry with me? I tried to help you. I'm sorry your baby died. You'll never know how much I wanted to help you wash your tiny boy and wrap his little body for burial. He was so beautiful! I wanted to walk by your side as you pressed him to your heart that day in the funeral procession. Elkanah said he would explain it to you—that because the child I carry is a Nazarite, I had to refrain from contact with death. You do understand, don't you, that as long as I carry him, I must observe the rules of the Nazarite for him? Or are you very angry? How will you act when my baby comes? Will you hate me again? Will you hate my son?

As the time of my delivery had grown nearer, I finally wanted to hear the stories of childbirth. Peninnah rated as an expert. But now she remained bound in her silence, unwilling to boast and warn. Nor could I ask her questions, because now "babies" fell into the category of forbidden topics. I feared the very roundness of my body ripening with child insulted her without words.

Finally, just as we heard the chatter of the children returning with Elkanah, Peninnah spoke. "The children like you," she said.

Shocked at her interruption of my silent conversation, I couldn't think of anything at all to say in response. Not one word. Then the clan swarmed into the courtyard with sticky fingers and faces boasting the remains of grandma's chewy raisin cakes, full of stories to tell of their adventure.

I never forgot Peninnah's words. I mulled them over again and again, trying to ferret out her meaning. I must confess those words fell like rain on the anxious little seed of hope in my heart. But reality often sprouts up different from my hopes.

"So it came to pass in the process of time. . ."
1 Samuel 1:20a NKJV

CHAPTER

22

Bonding

Together we sat on our mat admiring our sleeping son. Gently my finger caressed the petal softness of his cheek. He wrinkled his face, trembled, and relaxed again. "Isn't he beautiful?" I whispered.

I'd expected to be pleased and excited with my baby, but the experience of bringing a new life into the world far surpassed my greatest expectations. Never had a baby looked so amazing to me! Never had I felt such awe! The birth of a child must be the greatest of miracles! Maybe because God allows humans to participate so intimately, using Elkanah and me to partner with Him in creating a new life. How could anyone not worship the Lord after the experience of birthing a child?

Elkanah shared my pleasure, but it couldn't be the same for him. He'd already had other sons and daughters. Besides, this child had never nestled inside his body, cradled under his heart. He never felt the wiggles and kicks, the hiccoughs, the tight crowdedness. Nor did he labor to bring the child from the dark comfort of the womb to the light of day. No way could he understand, after suffering the excruciating pain of being a barren woman, the awesome joy of motherhood. I felt glad to be me. That, because of who I was, I could experience this unique ecstasy.

We sat and watched for a long time, content to admire our son whom we named, Samuel, "asked of God."

"His eyes are like yours, Hannah."

"He has your mouth and jaw. Except for the beard!" I laughed.

The scuffle of feet at our door interrupted us. "Who is it?" Elkanah asked. He'd warned the children not to bother me during my weeks of isolation. Three-year-old Tohu peeked inside, guilt smeared over his sweet little face. "What do you want?" Elkanah asked firmly.

Tohu rubbed his eye and mumbled. "See baby."

"You know you can't come in," Elkanah reminded him.

Tohu nodded, his lower lip puckered and trembling.

"It's okay, Elkanah. Children are naturally curious. Take Samuel to the courtyard so they can look at him."

"Are you sure?"

I nodded.

Gently and firmly, Elkanah lifted the sleeping baby and disappeared with the grinning Tohu dancing at his heels. I wouldn't have been surprised if the older children sent him, realizing he could get away with more than they could.

Leaning back on the cushion, I closed my eyes. I felt tired from childbirth, but the excitement of being a mother made it difficult for me to go to sleep. Out in the courtyard I heard the children calling each other to come see the baby. After the patter of running feet, all grew silent. In my mind I could see the scene—the circle of intent dark-eyed faces, the dancing fingers reaching out to touch the swaddled child. I could hear low adult voices giving cautions. Even from my room I enjoyed their admiration of my son. Finally I heard an infant whimper and then cry. Elkanah returned with Samuel, wide-awake and hungry.

I loved the days of isolation, viewing them as a special gift—that time the mother rests from all responsibilities in order to bond with her child. As I nursed my son, I tried to absorb all the beauty, the pleasure of motherhood: my son's small warmth cuddled next to my skin, the amusing movements of his face, the rhythmic tug and soft gulping of his nursing, the milky smell of his breath, the unbelievable smoothness of his skin. *Remember! Remember everything. Store the memories away forever,* I told myself.

In all our discussions with others, Elkanah and I never mentioned the secret reason behind my vow. Everyone assumed my promise issued solely from the desperate heart of a barren woman, a woman desperate enough to resort to anything to move the hand of God. Neither did the two of us talk privately about our desire for our son to become an important influence in turning Israel from idolatry back to loyalty to the Living God.

Usually thinking of the responsibility I'd taken on brought me a sense of humility mixed with gladness. Humility because I felt unworthy, unqualified for such a task, but gladness because I knew the Lord and I worked together. But once in a while in those days, as I held Samuel at my breast or laid him down on his little mat, my eyes caressed the face of my son and a pang of grief clutched my heart. At those times, I resolutely refused to look into the future. *Samuel is just a tiny baby,* I told myself. *He needs to stay with me for now.*

During my days in isolation, I felt concerned for Peninnah, who, in spite of her grieving, had to assume all the household responsibilities in addition to watching her own children. But taking charge helped pull her out of her sadness. After my retreat ended, I fell into spending most of my time watching Peninnah's younger ones while caring for Samuel, and I loved it. Peninnah continued doing most of the household work and supervised the older children's chores. I wondered if Elkanah reminded her of how I took care of the housework while she tended her babies, because she never complained. But sometimes I saw the pain of loss in her eyes as she saw me nursing my child.

The second new moon after Samuel's birth, when we finished our evening meal, Elkanah began talking about the annual trip to Shiloh. The children chattered with excitement and anticipation, and Peninnah's eyes took on a little more life. But I felt uneasy. I couldn't figure out why. I had no reason to worry about the women's baby talk, now that I also had a child. And even if they didn't let me help, I'd have Samuel to occupy my time. I wondered if I might be dreading going to the Tabernacle where one day I would leave my son, but that didn't feel true. With all my self-examination, I came up with nothing. Yet, the desire to remain in Ramah increased day by day.

So, a few days later, I put Samuel down for his nap and told Peninnah I'd be gone for a little while. I headed toward the hills making my way through the gate in the new wall that bound new Ramah to the old city. The winter grass still dominated the hillside, brown and dry. It's music rattled under my feet as I climbed one round after another, cleansing my mind of the bustle of a busy household full of children. Puffy white clouds gave hope of an early rain that would raise the earth to life after its winter rest. I paused to enjoy the cool breeze that lightly brushed my arms and face. The heat of the sun nestled between my tunic and the skin on my back. My gaze wandered across the open hillsides. Out there somewhere Dan sat with his flocks. Farther beyond lay places I'd never been, a world I'd only heard of. I closed my eyes and breathed deeply of the fresh air.

What should I do, what could I do about the trip to Shiloh? A gust of wind tugged at my skirt carrying with it the scent of dryness, and a bird chirped excitedly to his friends. What if I stayed home? Just Samuel and me. Elkanah and the rest of the family could go without us. In those few years before I took Samuel to the Tabernacle, I could spend those two weeks alone with my child. The more I thought of it, the more peaceful I became, the more certain that this would be the right thing to do.

By the time Elkanah arrived home in the evening, I could hardly wait to talk to him. I wasn't surprised when he objected.

"But Hannah, we always go to Shiloh as a family. It's part of my vow. I've really looked forward to having you and Samuel with me this year."

"I know, Elkanah. But I feel very strongly that I need this time alone with Samuel, to concentrate without distractions on preparing him for the time we'll leave him at the Tabernacle."

Elkanah remained silent for what seemed a long time. "Okay," he said. "Do what seems best to you." But a trace of concern shaded his face. "Don't forget, Hannah. When he's weaned, you and Samuel must go. I'm asking the Lord to help you keep the promise you made to Him."

So that year I stood at the side of the road holding little Samuel, waving to the others as they started the long day's journey to Shiloh. Then my tiny son and I returned to the quietness of the empty house, and for sixteen days, I enjoyed having Samuel all to myself.

For the first time I told him my story, explaining to him detail by detail the circumstances that led to his birth. He lay there in my arms looking up at my face, and I knew the impossibility of a three-month-old infant comprehending anything I said. But, even then, I sensed its importance for me, because that Passover season I established the tradition we carried on together over the next three years. I used this opportunity to put into child's words the reasons behind my promise. I couldn't possibly count the number of times, day after day, I told him his story, past, present, and future—the story of how God had worked and would work in his life. I guess that's when I became a storyteller! Samuel never told me I talked too long, that I'd mentioned this or that before. He never became embarrassed or alarmed when my voice trembled or when tears flooded my eyes, even when the moisture dropped down onto his chest, cheek, or hair.

Very soon—too soon—it seemed, the others returned, and life slipped back into its normal routine, and it became easy to forget that Samuel differed from other babies—that he wasn't mine to keep.

Elkanah's sister, Serah, visited me often. By now her son, Liron, had learned to walk and she had a daughter two months older than Samuel. We sat together in the shade with our babies watching the older children play in the courtyard.

"I can't see how you'll ever do it." Serah shook her head sadly as she watched me teasing one grin after another from my son. "How will you ever give him away?"

"He's still little now," I said and kissed his curly head.

"But they don't stay little very long, Hannah. It seems my Liron was Samuel's age just seconds ago, and now look at him."

Jemima and Vina held Liron's hands so he could toddle around joining the other children in playing "Bedouin robbers attacking travelers." Although he had no idea what they were doing, he enthusiastically added his screams to the rest of the villagers who tried to protect the supplies they carried to market.

"Time goes fast, Hannah." I heard the concern in Serah's voice.

I looked at six-month-old Samuel sitting on my lap. "I know, Serah." A lump rose in my throat. "He's changed so much already!"

She remained silent for a time. "Are you really going to keep your vow?"

Her words pierced my heart. Tears sprang into my eyes unbidden. I swallowed them and nodded.

"But . . . how will you bear to give him up?"

I took a deep, slow breath. "There are many times I wonder about that."

"Are you sorry now you made such a promise?"

I looked up into the rustling leaves, thinking how many times I'd asked myself that question. "Never, Serah. I'll never be sorry I made my vow. Even when I release Samuel, I'll retain my memories. And I'll *always* be his mother."

Serah nodded, but she still didn't look convinced.

"There are some things people can't really understand, Serah—until they experience them," I said. "Like love, motherhood, and barrenness. Just believe me, Serah, and be glad you don't understand barrenness."

"But maybe you'd have become pregnant anyway, without making the vow."

"Maybe. But in ten years of marriage, I never once got pregnant. It's easier for me to believe the Lord changed something inside me, allowing me to conceive. Besides, look." I motioned toward all the excited children running back and forth in the courtyard. "Peninnah never had trouble."

We laughed.

"Well, I'm so glad you have Samuel," Serah said. "I just hope it won't be too hard on you when you give him up."

"Me, too," I agreed.

Often over the years, I've been grateful for Serah's insistent questions, her refusal to allow me to forget the pain I would face when I gave up my son.

But not all the questionings I received were so friendly; and not every day did I feel so certain that the memories of my joy would satisfy the yearning of my mother heart. I understood why people felt perplexed. I had to learn to be content with their lack of understanding.

As Samuel got older, I began telling him the history of the Israelites and how Yaweh took care of us. Even a child can learn the ways of the Lord from the stories of how He related to His people–and they to Him. Soon Peninnah's children noticed and asked to join us. So, a daily ritual evolved. After Elkanah left and we completed our morning chores, the children and I sat down under the almond tree and told stories. (Not this one, Jerusha. Our first one, the one we planted soon after Elkanah and I married.) Samuel listened well for a small boy, even when he was just over a year old. He tried to call out names, and his wide-eyed seriousness prompted the rest of us to smile at times. The older children mimicked Samuel's funny baby names until Peninnah and I forbade it, telling them they'd get him confused.

Each evening the children eagerly demonstrated their knowledge to their father, watching for the pride in his eyes, listening for his commendations, answering his questions. One night after an evening of child recitations, Elkanah and I lay together in my little room with Samuel already asleep near us. "I would never have believed it, Hannah. All of you work together so well. I can hardly believe what you've taught the children. Just think how much poorer all of us would have been if you didn't make that vow."

I knew it was true. But, while Elkanah's pleasure pleased me, my heart trembled with anticipation of what lay ahead. The pain of knowing the costliness of my vow, and that soon–in spite of whatever advantages came to me, our family, even the nation of Israel—I would have to endure the grief of separation. How would I bear it?

"The next year Elkanah, Peninnah, and their children
went on their annual trip
to offer a sacrifice to the LORD.
But Hannah did not go.
She told her husband, 'Wait until the baby is weaned.
Then I will take him to the Tabernacle
and leave him there with the LORD permanently.'
'Whatever you think is best,' Elkanah agreed.
'Stay here for now,
and may the LORD help you keep your promise.'
So she stayed home and nursed the baby."
1 Samuel 1:21-23 NLT

CHAPTER

23

Preparation

The year before I took Samuel to Shiloh—that was the one. The most beautiful, the most painful. During Passover, for the last time, I had my son to myself. I'd grown to love those special weeks in the spring. I planned for them, anticipated them, remembered them with joy.

Some things remained the same every year. Like the stories I told about my barrenness, my vow, Samuel's birth. Even though the stories stayed the same, the telling of them changed a bit each year as Samuel knew them better and became older. Above all, I wanted Samuel to grow up understanding his purpose in life. I wanted him to know that when I gave him to the Lord, it wouldn't be because I didn't want to keep him for myself. Nor could he believe I kept my vow solely for fear of God's judgment if I broke my promise. No, I wanted Samuel to know and understand the secret things, the things I didn't share with others. I wanted him to claim his destiny to serve the Lord to the very best of his ability all the days of his life.

So that year, as in the preceding ones, we played learning games, like "helping Eli in the Tabernacle." Samuel played himself and I, old Eli. Samuel would be busy playing, or even pretend sleeping, when Eli needed him, but always Samuel came without complaint, quickly and quietly at Eli's first call. Then we practiced cleaning chores: carrying a pitcher of water without letting even one drop spill, sweeping the floor of the courtyard using water sprinkles to avoid stirring up dust, lifting and dusting small lamps, pots, and jars and being careful to put them back exactly in their places. He learned to be quiet and still when he'd much rather talk and wiggle. I felt very proud of Samuel. He amazed me with how quickly his skills grew, how much he learned from one year to the next. For such a little child, he excelled as an eager and diligent student.

Samuel had grown to anticipate the special activities we repeated yearly, like eating Passover with one set of grandparents, alternating year after year. Almost every day we took a trip over the hillside to help Samuel's legs grow strong enough for the long walk to Shiloh. We talked about what we would see on the way and about the stories and games that would keep us busy. While we stopped for snack breaks or picnics, we reviewed stories, sometimes an incident in the history of our ancestors, other times an event relating to our own lives. One of our favorite spots to stop included the mandrake patches where I had come in hopes of finding a cure for my barrenness.

At three, Samuel no longer needed me to identify the plant for him. He ran ahead, pointing. "Look, Mama! Mandrakes!" Sure enough all around him lay the small dark green plants with their bluish-purple flowers and dangling yellow fruit.

As soon as we seated ourselves by the patch, the telling began. "Women who want to have a baby often eat these fruits," I said.

"But they didn't work for you, right Mama?"

"Right. No matter how many I ate, no baby grew."

"Are you going to take some home to eat now?"

"Why?" I asked, not sure what he might be thinking.

"Next year I'll be a big boy. I'll go away, Mama. You need another baby so you won't be lonely." His eyes widened innocently as he watched me. His candor touched the most sensitive spot of my heart. I couldn't imagine the loneliness I would feel; I didn't want to. How many times had I pushed such ideas from my mind, refusing to think about what it would be like when I came home without my little Samuel? Over and over again I planned all the other details—preparing Samuel, talking to Eli, getting Samuel settled in his new home, even to that final scene of bravely saying good-bye to my little son and walking away with a smile on my face, waving a cheery good-bye, and saying, "I'll be back to see you next year, Samuel! I'll bring you a new robe!" But I refused to allow myself to go beyond that point.

That beautiful spring day, I refused again. Following one of my unspoken rules, I refrained from saying or doing anything that might interfere with Samuel wanting to carry out his service to the Lord. I couldn't let him see how greatly I dreaded our parting. So I reverted to my habit of pasting what I hoped to be a cheery smile on my face and diverting his attention to something safer. "Remember Samuel, these fruits don't help me have babies. But we like them, don't we? Pick two for us to eat."

Immediately his mind shifted to finding the two nicest love apples, and soon we sat side by side, biting into the fragrant fruit. But *my* mind refused to be so easily diverted. Time and again the thought of "next year" surfaced. Time and again I pushed the thought away, promising to deal with it later.

That same year, the year Samuel was three, we could walk farther. I told Dan about my plan weeks before, and he agreed to work with me. We decided on a day that Samuel and I would meet him and the younger cousins on the hillside. Early in the morning Samuel and I began our walk, a long one for his little legs, over the hills just turning green after the first spring rain. How beautiful, beautiful! Samuel and I, hand in hand, danced our delight together. Finally, over on the hilltop we spotted Uncle Dan and his sheep. Samuel's waning energy revived. Soon bleating sheep and jabbering cousins surrounded him like chicks around spilled grain. The children vied for the opportunity of showing him all the exciting sights—the big climbing rocks, the newborn lambs, the brook in the valley with its little fish and menagerie of bugs hiding in the cool grassy edges.

The day passed quickly. I stood back watching—watching, remembering, and storing away memories. And reviving treasured recollections of my own childhood, times spent on the hillside, watching sheep with my brothers. Every child should know the pleasure of pastoral life, the closeness to nature and to the God Who created all things. *How can a person truly know God,* I wondered, *without spending time outdoors?* I doubted Samuel would have many such opportunities living at the Tabernacle, so this would have to do. Was he too young to remember? I hoped not.

Later, at Dan's call, the children clamored up on the big rock to watch the sun bid us farewell amid a magnificent display of red and orange. But the sun struggled in competition for our attention with the rising fragrance of Dan's lamb in its roasting hole, tantalizing and distracting us. My mother rated as a wonderful cook, and my skills deserved commendations as well, but no meal I ever ate matched those around the campfire. Adults and children clustered together, tearing off succulent morsels of tender meat with our fingers, slowly savoring each bite, licking the last of the sweet, sticky juice from our fingers before reaching for another tempting portion. Between bites the children relived the excitement of the day, laughing, recalling, correcting each other's stories. The snapping of the fire cheered them on, bidding them forget the howling of wolves on the distant hills and the bleating of sheep in the safety of the fold nearby. The happy glow of the firelight danced on the children's faces, making their eyes shine a glistening gold. *Soak in the memories Samuel, memories of home*, my heart cried out to my son as I studied his intent little face.

Dan waited until no one could eat another savory bite. Then he drew out his flute and began to play. Slowly, softly, so sweetly the music flowed forth. Delicate notes floated up, up into the cool night air, drawing away with them the worries of the world. Calm settled over us, wrapping us in a blanket of peace. Above us in the blackness of the night, the sky displayed hundreds, thousands of twinkling stars and streaks of milky clouds.

How long our spirits rested in the heavens with our Maker, I don't really know, but at just the right moment, the music began to change, gently pulling us back to earth, returning our awareness of the faces around us, of the joy we shared together. Dan nodded, and I took out my pipe and joined in the music. Many of the children also knew how to play instruments—pipes, flutes, tambourines, even simple harps—and they, too, followed Dan's cue. One by one we joined the song as it slowly built in enthusiasm. Bodies swayed to the music and the younger ones, who couldn't yet play, added their clapping, tapping, and stomping to the sound. Samuel watched and followed, a smile of pleasure wreathing his face. Music, of course, comprised an important part of our family life, so he felt delighted, completely at home. Finally the music transitioned again from the joyfulness of life to the sweetness of sleep. One by one the older children wrapped robes around the younger ones, and then they tucked away their instruments and snuggled down, looking up at the stars until their eyes, too, closed in peaceful repose.

Samuel, who fell asleep early after his long day, lay nestled by my side where I fondled his dark curls and stroked the soft roundness of his cool cheek. My pipe lay hidden under my belt, and I closed my eyes, listening to Dan's last slow mournful song until it dissolved into the music of the night.

Dan threw more kindling on the fire and sat back. The fire crackled and spit as it lapped at the new twigs, sending sparks flying into the darkness. Silently our eyes swept the cluster of children sleeping around the fire, until we both focused on Samuel—his childish lips parted in sleep, his breath soft and even. "One year left, Hannah."

I nodded. A lump rose in my throat and tears blurred my vision. "It's so hard Dan! So hard to hold on tightly to every moment and yet at the same time to be letting go."

"You'll manage, Hannah. You're a tough woman. In spite of your sensitivity, your spirit remains strong." I saw him smile in the firelight. "Sometimes too strong perhaps?"

I smiled in return.

"Remember, the same Lord who helped you through other difficult times in your life will help you again. Just keep on depending on Him, one day at a time." Dan stood. "I'm going to check on the sheep," he said, and disappeared into the darkness.

I lay down beside my son, and drew his small warm body close to mine. I tried to think of Dan's encouraging words, but only one thought remained clear. This time next year, I would be saying good-bye.

"But Hannah did not go up . . .
the woman remained and nursed her son,
until she weaned him."
1 Samuel 1:21&23 RSV

CHAPTER

24

Transition

Never did a year pass so quickly! Never. I know people say years go faster as you get older, but every other year of my life has felt longer than that one. Yet what a year packed full of life!

First, I continually reinforced all I'd taught Samuel, preparing him to serve in a manner honoring to the Lord. Second, I worked to squeeze a lifetime of childhood fun into that one tiny year. Always, I tried to maintain balance. Balance between learning and playing, between making certain Samuel understood the importance of his calling and making sure he would willingly serve others–rather than focusing on himself, feeling superior. Trying to balance between living a normal life and recognizing little Samuel's life could never be "normal."

I wasn't the only one who found this life confusing. Throughout that last year family opposition mounted again. My parents were as bad as Elkanah's. In addition to doting on him more than ever, my mother–when she felt the pain of her coming loss–got into the habit of throwing her apron over her head when she wept–so Samuel wouldn't notice, she said. Father, torn between his pride and his pain, kept telling Elkanah over and over again, that if he fathered ten million sons, there would never be another Samuel. My brothers, their wives and children, all of them became more and more focused on Samuel.

"Elkanah, whatever will we do?" I asked in frustration one night after a visit with my family. "I've told them to act normal around Samuel, but their always flooding him with attention. How can we stop them?"

In silence Elkanah laid the sleeping Samuel on his mat, tucking a robe around him. Then he settled himself beside me, and together we sat gazing down at the peaceful sweet face of our son. "Can you cause rain to stay on the side of a hill instead of running down to the low land?" he asked. "It's impossible, Hannah. Rain drains to the valley, rushes down the wadi. If it comes to you, all a person can do is keep his head above the current. You can't make it go away. You've done all you can do, Hannah, but a normal life's impossible for Samuel. He will always get more attention than ordinary people. However, I believe you taught him how to swim." Elkanah reached out and wrapped me in his arms. "Now, stop worrying about Samuel, and notice how he handles himself." He kissed my forehead. "He'll be okay, Hannah. He'll be okay."

So in the following months, I tried to do what Elkanah suggested. What I saw comforted me and gave me a growing assurance that, even at this young age, Samuel would be at home in the Tabernacle. The child possessed a solemn poise commanding respect, even from those much older than he. His quiet discernment (which he probably got from his father) seemed strange in one so young. Yet he remained a joyful child, caring and sensitive of others. He accepted attention graciously without pride or self-centeredness. So, I concluded, Samuel had indeed learned to swim, and he would survive.

One cold windy night in the fall before our trip to Shiloh, Elkanah and I spent our evening in our room playing music together. Samuel, as usual, fell asleep on his mat near us long before we exhausted the songs waiting to be released from our hearts. Finally, the cool of the night air creeping in encouraged us to lay aside our instruments and retreat to the warmth of our bed. But we were far from sleepy, so our minds wandered, as they so often did, to the time when Samuel would no longer sleep with us.

"I've been wondering, Elkanah, about the clothes Samuel will need when he lives at the Tabernacle. I need to get them ready."

"Good idea."

"But what should he wear?"

"What do you mean?"

"Well, when you go to minister at the Tabernacle, you wear the white linen robe of the Levites rather than the ordinary woolen browns of everyday."

Elkanah remained silent. "Are you thinking Samuel should wear a Levitical robe?'

"I don't know. What do you think?"

Elkanah considered the options. "His situation is entirely new. There's never been a boy ministering at the Tabernacle. However, all Levites on duty must wear the proper clothes. I guess Samuel, like the High Priest, will be on duty all the time."

Hannah nodded, thinking of her promise. Her son would never be "off duty." Samuel would serve the Lord all the days of his life.

"Being dressed as a Levite would distinguish him from other children, making his presence less confusing to people who don't know him. It would definitely be unusual, but I doubt anything else will work."

So it was decided, and I began gathering my supplies.

Making Samuel's robe occupied much of my private time. In fact, over the months I stretched the moments out as long as I could. Carding, spinning, weaving. Savoring each touch, realizing that this little garment would embrace my son's body day after day while he remained far, far away from me. Soon the little robe would carry the smell of his flesh, but right then, I hoped the fibers would absorb something of me into their essence, that when Samuel wore this robe, it would speak to him of the mother who loved him dearly. That he would always remember my love, the things we'd done together, all I'd taught him. Into the fabric I wove many invisible things—hopes, prayers, memories, dreams.

I'll never forget the night when I completed the robe and dressed Samuel up for his father. No little boy ever felt more proud.

"Look, Papa! I'm just like you!" His dark eyes glistened. "Now I'm ready," he said.

And he was. But I can't say the same for me. Or for Peninnah's children.

"Why does Samuel have to go?" whined Micah, Peninnah's youngest son.

"Stop asking that *same* question *over* and *over* and *over*," Elihu said as he rubbed his forehead. His voice sound irritated, but I noticed him blinking as if to erase tears from his eyes.

"But . . . but . . . ," Micah's lip trembled. He turned and ran to his favorite retreat in the east corner of the courtyard.

Jemima glared at Elihu and marched off to comfort Micah. Peninnah's baby, Vina, now nearly six, also gave him a look before strutting off after her big sister.

As the countdown continued, the rumble grew louder and louder, not only in our family, but throughout Ramah. Whenever I walked through Ramah, I heard their comments, sometimes directed to me, but often spoken to someone else–for my benefit I'm sure.

"It's not right, not normal. How could any sane mother give her only son away?"

"I heard about her vow–long ago–but I never believed she'd actually keep it!"

"Do you *really* think she'll leave him, I mean once they get there?"

Finally that long awaited departure day arrived. Our families and many of the people of Ramah gathered to see us off. Some critical, some curious, but most honestly seeking a chance to bid Samuel good-bye. As the time for him to leave drew nearer, he'd become a celebrity, an extension of Ramah, a source of fame.

"We'll come and see you in Shiloh," one after another promised. They pelted him with kisses and pressed little cakes, dried fruit, and nuts into his small hands.

Peninnah knelt beside him, taking the gifts one after another and laying them carefully in a basket to prevent their being crushed or dropped. I never knew if Elkanah, or perhaps his mother, assigned her that responsibility, or if she took it upon herself. Even in that most intense moment, as I saw her kneeling there beside my Samuel, I couldn't help thinking of how much she'd changed.

For a while I thought we'd never get down the road away from Ramah, away from the weeping women and cheering men behind us, and finally the last of the children who trailed us all the way to the bend leading north.

"Look, Mama!" Samuel said some time later in his excited high voice. "Way over there. See? The hill with the one lonely tree. Is that the place where we stop for our first rest?"

So the day continued, with Samuel searching for the landmarks I'd described to him on our pretend trips. Each time we arrived at a resting spot, he asked Peninnah to spread out his abundant supply of snacks for the family to share.

"You should save some for yourself, Samuel," I insisted. "Nuts and dry fruit keep quite well."

"That's okay, Mama. Jemima likes nuts, and Giddel and Tohu especially like dried figs."

In spite of Samuel's generosity, after the first serving, Peninnah packed away the best portions to save for Samuel, making certain nothing she saved contained raisins.

Fun filled our journey: the children informing Samuel of incidents from other trips, Elkanah telling a story as he always did, Samuel delighting in the adventure of his long anticipated trip. Surprisingly, even I felt happy. Then we arrived in Shiloh, and Peninnah's family welcomed us with an abundant feast. Although this time I, too, had a son, I couldn't help wondering whether I'd be out of place, like that cucumber plant that once grew among the stocks of corn.

Elkanah decided it would be best to wait until the day before we left for Ramah to give Samuel to Eli. So while Elkanah served at the Tabernacle, Samuel was to stay with me at the home of Peninnah's family, getting to know his Shiloh cousins. As usual, on the first Sabbath, we went as a family to give our sacrifices to the Lord. For the first time Samuel brought his portion, since Elkanah had offered the sacrifices for Samuel and me during the years we remained in Ramah.

For the first time Samuel saw the Tabernacle. I'm afraid I didn't worship much that day. I was too intent on watching my son. What if the activity at the Tabernacle frightened him? After all, we came from a small village, living quiet, unexciting lives. At the Tabernacle, people of all sorts constantly came and went, bringing their sacrifices with them. How would he handle the sight and odor of blood, the smell of burning flesh mixed with the sweetness of the incense, or the bleating of animals combined with the Levites' singing? No wonder many sensitive children found their first experience overwhelming! Would Samuel be afraid to stay, to make this strange place his new home?

His wide dark eyes moved constantly about the Tabernacle. His eyes searching, then stopping and widening as if in delighted recognition. Then searching again. His face reflected the same excitement I'd witnessed on our journey to Shiloh. In the last months before our trip, Elkanah had spent a great deal of time explaining the ways of the Tabernacle to Samuel, and now Samuel seemed to be trying to fit together all the pieces of information his father had given him.

"Come, Samuel," I said before we left the Tabernacle that day. "See this place?" I pointed. "I stood right here when I asked God for a very special son." There, in low murmurs, we recited together the commitment I made to God.

Each day thereafter Samuel grasped my hand and drew me to that spot. "Right here, Mama. You talked to God right here." Then he whispered the story I'd so often told him.

On our journey, Samuel had expressed his excitement without inhibition, but in the Tabernacle, he restrained himself as if in reverence for this holy place. Not until we walked together through the streets of Shiloh toward Peninnah's family home, did he allow his pent up excitement to burst forth.

"I heard them singing your songs, Papa," he said. Pride glistened in his eyes.

Elkanah smiled.

"Sometimes," Samuel said thoughtfully, "the songs carry us up close to God. Other times they bring Him down to us. Both are nice."

Elkanah looked at me. A lump rose in my throat.

"But first we have to be clean, right Papa? That's why we bring sacrifices." His eyes lost their sparkle and took on that look of a black bottomless pool. He shook his head, and his eyes filled with tears. "I'm sorry for my sins." He looked up, first at his father, then at me. "When I do bad things, it makes God very sad. Sin hurts people, doesn't it? Like when I get into my brothers' things after they ask me not to. Or when I pretend not to hear when you call me. Or when I don't tell the truth because I don't want to get into trouble." He shook his head. "I'm glad God made a way for us to get rid of all those bad things." He smiled.

We walked along in silence. Perhaps Elkanah also felt unable to speak.

"I'm glad I get to work in the Tabernacle." Samuel reached out and slipped his hands into ours. "Helping people to be close to God is important," he said. "But God's helpers must be very clean." He looked up at his father. "I saw that big laver with the shiny mirrors you told me about. I looked to see if anything was wrong with me."

I smiled, remembering Samuel standing there, examining himself.

"I saw my nice white robe. It was clean. But there was some dirt on my cheek right here, wasn't there, Mama? I didn't even know it was there. That's why the mirrors are important, right?"

I nodded, recalling how Elkanah had taken water from the tall laver and helped Samuel wash the smug away.

"But," Elkanah said, "dirt on the outside is not as important to God as bad thoughts and actions, Samuel. Only God can help us see those, not the mirrors."

Our time in Shiloh passed too quickly. Every day I took Samuel to the Tabernacle, so he would begin to feel at home there. Each day Samuel looked for old Eli and greeted him on the way in and out of the temple. "I like Eli," he whispered each time as we walked away from him. I never spoke to Eli. I wanted to save that for the day I would give Samuel into his care.

Other than our trips to the Tabernacle, the incident that impressed Samuel most occurred on one of our walks around Shiloh. Often Samuel and I took walks alone, but one morning Peninnah and her children accompanied us.

"I lived all my life in Shiloh until I married your father," Peninnah explained to the children. "As the only girl, I had to help my mother with cooking, take care of my little brothers, and doing housework, so I didn't have much time to play."

I forced myself not to stare at Peninnah. After all these years, that was the first I'd heard her mention her childhood.

"Did you ever go to the fields with your brothers?" Elihu asked, and I suspected he was remembering the stories I'd told him of my experiences with my brothers.

"Only when my father sent me to check on them after they'd been gone a long time."

"Was it fun?" Tohu asked eagerly.

"Not really." She looked down and pinched the opening of her tunic tight around her neck.

"Were you scared of the wild animals?" Milcah whispered. *He* was.

Peninnah smiled and shook her head. "Not as must as the people." Abruptly she turned and pointed to a hill nearby. "Look!" her voice rose emphatically, reminding me of her days of drama. I've always wondered if she intentionally drew their attention from an uncomfortable topic. "See the big stone up on the hill over there by the trees? That's a place people go to worship the gods of the Canaanites."

Samuel frowned as he lifted his chin to gaze at the scene. "They worship idols there?" he asked pointing, his eyes growing wide and dark.

"Yes."

"But only the Canaanites, right? Not *Yaweh's* people."

"No, Samuel, Israelites worship on this hill, mostly people from Shiloh."

"But why?" Samuel asked. "The Tabernacle's right here in this village. Why don't they worship the Lord instead?"

Peninnah shrugged. "Perhaps the God of Israel didn't do what they wanted, didn't satisfy them somehow."

Samuel frowned. He murmured something to himself, but I couldn't distinguish what he said.

For nearly an hour Peninnah kept us tromping over the hillside, pointing out good lookouts and rocky ledges great for climbing. I saw for the first time a new side of Peninnah. I wondered if she'd taken her children on hikes such as this on the years when Samuel and I stayed at home. But none of the children mentioned having been there previously. I was so glad she included Samuel and me. Maybe she'd done it because she knew this would be Samuel's new home and thought he might get lonely for our trips through the fields. I'll never know.

We returned to her father's house weary and warm, but all our adventures failed to erase Samuel's memory of the Cannanite altar. As soon as his father arrived, he questioned him about Israelites who worshipped other gods.

A few days later I overheard Samuel talking to his older siblings and cousins. "We must *always* be loyal to the Lord. He's the only True God. He loves us very much!" His face broke into a huge smile. "God's rules are good rules. They help us live the right way. So we won't hurt ourselves. Or other people." Then he frowned. "Don't *ever* worship other gods! Never!" he said with a frown, wagging his small finger emphatically.

Their rapt attention impressed me. *Please, Lord, let them take his words seriously even though he's so young.* Back in Ramah several times during the following year, I overheard

Peninnah's children reminding each other of what Samuel said that day.

Two days before we went home, I took Samuel to visit my mother's sister who lived in Shiloh. "We'll keep a close watch on Samuel," her husband promised. "We go to the Tabernacle nearly every day, and we'll look for him whenever we're there."

"I'll take him special treats sometimes," my aunt assured me. "And, don't worry, I'll remember. No raisins!" With each word she struck her finger emphatically in the palm of her hand.

My uncle smiled down at Samuel who stood quietly beside me observing our conversation. "Hannah, it's a great honor to our family to have a Nazarite serving in the Tabernacle!"

We took the long way around the outer edges of Shiloh to enjoy the countryside on our way back to the house. On the way Samuel reached out and took my hand in his own. "Mama?" Samuel asked, his dark eyes looking seriously into mine. "You love me very much, don't you?"

A lump rose in my throat. I stopped walking, and, while determinedly holding back the tears, I knelt in front of my child. Gently, I surround his face with my hands and caressed him with my eyes. A firm courageous jaw, but still round and soft with the fullness of childhood. "Yes, Samuel, my son. I love you very much."

"You love the Lord, our God, too." His dark eyes peered into the depths of my soul. "You love Him, very, *very* much?"

"Yes, Samuel, I love our God very, *very* much."

A breeze lifted the hair over his forehead, and birds chirped in the bushes nearby.

"Mama, why do you love the Lord so very much?"

The beauty of his innocent cherub face tugged at my

heart. I drew him to myself, but I refused to squeeze him as tightly as I wanted to. I kissed his forehead. Rising, I took Samuel's hand and led him to a grassy spot beside the road. "Come Samuel, let's sit here and talk."

After we sat down side by side, I took his hand in mine and smiled into his eager face, willing my tears to stay stored away. "I began to love the Lord Almighty as just a little child, like you did. I remember my father telling me stories about our great God, a God who is very powerful, but also a God who loves and cares for His people. The more I learned about our God, the more I came to love Him."

I wished I could explain it better to Samuel. But how could a little child so fresh and new, so inexperienced in the suffering of life, understand the way faith struggles and grows through the difficulties it faces? Why *did* I love Yaweh so much? Well, He'd rescued me from the pit of despair. He gave me hope for a meaningful life—even if I never had children. In my times of greatest weakness, He'd given me strength.

But my love for the Lord hadn't begun there. In that moment I felt again the adoration for God I had as a young child. The passion of an innocent heart, the pure uninhibited love, love without fear, reservation, or questions. I felt again its pure joy. There were no words to explain it. So I only smiled.

But Samuel's little face lit up with understanding, and he nodded enthusiastically. "I love Yaweh, too. He's a good God. I love Him very, *very* much."

In that moment I realized how wrong I'd been during those years of darkness to depreciate the faith of my childhood. It's true, my faith had to grow to meet the challenges of my adult life, but that day, sitting on the grass beside my little son, I came to understand that all stages of faith are precious in God's sight, each beautiful and appropriate in its time.

"I know you love the Lord, Samuel." As I smiled at my

son, there appeared in my mind the picture I saw the night I made my vow to God—the picture of the man God could use to bring Israel to Him. My heart flooded with joy as I looked into Samuel's upturned face. The fulfillment of that hope had already begun! In that moment, I had no doubt. God would continue to carry out His plan for the life of this child of promise. And I was glad.

But I had no idea how difficult the task would be—not just for me, but for him.

Then finally the day arrived, the day I'd anticipated for all of Samuel's life.

". . . his mother made him a little robe. . .
After he was weaned, she took the boy with her,
young as he was,
. . . and brought him to the house of the LORD at Shiloh."
1 Samuel 2:19 and 1:24 NIV

CHAPTER

25
The Gift

The events of that day stand out as clear in my mind as the day they happened, scene after scene preserved forever in my memory. The first occurred before dawn. I'd tossed restlessly all night. The excitement, the magnitude of this day of my life, the desire to savor each moment pushed sleep away. In the darkness of the early morning I reached my hand out from the warmth of the blanket where I lay beside Elkanah and gently touched the cold curly hair of my son laying beside me on his mat.

I remember thinking, "Only a few more hours, and Samuel will no longer be mine." But as I let the soft curls twist around my fingers, I realized Samuel had never really been mine. Even before his birth, he belonged to God. Yes, the Lord granted me the wonderful privilege of being his mother, but Samuel never *belonged* to me.

My thoughts returned to the days before my vow. But they seemed so far away, like the life of a different person in a time long ago. How could the overwhelmed Hannah who ran out the door to escape Peninnah's torment be the same woman as Samuel's mother? What would my life have been like if I had never had my son? What would it be like when he was gone?

Elkanah must have noticed my slight movement because his arm tightened around me. But, rather than sinking toward my husband's body, I kept my hand on Samuel's head. Elkanah relaxed his hold and began caressing my shoulder. He knew. He knew as well as any human could, the struggle I felt. In spite of my joy at having accomplished what I set out to do, a mountain of heaviness lay on my chest.

"What will my life be like after Samuel's gone?" I whispered around the lump in my throat.

"God will provide the strength we need," Elkanah said.

We lay still, each absorbed in silence. Then at the first sign of dawn, Elkanah rose to pray. "The Lord is my strength and my song; he has become my salvation." The familiar words comforted me. "He is my God, and I will praise Him, my father's God, and I will exalt Him. . . ." I rose with the words ringing in my heart, determined to make them mine for that particular day.

A million pictures flash through my mind, Jerusha, as I recall our day of separation. Last time pictures. First time pictures. Once-in-a-lifetime pictures. My hands combing Samuel's curly dark hair. Samuel eating breakfast surrounded by his siblings. His dark solemn eyes meeting mine as I straightened that tiny Levitical robe the morning we took him to the Tabernacle. I could list them all—every one. But I won't.

We walked to the Tabernacle that day, Elkanah leading a three-year-old bull he purchased as a special sacrifice to God, and Samuel and I following with a container of flour and a skin of wine for our offering. This time Peninnah and the others remained behind. Elkanah and I smiled at Samuel's enthusiasm, silently held in check, but evidenced by the alertness in his eyes and the way he bounced on his left leg as he walked. When we reached the Tabernacle that day, a holy stillness settled over all of us. Never have I felt the presence of the Almighty as I did that day as Elkanah offered our sacrifices to the Lord—a simmering of peace and joy mixed together . . . and an awesome awareness of HIM.

When we finally walked out the Tabernacle gate toward the pillar where Eli sat on his chair, I wondered if I'd be able to speak. But Elkanah and I had planned everything and rehearsed it so many times with Samuel, that I doubt anything could have disturbed our routine. As one, we walked to Eli and paused before him, just as we practiced. But this time it was for real. Eli squinted at us as if trying to see who we were.

In that moment, a joyful confidence overtook me. "My lord," I said respectfully with a slight nod, surprised at the calm assurance in my voice. "I'm the woman who stood here beside you praying to the Lord five years ago. I prayed for this child." I laid my hand on Samuel's curls. "The Lord granted me what I asked of Him. So now I give him to the Lord. For his whole life he will be given over to the Lord."

We may have prepared ourselves for Samuel's transition into the Tabernacle, but we took poor Eli completely by surprise. Funny how I never once thought of how he would respond to Samuel's arrival. To say he appeared shocked puts it mildly.

For a long time he said nothing. He blinked repeatedly and then swallowed, cleared his throat, and swallowed again. "I . . . remember you," he finally said with a nod, "I'm glad the Lord answered your prayer, as I asked Him to do." He grasped his white beard near his chin and his thumb stroked frantically. "But . . . but, well . . . don't you think this child is a little young to be serving the Lord?" He leaned forward and peered at Samuel from the distance of a hand's breadth. "He's still a baby. The Tabernacle's no place for one so young. Maybe when he gets older. . . . Twenty-five is plenty soon to begin service." His drew back as his voice trailed off.

"With all respect, my lord," Elkanah said, "I understand your concern. Perhaps you remember me, Elkanah from Ramah?"

"Oh, yes. Yes, of course," Eli said. From the relief in his voice, I suspected he'd rather deal with a rational father, someone he knew and respected, than a potentially emotional mother.

"I know my wife's vow is highly unusual. I can see why you'd be concerned about the age of our child. But this is a unique situation. She promised that if God Almighty would give her a son, she would give her child to serve the Lord as a Nazarite for 'all the days of his life.' And, as you see, the Lord kept His part of the bargain." Elkanah reached out and laid his hand on Samuel, who looked up into his father's face and beamed. Elkanah returned his smile and continued. "Since the boy's birth, Hannah has diligently trained him to be of service. Both of us have made sure he knows the stories of our ancestors and that he understands and reverences the Lord. I also taught him the ways of the Tabernacle. My lord, I assure you, if you allow Samuel to stay with you, you'll not be disappointed."

Eli studied Samuel from a distance, and I wondered what he tried to see. But those thoughts revealed themselves much later.

As we waited, Samuel spoke up. "Don't worry, my lord. I'll be good. Here, let me show you how Mama taught me to lead you around." Samuel stepped forward and took hold of Eli's hand. "Now first, you have to stand up."

Old Eli, taken by surprise, did as Samuel instructed, struggling to lift his massive bulk from his chair. Samuel turned around, placing his right shoulder under Eli's left hand. "Just hold on here," he instructed, patting Eli's hand. "Now, where, my lord, would you like to go?"

Elkanah and I watched in amusement as Samuel and Eli played "taking Eli around the Tabernacle." Two years back I'd asked Elkanah to make careful note of the layout of the Tabernacle and all its furnishings, measuring it out in steps so I could make a drawing in the dirt and teach Samuel his way around. In the previous weeks during our visits to the Tabernacle, Samuel checked everything, seeing with his eyes things he'd seen only in his imagination: the lamp, the table, the door to Eli's personal room, the women's court, the entrance to the men's court. As they moved about the Tabernacle that morning, I noticed people staring at Samuel in his Levitical garb as he led the High Priest from place to place. Next to Eli's bulk, Samuel looked tinier than ever.

Finally as Samuel and Eli stood near the doorway leading from the women's court into the area for the men, Samuel paused. He stood as close to the Holy Place as he was allowed to go. Without warning, he dropped their game. Lifting his hands and face, Samuel began to worship the Lord. "Who among the gods is like You, O Lord?" As his childish voice rang out, silence settled in the women's court. Several men appeared at the door of the men's court to see what was going on. Samuel remained unaware of anyone but the Lord. "Who is like You — majestic in holiness, awesome in glory, working wonders? . . ."

Tears caught in my throat as I watched him. Thankfulness welled up in my heart. My dream. The vision. Already, it was coming true. Around us women and children, as well as men, witnessed with amazement our child's simple, pure adoration of the Almighty Lord. Tears of joy rose up in my heart.

"In Your unfailing love You will lead the people You have redeemed," Samuel continued, and a strange confidence rang in his voice. "In your strength You will guide them to Your holy dwelling. The nations will hear and tremble."

As Samuel's voice ceased and his head bowed in reverence, I could contain myself no longer. "My heart rejoices in the Lord . . . " I, too, followed my son in raising my hands in joy. "There is no one holy like the Lord; there is no one besides You; there is no Rock like our God." Those were the words of the song Dan taught me during my time of deepest darkness, during the time I came to believe in the right of the Lord to rule in His sovereignty. Before the time of Peninnah's arrival. Before the time of my vow. "She who was barren has borne seven children . . . " In that moment, I realized that the God of Israel had completely satisfied my longings, as if in truth, my home were as full of children as the week is full of days.

Then, I understood. If God had never allowed me to experience the anguish of barrenness, I would never have made my vow. I might have produced six children, like my mother and grandmother, or seven like Peninnah, or even more–but I'd never have raised one to be like Samuel. I'd never have possessed such a gift to give to the Lord, to the people of Israel. "The Lord sends poverty and wealth; he humbles and he exalts. He raises the poor from the dust and lifts the needy from the ash heap; he seats them with princes and has them inherit a throne of honor. . . . "

Most of that day Elkanah and I stayed at the Tabernacle talking to Eli, making sure Samuel felt comfortable in his new home. It was obvious that the news about Samuel traveled quickly through the Tabernacle, spilling out into the streets of Shiloh. Before long "worshippers" crowded the Tabernacle, all peering at the new little Levite.

For the first time I met Eli's sons, Hophni and Phinehas. By the time they arrived, Eli had decided to keep Samuel and had invited us into his personal quarters. "I know of just the place for you," he assured Samuel just as his sons walked in.

With a quick glance, their eyes swept coolly over me. They nodded to Elkanah and briefly studied our little Samuel. Then the taller big one turned and addressed his father as if the three of us ceased to exist. "So, Father," he said. (I found out later he was Hophni.) "What's this we hear about a child moving into the Tabernacle?"

"Yes, well, this woman here . . ." Eli nodded toward me, speaking very slowly as if gathering his thoughts to prepare for an argument he knew lay ahead, "Well, several years ago, she prayed that God would give her a son. . . ."

The shorter one (Phinehas), also quite heavy, briskly brushed aside his father's words. "We know, Father. *Everyone* knows the story by now." His lips curled and disgust covered his face. "Don't tell me you're willing to agree to this ridiculous plan!"

"You," his brother added, looking down on his father with a dark glare, ". . . you of all people, should know the one thing we *don't* need in the Tabernacle is children!"

They took turns arguing, and, Eli, without attempting to interrupt them, sat down. His rested his hands on his knees, rocking back and forth as he gazed expressionlessly at the floor, then at Elkanah, Samuel, and me, and back at the floor again. Although Eli seemed disinterested in their concerns, I listened carefully, trying to see if, in spite of my assurance that I'd done the right thing, I'd overlooked something important. In the midst of the excitement, Samuel slipped out of the room, and none of us noticed until he returned. He walked up to Eli's sons and held up two cups of water.

"Talking makes people thirsty," he said as he smiled at each of them in turn.

Surprised, they wordlessly accepted Samuel's offer.

"Now, I've been thinking," Eli said when his sons put the water to their lips, "the storage closet next to my room can easily be made into a place for the child. You two are not to have anything to do with him. He will answer *only* to me. I think having a quick pair of legs and observant eyes at my side may be a great blessing for a slow old blind man. Now hurry. Send some of the Levites to prepare Samuel's room."

Dust flew and before we left, the closet sparkled. I helped Samuel roll out his mat and find places for the few possessions we'd packed in his bundle.

Smiling happily at his new home, Samuel ran to me for a hug. "You can go now, Mama. I'll be just fine here." He kissed me firmly and gave my neck a squeeze before turning to his father for a hug and kiss. Then Elkanah stood, took my hand, and led the way out with Samuel following and Eli shuffling along with his hand on Samuel's shoulder. Samuel and Eli stopped at Eli's post near the door while Elkanah and I walked on toward Peninnah's parents' house. But, I must confess, we stopped often to turn and look back. Each time Samuel smiled with delight and waved to us, until finally we rounded the bend out of his sight. Then Elkanah halted in the road.

"Hannah," Elkanah's voice thickened with emotion, "let's walk outside town before going home."

I nodded, knowing I couldn't speak. Our pace quickened as we headed west toward the setting sun. Sometimes I wonder how a person can feel so much emotion, profound joy and deepest sorrow, both at the same time. Yet the universe remained unchanged. As always, the sun set on the shining waters of the Great Sea far to the west, and as darkness settled, millions of stars sprang into the night sky. We talked little, cried and hugged much. We endured the chill as long as we could, then returned to the house and crept in without talking to anyone.

The next morning brought an emotional freshness that surprised me—the clinging and crying feelings gone, replaced by a peaceful calm. I rose with Elkanah, dressed, and gathered our belongings, tying our bundles for our trip home as Elkanah finished his prayers. Then we joined the family for breakfast and the whole clan headed to the Tabernacle with us.

Samuel, who was standing at the pillar next to Eli when we arrived, joined us for worship, and then we said our good-byes. Both Elkanah and I focused on trying to make this as pleasant and painless an experience as possible for all the children. Although a few tears leaked out of Peninnah's brood, Samuel, in his clean white robe, seemed delighted to remain behind to fill his new position.

That trip home was the quietest ever. Oh, Elkanah did his best to make things normal, but no one was fooled–not even Vina, who sucked her thumb until it was sore. I'd be lying if I said it was easy. I kept reminding myself of the lessons Dan taught me. Rather than trying to imagine how it would feel to have Samuel gone, I worked at being thankful, remembering all the good things I'd enjoyed on the trip. Carefully, I reviewed each event in precise detail, tucking away each memory to enjoy over and over in the coming days. Besides, by now I'd learned that my imagined projections of the future rarely resembled reality. For the first time, I felt content to let the future remain in the hands of the Almighty.

"When they had slaughtered the bull,
they brought the boy to Eli, and she said to him,
'As surely as you live, my lord,
I am the woman who stood here beside you
praying to the LORD.
I prayed for this child,
and the LORD has granted me what I asked of him.
So now I give him to the LORD.
For his whole life he will be given over to the LORD.'
And he worshiped the LORD there.
Then Hannah prayed and said:
'My heart rejoices in the LORD. . . '"
1 Samuel 1:24-2:1 NIV

CHAPTER

26

The Interim

Elkanah was right. The Lord did give us the grace we needed. I shouldn't have been surprised, but I was.

Grace. I became curious about that word when I was nine, perhaps. I remember asking my father what "grace" meant. "It's a good word, Hannah," my father told me, "a word worth understanding. Grace is a marvelous gift from the Lord that takes us beyond ourselves, our human limitations. God's grace is something divine. It's what enables us to desire to do God's will rather than our own. Grace also gives us the ability, in addition to the desire, to do God's will."

Often during that year, I remembered my father's words. You see, no matter what I had told myself about being brave, there always lurked in the corner of my mind the fear that the loss of Samuel–in spite of all my good intentions–might throw me back into the pit of despair.

But in that first year without Samuel, I gained a new appreciation for my years of great sadness, all I'd learned then. "Focus on the beautiful things rather than your suffering. . . . Praise God through music." I found that the exercises Dan required of me in those dark days prepared me well for

Samuel's departure. In fact, that first year without Samuel shocked me with its joy.

Another thing that surprised me was how little my life changed. I continued doing the same things in the same way, but this time with Peninnah's children–and later including other children in Ramah after Peninnah's clan bragged to their cousins and friends about our story times. One day when I took Peninnah's children on a special outing to visit Dan and the sheep in the fields, I learned that, once again, the talk of the village focused on me. This time, for a change, the talk was positive.

"Moselle says you've become known as an expert in telling the stories of our heroes to the children," Dan said, as we watched the young ones hiding from one another behind rocks in the meadow. I'd always liked Dan's wife, Moselle. Sweet and sincere, Moselle matched Dan in her optimistic perspective on life, even though, she, too, had struggled with the death of their son. "She says you rarely do housework anymore because you're too busy spending time with other people's children." His eyes smiled at me.

He said it in a teasing way. Although we both knew he exaggerated, I heard an unexpected ring of truth. Dan's comment caused me to wonder. Could it be that I filled my hunger for Samuel by loving other people's children? I began watching myself more carefully, and I saw that reaching out to someone else who seemed lonely, especially a child, had become a common way of quickly filling the empty spot Samuel's absence created in my life. So—even on the nights I slept alone—I fell asleep quickly after a busy day, sometimes even before finishing my prayers for Samuel.

I was surprised, too, at how often we received news about Samuel. People returning home from a trip to Shiloh constantly stopped at our home. Some we knew; others were strangers—like the family that stopped in after dinner one night.

"Are you the mother of the boy Samuel, the one who lives at the Tabernacle in Shiloh?" I overheard the father ask Peninnah as he stood surrounded by a cluster of wide-eyed youngsters and a weary-looking wife.

"No, she's over there with the children," Peninnah said, nodding to where I led the young ones in demonstrating to Elkanah their knowledge of Gideon, a judge in our past who the Lord used to bring salvation to his people. "You're welcome to join them," Peninnah said. "They'll be finished soon."

Although the family seemed quite willing to listen, I cut our presentation short so Elkanah could focus on the strangers.

"We bring you greetings from your son, Samuel, and the old priest, Eli," the man began. "We're on our way home to Bethlehem. We met your son when we went to worship in Shiloh. You can be very proud of him."

The woman nodded enthusiastically. "I've never seen a better behaved child. His love of the Lord is amazing! We were so glad our children got the opportunity to know him. It's had a great impact on them and their understanding of the Almighty."

Elkanah smiled. How many times had we heard these same comments? And of course, since it was late, Elkanah invited the family to stay for the night—as he always did. I offered to make them food, but they, like many of the others, made sure they had eaten before appearing at our door. So, the family joined us in the courtyard, and the stories began. Much information we heard repeated time after time: Samuel appeared to be very happy; Eli spoke highly of him, seeing him as a special gift from God; Samuel's unbridled devotion to the Lord inspired the people at the Tabernacle to reach out to God. Even though we rarely heard anything totally new, my mother heart savored hearing the tales over and over–each version with its own peculiar seasoning, occasionally embellished with something new, like a particular conversation or encounter.

I wish now I would have noticed that Peninnah, during that year, gradually withdrew more and more from the cheerful gathering in the courtyard—usually by herself, sometimes taking her protesting children with her.

Not all the reports came from travelers. During Samuel's first year at Shiloh, it seemed half the families of Ramah decided to make the journey to the Tabernacle–whereas hardly any had gone before. Of course, when they returned, almost every family stopped by to tell us about their visit with Samuel. Dan and his clan were one of the first to go. He never said, but I've always believed Dan went early just to make sure Samuel had adjusted well. Who knows? I wouldn't be surprised if my family instructed Dan to bring Samuel home if he seemed traumatized by his separation. But Dan's clan returned with enthusiastic reports of Samuel's well-being.

The cousins could hardly wait for the adults to finish talking so they could add their observations.

"Did you get to see Samuel's room?" one of the cousins asked Peninnah's children.

Elihu and Giddel, Peninnah's two oldest, looked at each other. "No," Elihu said, disappointment in his voice.

"We did!"

I glanced over at Elkanah, wishing we'd thought of taking the children to see Samuel's room. But the morning we said goodbye to Samuel had been much too tense with emotion to think about such details.

"Does Samuel stay at the Tabernacle all the time?" Tohu asked.

The cousins shook their heads. "He went on hikes with us while we were there."

"He took us all around to see many of his favorite places."

"And he showed us the hill where God's people worship other gods," little Lisha said solemnly.

Her mother, Moselle, leaned toward me to whisper, "Samuel's pain at the unfaithfulness of God's people made a big impression on her—and the others, too."

"Does he have friends?" asked Milcah, Peninnah's youngest boy, and the one who'd played with Samuel the most.

"Oh yes, he has lots of friends!"

"*Everyone* knows him."

"And he knows everyone—even their names!"

"All the people come and talk to him, especially the kids."

Dan reached over and lifted Jemima onto his knee. "Eli says Samuel gets lots of invitations to spend time with families. Sometimes he visits your grandparents, sometimes our Aunt Abigail. And Eli's clan considers him part of their family, too. Eli said he'd never see Samuel at all if he accepted all the he gets."

"Does he sleep with them?'" asked Vina after popping her thumb from her mouth.

Dan shook his head.

"Hardly ever," Moselle said, drawing Vina close and smoothing the hair from her face. "Eli thinks Samuel wants to be close to him just in case he needs him during the night. The two of them, old Eli and little Samuel, have become quite a pair, nearly inseparable."

"Well, I hope Eli doesn't feed him any raisins!" Jemima said emphatically.

Dan smiled down into her serious face. "I think everyone is careful what they feed Samuel. But you don't have to worry. If someone were to forget, Samuel wouldn't. He always asks before he eats. You'd be proud of him, Jemima."

She sighed as if relieved and smiled contentedly. Obviously, she missed her job as Samuel's oldest sister.

After the clamor settled and the children began playing "visiting Samuel at the Tabernacle," Moselle reached out and put her hand on my knee. "Hannah, there's no need for you to worry. Samuel talks about you often. It's obvious he loves you dearly, but he's very happy in his new home."

Dan nodded. He leaned back with his hands behind his head. "When I first heard of your vow, Hannah, I didn't know what to think. I really wanted to support you, especially when you faced so much opposition, so I didn't voice my concerns–as the others did." He smiled, and I returned his smile, remembering those days well. "But now, having seen Samuel in action, a tiny boy ministering before the Lord—already having an impact on those who come to the Tabernacle—I know you did the right thing. Who knows what long term effects your promise will have?"

Later on my parents, and then my four older brothers and their families, made trips to Shiloh, each going at a different time rather than in groups as they usually did. Each time they returned with glowing reports of Samuel and how proud they were to be his family. It seemed strange, after all the years of having been the focus of so much criticism—from the people of Ramah and our families—to now be showered with admiration. I couldn't help wondering how long it would last.

Perhaps the biggest shock of all came from Timara. One day a few months before our first return to Shiloh, she came over with her children so they could listen to story time and play with Peninnah's bunch. Just before they left she said, "I've been trying to get Dermot to let us make a trip to Shiloh, but so far, he hasn't consented."

Timara asking to go to Shiloh? I couldn't believe it. I'd been surprised at how often she and her little ones just happened to come by at the time we set aside to talk about Yaweh and his friends. She watched and listened as intently as the children, and I wondered what she thought. I hoped she was learning to love the Lord who loved her so much. I never felt comfortable asking.

Wordless, I looked down, caressing her daughter's dark curls—curls so much like Samuel's. "I want to go see Samuel," the little one said, looking up at me with her big round eyes.

I smiled. "Maybe someday you will."

Later as I nestled down alone for the night, I thought about the number of people Samuel had already influenced. How many people—even those who'd neglected the Lord for years—decided to go to the Tabernacle just to see Samuel? How many, once they got there and saw his pure devotion to God, were challenged to evaluate their relationship with the Almighty? How many moved closer to God because of him? Oh, I knew this was only a little thing, not anything like the big turning I'd imagined and still prayed for, but at least people were moving in the right direction. That night, once again, I fell asleep praying that the Lord would protect my child and help him live a life pleasing to the Lord.

"Then Elka'nah went home to Ramah.
And the boy ministered to the LORD,
in the presence of Eli the priest."
1 Samuel 2:11 RSV

CHAPTER

27

The Unveiling

There were some dark spots amid the bright reports about Samuel. How could it be otherwise? Occasionally, someone from Ramah or a traveler would express shock and disapproval at what I had done, often right to my face.

"Giving away your son is totally unnatural."

"How can you sleep at night knowing you relinquished your child into the care of a blind, old man who can hardly get around?"

"The Tabernacle is certainly no place for a child to grow up!"

"Right now Samuel may be too young to resent what you've done to him, but one day he'll hate you. That's for sure!"

"You'll be sorry. You'll see. . ."

But the innocent, curious questions of the children hurt most.

"Why did you give Samuel away?"

"Don't you love him?"

"I'm glad my mommy didn't give *me* away."

Then one day about seven or eight weeks before we returned to Shiloh, Diza's family visited the Tabernacle. I should have realized something amiss when Peninnah returned home from the well the morning after their return. Something about her reminded me of the Peninnah years ago—the swagger in her step, the tilt of her chin, the hard thin line of her lips, the evasiveness of her eyes. But the children and I had plans for the day, so I ignored the observation.

As quickly as possible I finished my task. "I'm taking the children to collect brush for firewood," I called to Peninnah just before turning to follow the children onto the road.

I nearly collided with Serah. "Oh!" I said. At the sight of her face, my smile faded. Never before had I seen Serah's eyes glare or her lips take on that hard disapproving look I'd seen in her mother.

She backed up only enough to give me room to get through the doorway. "We need to talk," she whispered in a low, stern voice. "Right now. Without her." She tossed her head toward the courtyard were Peninnah kneaded bread.

I swallowed, recalling the change in Peninnah I'd throw aside. What was up, I didn't know, but it couldn't be good. "Can you come with us to gather kindling?" I asked.

"Sure," she nodded. Her youngsters ran off, eager to catch up with the others, and we followed. I tried to carry on a normal dialogue as we traipsed over the hills, pointing out how the dryness of winter would soon be replaced by the beauty of spring. But our conversation seemed forced and artificial. Finally when the children scattered in all directions in their search for dried brush, we sat down on a rock where we could keep watch as we talked.

"What's wrong?" I asked, not knowing if I wanted to know or not. Since the night I made my vow to God, returned to the house and told Peninnah to get me something to eat, my relationship with her had drastically changed. Not that we were friends, but ever since then she'd shown me a new level of respect. But this morning? That's what was different. Respect.

But why? What had I done? On the way following the children across the hills, as I talked to Serah, I'd searched my mind for clues, but found none.

"Diza's at the well talking . . . about you." Serah paused apologetically.

"And?"

"They just got back from Shiloh."

"I know."

"Well," Serah ran her finger under a wisp of hair laying over her cheek and tucked it behind her ear. "Well," she paused before blurting out, "she's saying you were wrong to leave Samuel at the Tabernacle. It's no place for a child."

"We've heard that from other people, Serah. You know that." I sighed. It would take more than that to influence Peninnah. "What else did she say?" I needed to know.

Serah lowered her eyes and went through the motions of fixing her hair, although nothing hung loose this time. She looked up, the anger I'd seen in her eyes when we bumped into each other at the courtyard door, replaced by sadness. How like Serah, unwilling to say words that hurt those she loved.

"Go on, Serah. It's better if I know."

She swallowed and then licked her lips. "Diza says that you're willing to ruin your son's life just to get attention for yourself. That all you want is people's admiration. She says that you think you're better than the rest of us—that you don't care *what* you have to do to get everyone to think you're someone special."

I looked at her, speechless.

"I . . . I know it's not true . . . but . . . I can tell some people like to believe her. You know how Diza is. She's good at talking." Serah pushed her hair back, on the other side this time, and glanced up at my frozen face. With a deep breath, she began again. "Diza talked about all the strangers that come here and make over you. About the people at the Tabernacle, and how they keep telling everyone about your vow—making you into a national heroine. And . . ." she lowered her eyes and waited as if gathering her strength before continuing. "And she says you planned this just so you could take advantage of Peninnah, put her in her place. She says you like feeling that you are better she is–than *all* of us. And . . . " Serah let her eyes fall. "She says now you're trying to steal the affections of the children of Ramah, making them love you better than their own mothers."

For a long time we sat in silence.

I couldn't believe it! I'd never heard of anything so bizarre—at least not since Peninnah's crazy days. Give away my son to get others to admire me? Never had such a thought crossed my mind. Yet, as I recalled the multitude of visitors over the past year, their abundant praise of my son—and me—I began to see how Diza could weave a tale that gave the appearance of truth. So I said nothing.

Neither did Serah.

Finally the children returned, comparing and boasting of their finds. I herded them together, and we headed home, but this time Serah and I trailed them in silence.

As we neared Ramah, Serah said. "I'll go home from here." Her eyes begged me not to blame her for the message.

I smiled and gave her a hug. "Thank you for telling me," I whispered in her ear. "Thank you for being my friend."

Why did life have to be so difficult? Especially when I tried to do what was right? A whirlwind of thoughts and emotions invaded my mind. Anger at Diza and her false accusations. Anger at those who so easily believed her. Anger because she'd poisoned Peninnah's mind. I had no idea where *that* would lead—but it couldn't be anywhere good. Anger because I felt trapped again, not knowing what to say to Elkanah. Knowing he would be hurt no matter what I said.

Just when things were going so well. Just as my excitement about going to see Samuel mounted higher every day, Diza spun a web of lies! How could she? Why would she? What was I going to do?

By the time we reached home, I knew the first part of my plan. After helping the children deposit their kindling, I told Peninnah I'd be gone for the afternoon and would she please get dinner ready. Ignoring her scowl, not even attempting to understand what she mumbled under her breath, I hurried into my room, tucked my pipe into my belt, and headed for Dan's house.

Moselle's awkward silence when she saw me eloquently declared that she, too, had heard Diza's accusations. I said nothing about it, only asking where Dan had taken the sheep. Rather than giving instructions, Moselle called Yaron, their youngest son to escort me to his father. As I turned to leave, she reached out and embraced me firmly and then kissed my cheek. Tears sprang to my eyes, but I held them back as I hurried after Yaron. A kiss. A solemn pledge that she would always be my friend, no matter what. Without a word, she'd promised she would never betray me.

Together Yaron and I tramped across the rolling hills. The warmth of the sun covered my back, the gentle breeze caressing my face as if to comfort me. At my side the bouncing child stirred up longing for my son. How could anyone dare suggest that the compliments I received could ever make up for my loss?

As I hoped, being with my brother provided the freedom I needed to be myself. I could speak without the need to edit anything, knowing that he'd overlook all my emotional exaggerations and accusations, listening with compassion to my frustration and pain without condemning or criticizing me—or taking me too seriously. Then I wept, and he held me until I became silent and still. Next we waited, sitting side by side on the rock near the big tree, listening only to the gentle stream running down from the brook, the bleating of the sheep, the call of birds, and voices of his sons on the far hill. Only then did my brother speak. Only then could I listen.

"Diza's a difficult case, Hannah. But being angry with her won't help. She's the kind who feeds on anger. Trying to fight her won't work either."

He was right. I'd seen enough instances over our years of growing up together. She and Timara had a confrontation once, and even to this day they've hated each other.

"Anger, hatred, revenge—those eat up our creative energy, Hannah. They embitter and harden the nicest people." Dan reached down and scratched the head of the sheep that insistently rubbed against his leg.

"There's something I think I should tell you," he continued. "Many years ago, just after your engagement to Elkanah, I heard Diza's brother tormenting Diza, taunting her for wanting to marry Elkanah, claiming she was jealous of you. From the expression on her face, I believe what he said was true." Dan reached over and rubbed the head of another sheep that had come to join his friend. "We both know Diza hasn't had a wonderful marriage, being a second wife and all.

"I guess what I'm trying to say is this: trying to fight her jealousy head-on is doomed to fail. I'm sorry, Hannah, but I really don't know how to advise you. Maybe you'll just have to hold tighter to God and rise above the situation. One thing is sure: you must talk to Elkanah. Right away. It's his right to know and his responsibility to deal with Peninnah."

Dan smiled sadly, reached over and slipped the shepherd's pipe from my belt and handed it to me. Together we reached up to God Who alone can understand the agony of the heart. Before I left, Dan and I both lifted up my dilemma to the Lord, asking for His wisdom and guidance.

As I walked home, over the rolling hills, I continued to talk to the Almighty, and by the time I returned home I knew the next part of my plan. Not exactly how it would work out, of course, but I knew I would take Dan's advice and be honest—with Elkanah and Peninnah. I wouldn't bow to Diza's accusations, either by ignoring them or by fighting them with my own. Somehow, I knew, the Lord would guide me as I listened for His direction.

That evening, when Elkanah arrived, Peninnah had dinner ready, and we all sat down as usual. Tension polluted the atmosphere. Elkanah gave me a questioning look, but I only lowered my eyes. "So, tell me about your day," he said in a cheerful voice, inviting anyone in the circle to answer.

"In the morning we got firewood," Giddel volunteered.

"That sounds fun."

"But after lunch we couldn't do anything." Jemima said.

"Oh?"

"Mommy was grouchy," Micah said innocently.

I saw Elkanah turn his eyes to Peninnah, but she refused to meet his gaze.

Elkanah dipped his bread into the stew. "Was something wrong, Peninnah?" Elkanah asked before putting his bread in his mouth.

Peninnah turned to him, her eyes brimming with tears. "Hannah was gone all afternoon, leaving me to prepare the dinner *and* supervise the children. I didn't mind being left with all the work this morning, but she has no right to treat me like a *slave*." As her voice rose and felt dramatically, her children stared at her wide-eyed.

My heart sank.

I thought Elkanah would question me, but he immediately turned his eyes to the children while speaking to Peninnah and me. "Well," he smiled brightly and patted Vina who'd begun to whimper, "we grownups will talk about that later." He smiled again, his eyes sweeping around the circle of children. "I found something for each of you on the way home. Do you want to have it now or after we finish eating?"

"Now!" they shouted in unison, except for Vina who echoed their cry. Immediately they closed their eyes and held out their hands, well versed in Elkanah's way of distributing surprises. He often brought home special leaves, twigs, or seeds, pretty rocks or, sometimes, something more unusual, like the discarded skin of a snake, and once a live lizard. Today each hand received a small stone, and, in their excitement, comparing their treasures and storing them away, the children seemed to forget Peninnah's outburst, but I'm sure none of the adults did.

After our meal, I cleaned up and Peninnah put the children to bed before we joined Elkanah in the courtyard. I carried out our robes, because, although real winter had passed, the night breeze still got very cool. Peninnah brought an oil lamp from her room and set it in the center, making it possible to dimly see one another's faces when we seated ourselves in a tight circle. I'm sure it wasn't long before Elkanah opened the conversation, but it seemed like forever to me.

First, he asked Peninnah to explain her "concern." As I listened, I thanked God that Serah came to me so quickly. How much better for me to hear Peninnah after processing my emotions with Dan and spending time listening to the Lord! Using all her skills, Peninnah drew herself as innocent and abused, and me as darkly egotistical and selfish. Elkanah listened patiently, letting her have all the time she wanted. I must confess, I felt impatient to have my turn, wanting to point out the foolishness of her words.

Just when I could hardly stand it any longer, Elkanah reached over in the semi-darkness and took my hand, giving me a gentle squeeze. "Just wait, Hannah," he seemed to say. "If you give her time to talk, it'll be much easier for all of us."

So I relaxed and waited. For the first time, I began to perceive Peninnah's pain.

Later, as I looked back on that experience, I came to believe that in that moment, the Lord in his grace, allowed me to hear. Not Peninnah's crazy words–but her aching heart. What I heard went much deeper than the dramatic tears and complaints I learned years ago to distrust. The weeping I heard was inaudible—the heartbroken sobs of a child.

With a sense of shock and embarrassment, I realized that all throughout that year—a year of special grace for me—never once had I stopped to try to imagine Peninnah's feelings. I'd focused on my pain, my joys, my need to cope. I'd done many things right. I called out to God for help, and He had given me strength and courage. I'd allowed my loneliness to motivate me to reach out to others—many others. But I'd never thought of Peninnah. How had she felt when I spent time with her children? Did she fear they loved me as much as they loved her? How did she feel when so much conversation in our household centered around my absent son? When, one after another, people applauded me and Samuel–ignoring her and her children? When our family and friends, including Elkanah, focused a great deal of attention on me, trying to make this year of transition more bearable?

I felt my cheeks burn with shame. Diza's accusations? In a way they were totally false. But in another way? Was the Lord showing me my self-centeredness? Certainly, I hadn't intended to ignore Peninnah and her needs, but I had.

Peninnah had been good to my son when he lived with us. She'd been cooperative and allowed me time with him. Yet somehow, I felt I deserved it because I would have my son such a short time. I'd failed to appreciate her sacrifice. Then even when Samuel was gone, life in our home still revolved around Samuel, and around me.

Suddenly I understood. Diza's words–whatever motivated them–like a spark of fire, ignited very dry twigs. Peninnah, I felt sure now, had felt untended, unwatered, and unappreciated for a long time or Diza's words wouldn't have affected her so quickly. She'd been overlooked, largely because of me. As I sat there in the flickering lamplight, all I'd planned to say to vindicate myself turned worthless.

Finally Peninnah fell silent, empty of all her words.

Elkanah turned to me. "Hannah, do you want to say anything?"

Nothing would come from my mouth. A lump rose in my throat and tears in my eyes. I dropped Elkanah's hand, leaned forward and crawled toward Peninnah. Reaching out, I embraced her and began to cry. At first she sat rigid and unresponsive like a tree. "I'm sorry," I whispered. "I'm so sorry for not thinking about you."

Soon we both wept, hugging each other.

It was so strange–that night. I'm sure Diza believed her words would devastate our family, steal away our joy. They could have. All of us knew they could have. Instead, God used them to reveal truth and bring us closer together, closer than we'd ever been.

"Then Elkanah and Hannah returned home to Ramah without Samuel."
1 Samuel 2:11a NLT

CHAPTER

28

The Return

But problems still remained with others in Ramah. As always, people took sides. Some mothers stopped letting their children visit, at least for a while. The children themselves seemed confused about the changes. Some repeated the mean things they heard their parents say. Peninnah's older boys, Elihu, Giddel and Tohu got into a number of fights protecting my name. Even Jemima, we heard, got into some verbal battles in my defense. But, with things resolved between Peninnah and me—or so I hoped—I had little interest or energy to invest in worrying about what others believed.

After all, time for our trip to Shiloh continued to draw nearer and nearer, so I doubt anything could have detracted me for long. I can't say I began counting the days. To be truthful, I'd been counting since the day we left. Yet, I'll admit that as the time grew closer, my anticipation mounted and made it difficult for me to concentrate. At times Elkanah found my forgetfulness amusing, but I felt annoyed with myself and embarrassed as well. Every day I reminded myself to be mindful of Peninnah, not to allow myself to become self-absorbed.

But, in spite of all my efforts, I must confess that nothing took my thoughts off Samuel for long, day or night. During the month before we left, when I lay down on my bed, I held Samuel's new robe close to my heart as I prayed for him before falling asleep. All night his robe lay in his vacant spot, where his mat had been, and sometimes I'd reach out and caress it as I had my son's hair.

On the nights Elkanah spent with me, we made plans. "I think we should go to Shiloh a few days early," Elkanah said seventeen days before our scheduled time for departure. "That way we can spend time together as a family before I begin my two weeks of service in the Tabernacle."

My heart leapt with joy! I would see Samuel sooner than I thought.

"The first day after we arrive, you and I will spend the morning alone with Samuel." Just Samuel, Elkanah and me? I could hardly contain myself! "Then in the afternoon all of us can go on an outing," Elkanah said. "The second morning, you and I will spend at the Tabernacle letting Samuel show us around. Then in the afternoon we'll do something with our whole family again. You can come up with some ideas for the third day." He stroked my hair. "How does that sound?"

I tried to contain my excitement, to sound like a mature woman, but it was hard. Especially considering the apprehension I'd begun to experience as I thought of staying with Peninnah's family. Of course, it would be different than before I had Samuel, but I didn't want to be bound to them. I wanted some space. So I was glad to discover that Elkanah also craved times to be alone with Samuel and with our own family. For those last fourteen days, my mind whirled with endless options for the third day, but settled on none.

Finally the morning of our journey arrived. The previous day I made myself work hard cleaning my room. It felt as if I'd explode if I didn't do something to dissipate my exhilaration. I hoped that if I worked hard all day, I'd be tired enough to fall asleep that night. Maybe it helped a little. But I awoke before dawn filled with anticipation, and I knew I'd never fall back asleep. For a while I avoided disturbing Elkanah, but . . . well, it was impossible. So we lay together, wrapped in each other's arms, and Elkanah patiently let me talk, and wonder, and imagine, and plan.

Never did a journey to Shiloh seem so long, yet I remember nothing of what happened on the way. My anticipation became painful. Finally we arrived. But nothing, nothing, prepared me for my first glimpse of Samuel. My baby was gone! The soft roundness at his wrists had disappeared. His arms and legs seemed so long and straight. His curly dark hair nearly touched his shoulders. But when he ran to meet us, his eyes hadn't changed at all. They still sparkled with love for us and eagerness for life.

I knelt down and held out my arms, hardly knowing how to greet him. How would he respond after all this time? He ran up and hugged me as if we'd been apart only days. I waited for him to release me, savoring every second of having him pressed close to my heart, yet not wanting to cling to him. Oh, how I'd missed him! Encouraged by his willingness to bridge our year apart in one moment, I reached up and smoothed his dark ringlets. The curls, as always, grasped my fingers in response. I suppressed a sigh of contentment. "My, how you've grown," I said, smiling and trying to keep the tears out of my eyes and voice.

But Samuel reached over and gently touched the side of my eye, releasing drops hiding along the rim. "Are these the happy kind of tears?" he asked.

I nodded.

"I thought so," he said, and gave me an eager hug and a kiss before turning his attention to his father and then the rest of the family.

While he greeted each one, I devoured him with my eyes. His legs protruded from beneath that first little robe I'd made for him the previous year, and I was glad I'd taken my mother's advice about the one I brought with me this time. "Make that robe plenty long," she'd warned me. "Better to raise the hem than to have him wear something too small for a whole year."

On top of his Levitical robe, I noted with surprise, Samuel wore an ephod. The apron, made in two parts connected at each shoulder by a peg, hung down to his knees and was bound at the waist with a wide golden belt. It looked striking similar to the garment worn by, Eli, the High Priest. But I lay aside the observation in preference to watching my son.

I'm very certain I could tell you, almost moment by moment, all that happened in those weeks in Shiloh. *You must remember everything,* I'd instructed myself over and over in the months and days before our trip to Shiloh, as well as a seventy-seven times each day of our stay. *Never forget anything,* I reminded myself again each night as I rehearsed all that had happened. Of course, the hours Elkanah and I spent sharing our experiences and observations also helped solidify these memories in my mind.

That first night, after a celebration meal with Peninnah's family, Samuel slept beside me. I can't count the number of times I woke up in the night just to peer at him in the dim light. I wanted so much to caress his curls, but I was afraid that after sleeping alone for a year, my touch would waken him. So I just looked, thankful for the small lamp in the corner that gave just enough illumination to let my eyes drink in the beauty of him. In sleep, he didn't look quite so grown up.

The following morning, according to our plan, Elkanah, Samuel, and I left early, taking our breakfast with us. If we hadn't promised to take Peninnah's children on an outing in the afternoon, I think we would have witnessed many tears. But Peninnah enticed them with the prospect of playing with their Shiloh cousins, so they waved bravely, calling to Samuel until we turned a corner and were hidden from sight.

I'd wondered if Samuel would feel like we were strangers. But our return appeared to be just as natural to him as recognizing the Tabernacle had been the pervious year. After all, one of the games we'd played in preparation for his move to the Tabernacle was "Papa and Mama return to visit Samuel." As soon as we reached the open hills, Elkanah took off running, challenging Samuel to catch him. Immediately Samuel sprang to life, his eyes sparkling, as if he remembered the many times he'd chased his papa over the hills around Ramah. Most of the morning we spent enjoying nature, laughing, and romping together, and of course, making music. Elkanah, who remembered to carry at least a few small instruments on his person wherever he went, handed me a flute. First, Elkanah and Samuel sang while I played. Then Elkanah gave Samuel a new flute, a little larger and more complex than the one he'd given him last year.

"Thank you, Papa," Samuel said, his eye shining. He ran his finger over its smoothness, examining each hole before looking up. "You made it for me, right?"

Elkanah smiled and nodded as he moved closer. He put his arms around Samuel, one arm on each side to guide him in getting used to his new flute. I sat back watching, delighting in observing them working together. With their faces cheek to cheek, anyone could identify them as father and son. Before long, I saw Elkanah glance at the sky, and my gaze followed his. My heart squeezed painfully. The morning had passed much too quickly!

"Let's go back and get your brothers and sisters." Elkanah's voice displayed none of the reluctance I felt. He smiled, tucked Samuel's flute into his belt, reached down and swung Samuel high into the air above his head. My eyes held onto them, storing the image away deep in my memory—father and son silhouetted against the azure blue background. My ears soaked up their laughter; my soul—their smiles, their joy.

Once I heard someone say that the Almighty has a special place in heaven where He keeps the tears of His friends. That morning as we walked back to get the others, I felt sure that God also created a special place inside each of us where we can hide our most precious memories, not the every day kind, but the ones that press into the deepest core of our being and form our future.

But I took no time to contemplate then. I was much too busy gathering raw materials, storing away fresh memories to be enjoyed over and over in the year ahead—so many different memories, like a lovely bouquet of wildflowers in a wide range of fragrances, shapes, sizes, and colors. Like that one night I spent with my son. The few moments we had alone. Experiences we shared with Elkanah, with our whole family . . . with Peninnah's family. There were our times in the Tabernacle, worshipping, visiting. Then walking, out on the hillside and through Shiloh. What memories! I eagerly collected them all.

Day after day people accosted us, the villagers of Shiloh and Israelites who came to the Tabernacle to worship. "Samuel is the best thing to happen in Shiloh in my lifetime," one old man told me in a shaky voice. "After the wicked behavior of the High Priest's sons, it's refreshing to see one so young with a heart to please the Lord."

"For years now attendance at the Tabernacle has decreased," a grandmotherly woman said. "But since Samuel arrived, this place sprang back to life!"

Most were positive comments, but not all. With the experiences I'd had, I'd moved beyond the stage of being surprised by opposition, but I still hadn't anticipated Diza's handiwork. But, at least when people looked at me with disgust, drawing their garments away or murmuring to each other behind their hands, I could guess the source of their displeasure. That first morning after we returned to Peninnah's parents' house to get Peninnah and the children, I first noticed an uneasiness. Maybe I'd been too excited to sense it the night before, I don't know. But that morning, there is was. Poison. Polluting the air, like the foul, stinging smoke from rotting flesh. In spite of having dealt with Diza's accusation back in Ramah, some of the stench clung to Peninnah that morning when we first left the house. I saw it in the straight hardness of her mouth and the aversion of her eyes. But out on the hillside the wind must have blown it away.

That night when the mothers began to settle their children for the night, I reached out and took Samuel's hand. Instead of coming with me, he held me firm. Surprised, I looked down into his upturned face, his serious dark eyes. "Mama," he said softly, "I love to sleep with you and Papa. But at night Eli needs me to be with him. Sometimes he has to get up. If I'm not there he might fall."

A lump choked me, and tears pooled in my eyelids. I don't know which impacted me more, my sadness over losing sleeping time with my son or the pride I felt in him. But, that night Elkanah and I began the tradition of walking Samuel to his own home at bedtime.

On our return to Peninnah's parents' house, Elkanah and I reviewed the highlights of our day. As we neared the doorway, Elkanah paused. "I need to talk to you and Peninnah."

The seriousness in his voice left me anxious. *Please don't let anything ruin my few days with Samuel,* I pleaded as we sat down together in my room.

"Tell Hannah what your sisters-in-law told you," Elkanah

began.

"It's Diza," Peninnah said as she looked down at her hands and rubbed her thumb. "While she was here, she talked a lot–to my family, to everyone."

"What exactly did Diza say?" Elkanah prodded.

Peninnah's eyes swept to the left as if trying to find the words. "Well," she took a deep breath, "she said Hannah is proud and thinks she is better than everyone else. You know, like she said in Ramah."

"And?" Elkanah prodded. Later as I thought about it, I felt amazed and grateful for how far he'd come in dealing with the problems between us.

I thought I saw the glint of a tear in Peninnah's right eye, but in the dim lamplight, I could have been mistaken.

"She said you caused me to lose my baby." I'm sure I didn't imagine the tremor in her voice. "She also said the Philistines are going to attack, and it will be because of what you did to those boys."

My stomach tightened. "That's crazy," I said. "*They* attacked first. How could that be *my* fault?" I looked from Peninnah to Elkanah.

Elkanah sighed. "When people want to stir up trouble, what they say doesn't have to make sense. But I felt, Hannah, that you need to know. So you'll understand people's responses."

And so I'll pray even more diligently that the Philistines don't attack, I thought.

Later as we lay down for the night, I couldn't help asking Elkanah, "Why would Diza say such things? I always tried to be a good friend to her."

Elkanah's silence stretched longer than usual. Finally he spoke. "Jealousy, Hannah, is a very evil thing. It can destroy the closest relationships."

I didn't have many words that night, or even orderly thoughts, at first at least. Soon I heard Elkanah's soft even breathing. I stared at the dark corner where the flicker of the tiny lamp failed to tickle the ceiling beams. To say Diza's comments had no effect on me would be a great overstatement, but, thank God, I no longer allowed them to control the reins of my mind. By now I'd learned a new strategy. I'd learned to ask the Lord what He thought about the words people said. Then I'd listen, waiting for Him to tell me if they were true or false. The true ones I kept, but the false ones I threw into His burning rubbish heap while saying a prayer for the one who said them. That's what I did that night.

The next morning, I began a personal tradition that I repeated each day when I was in Shiloh. I never knew if the events of the previous night had anything to do with it or not. But each morning after that, when I went to the Tabernacle, I returned to the exact spot where I made my vow to God. Somehow the very place seemed sacred to me as if it still remembered, held firmly in its possession, the words I'd spoken to Yaweh six years earlier.

Often when I stood there, I just listened. Not to the things going on around me, but to the silence within. I think that was when I learned that silence speaks. Or perhaps it's more accurate to say, God speaks in silence–often without words. Sometimes silence communicates more clearly, more profoundly than the best conversation with a human. In order to communicate with people, Jerusha, we have to translate what's in our hearts into words–and hope others interpret them accurately. But, with the Almighty, when we really quiet ourselves before Him and open up our hearts, He hears. He hears not just what we say (whether we use words or speak only with our hearts), but He also hears what we are–not just on the surface, but in the deepest parts of our being. He hears with complete accuracy, understanding us so much better than we understand ourselves. Then He speaks.

Mostly the Lord speaks to me of his love. He accepts me. Comforts me. Assures me. He doesn't promise me life without pain or disappointment. Yet, He says He will be with me always and give me strength. Standing there, I couldn't help wondering why so many people willingly exchange this kind of relationship with Yaweh for the cold, indifferent power claims of false gods, and the temporary highs they dole out.

One day when I was standing in God's presence, in the silence, listening, I became aware of someone standing near me. Turning, I saw the High Priest, Eli at a respectful distance behind me.

"Hello," I said. "Would you like to talk to me?"

"If you're finished."

"Yes, I am."

I followed him as he shuffled away, not to his usual post at the pillar near the entrance, but to a corner out of the way of those coming into the Tabernacle. As I watched, he reached out and ran his hand along the bench before slowly lowering his heavy bulk.

"It much easier for me to get around when Samuel's with me," he said with a smile, "but I want to speak to you alone. Sit down." I did, and after a moment, Eli began. "I'm sure you must realize that your first announcement about leaving your little son with me caused me great concern."

I nodded. Then, remembering he couldn't see, I said, "Yes, I could tell."

"Well, I've known many boys in my day," Eli continued, "and the thought of one of them staying at the Tabernacle left me exhausted. An old blind man certainly doesn't need a child under his feet. But on the day Samuel showed me around the

Tabernacle, I knew immediately he was different than all the rest. Dear woman, I have no idea how you did it, but you taught that boy exactly how to help me and how to make himself useful in the Tabernacle. I have never seen such a content child. Nor one who loves the Lord so deeply. It's truly amazing in one so young. Now I hate to think what I'd do without him." He sighed and stroked his long white beard.

"My lord, I have a question I'd like to ask you, if I may."

He nodded. "Go ahead."

"I noticed that Samuel wears a ephod, very much like yours."

"Ummm," he nodded again. "That was my idea." He took a deep breath as if gathering his thoughts. "I don't know how you came up with it, but the idea of having Samuel wear a Levitical robe was a very good one. Though I admit it shocked me when I first saw him." He smiled. "I'd never seen such a miniature Levite. His uniform saves answering a lot of questions. Very few visitors arrive at the Tabernacle without having heard about the new little Levite boy serving here. Yet his garment makes it easy for them to spot him without bothering anyone.

"But, back to your question. My difficulty came from the Levites really. Samuel's clothing led them to consider him to be 'one of them,' and they felt free to include him in their activities whenever they wished. That was all well and good, except that very soon I couldn't find Samuel when I needed him. So, I decided to have the woman who makes my garments make an ephod for Samuel—but plain white, rather than the High Priest's blue, scarlet, and purple, and without the gold embroidery of the High Priest. Of course, he has no turban or breastplate."

He paused and stroked his white beard with his thumb before continuing. "My sons opposed my idea—as I assumed they would. They've had some difficulty adjusting to the thought of my having Samuel as my personal assistant. '*We*'re your assistants,' they told me. But anyone who works at the House of the Lord will assure you that assisting me is certainly *not* their top priority. Whole days pass without either of them speaking to me. When they do, it's rarely, if ever, to assist me." Eli sighed. "The ephod solved my problem. So it remains. It marks Samuel as a unique breed. A Levite associated with the High Priest."

Then he told me again of his gratitude for Samuel. Sometimes I recognized the exact wording someone had passed on. "Eli said . . . " But I valued hearing the words from Eli's own mouth.

Then the day before we left Shiloh, Eli asked to speak to Elkanah and me together. "I want to give you a blessing before you leave," Eli said. I heard a tremor of emotion in old priest's voice, and an inexplicable expectancy settled over me—as if my spirit stood on tiptoe, anticipating something that lay beyond the scope of my comprehension. Eli raised his hands toward us in a sign of blessing, and I bowed my head, still wondering what was going on inside me. "May the Lord give you children by this woman to take the place of the one she prayed for and gave to the Lord," he said.

As his words entered my ears, an intense calm descended on me, then my heart became light, as if floating with a kind of joy more concentrated, yet less bulky than normal joy. It took a while for the words to break through to my mind. ". . . give . . . children . . . by this woman . . . " Then my knees became weak, and I felt Elkanah reach out to steady me. Wonder overwhelmed me.

Never would I have asked the Lord for another child! Yet, Eli had done it for me. Little by little the realization of his prayer sank in as I heard Eli's words repeated over, and over, and over again in that deep place in my heart. "May the Lord give you children by this woman to take the place of the one she prayed for and gave to the Lord."

" Now Samuel was ministering before the LORD,
as a boy wearing a linen ephod.
And his mother would make him a little robe
and bring it to him from year to year
when she would come up with her husband
to offer the yearly sacrifice.
Then Eli would bless Elkanah and his wife and say,
'May the LORD give you children from this woman
in place of the one she dedicated to the LORD. . . .'"
1 Samuel 2:18-20 NASB

CHAPTER

29

The Reward

This time, unlike the first time, I noticed immediately the signs of my pregnancy. My emotional response differed, too. The first time, the bundle of feelings included the exuberant joy only a barren woman can know, the thrill of a long-awaited dream come true, the anticipation of entering a new life of motherhood, and a solemn assurance that I had indeed encountered God and He had handed me the assignment for which I volunteered. But this time, the joy came more quietly, like a warm sensation glowing deep within. A peaceful joy, warm like milk taken from my nanny goat, soothing and sweet like honey. This time it felt as if God put His hand of blessing on my head and gave me a reward, not an assignment.

Both times I conceived quickly. Friends and family were still coming over to hear stories of our visit with Samuel when I found out. As I sat there with my hand on my abdomen, I tried to keep the realization of my pregnancy from detracting from the fun of hearing the experiences and observations of other members of the family. It amazed me that even with all my attentiveness, I'd overlooked things someone else saw or heard. Even Peninnah's children gathered information I'd missed.

"I wish we could've stayed longer in Shiloh," Giddel said

one night as we sat in the courtyard enjoying the evening breeze as we watched the clouds changing colors and shapes.

That night Giddel and Tohu enjoyed the privilege of sitting on Elkanah's lap. Elkanah teased them about being too old, at nine and eight years of age, but neither accepted his judgment. The night before, the two oldest had their turns—Elihu, who would become twelve the next year, chose to take his place at his father's right side, and Jemina delightedly possessed Papa's lap all for herself. The next day the two youngest, Milcah and Vina, would enjoy their privilege. With Samuel gone the rotation came out even, but Samuel had not evaporated from our thoughts.

"Yeah, if we stayed longer we could've gone up on the hills with him and Ahitub."

"Ahitub?" I asked. "Who's he?"

"Samuel's best friend," the children chorused.

I looked over at Elkanah, wondering if he knew anything about this friendship.

He raised his brows and turned to Elihu. "So who's Ahitub—besides being Samuel's friend?"

"Eli's grandson, the son of Phinehas."

Later that night as Elkanah and I lay together in the dark before going to sleep, my mind wandered back to our conversation. "Do you know anything about Ahitub," I asked.

"No, not really. But when Elihu said who he was I remember seeing him once. He's probably just a few years older than Samuel, I'd say."

"I hope he's not a bad influence on Samuel."

"I hope Samuel's a good influence on him," Elkanah countered. "We need improved quality in the priestly line."

I considered his words. That was, after all, what I prayed for, wasn't it? To have a son who would have an impact on others for good? But I wasn't naïve. I knew that older boys most often have influence on the younger, not vice versa. I thought about all that had been in my heart at the time I asked for Samuel, about the vision I had for him. *Why am I afraid?* I thought. *I trusted God, believing He was powerful enough to enable me to produce a son. Why should I doubt that He's powerful enough to grow Samuel into the kind of man he needs to be?* When I made my vow I felt certain, although I heard no audible voice, that the Almighty and I agreed on the quality of the man needed to help Israel. So, I decided, the best thing I could do would be to continue praying for my son and trust the Lord to do His part—even better than I'd done mine.

"Maybe this will comfort you," Elkanah interrupted my thoughts. "Samuel shows an amazing sensitivity to right and wrong, insight far beyond his years. Remember, our first night in Shiloh? Did you notice that Samuel didn't eat any meat at the meal? I was puzzled because his Nazarite vow places no limitations on eating meat. So the next day I asked Samuel about it.

"'Why didn't you eat meat last night?'

"He looked down and was quiet for a long time before answering. Then he looked up at me. 'Papa, did you know that Eli's sons steal God's offerings and serve them for dinner?'

"I can't tell you how shocked I was, Hannah. I wondered how he had such a clear understanding of the situation. I felt certain he couldn't have heard it from Eli since everyone knows how Eli enjoys eating roasted meat. So I asked him, 'How long have you known this?'

"'Almost since the first.'

"'How did you find out about it?' I asked.

"'When I'm in the Tabernacle I hear lots of things.' Again, Hannah, he looked down for a long time. 'I hear what the people say as they're leaving. Some of them are very angry. Do you think God is angry, too?' Even before I could answer he said, 'I do. I think He's *very* angry. That's why I don't eat any of their meat.'

"I nodded. 'I understand,' I said. 'But if you want to eat meat with other people, like Peninnah's family, I think that would be okay. You don't have to, but you could. I don't think God would be unhappy about that.'

"I noticed the next night Samuel took a little meat and glanced up at me and smiled.'"

Elkanah turned toward me and drew me close. "Hannah, God has given Samuel a discerning spirit—wisdom that comes from Him. I don't understand much about how that works, but I believe we can trust God to take care of Samuel when we can't be there to help him."

So we both came to the same conclusion in entirely different ways.

That year seemed much less stressful than the year before. Within a month after our return, interest in Samuel had died to a trickle. Even the number of visitors who dropped in to visit us in Ramah dwindled to less than a fourth of what it had been. Life became more normal, focusing on those of us who lived at home.

It surprised me how little my second pregnancy impacted our village. "Did you notice that our parents weren't any more excited about my second child than they were about Peninnah's children?" I asked Elkanah one night as I worked on weaving Samuel's new robe.

"I think once a woman has a baby, people tend to believe she could have another." He went on working on the new flute he was making to take to Samuel.

"But I never expected to become pregnant again. Samuel was a miracle in answer to my vow; I knew he'd be the only one."

Elkanah blew on the flute he was making. "I agree. I'm

certain this child is a gift in response to Eli's blessing. But, Hannah, it's all right if no one else knows."

And it was. Keeping some things secret makes life a lot easier. But not everything can be kept secret.

A few months before our trip, just three days after the end of my time of isolation following Jeroham's birth, a visitor stopped in. Peninnah went to put the children to bed, but I continued to sit outside holding Jeroham, enjoying the outdoors immensely after spending thirty days in my little room. The visitor, a Levite returning from the Tabernacle after being on duty two weeks, gave us news about Samuel–how indispensable he'd become to Eli, how devoted to the Lord, how respectful and modest. I'd only met Hod once when he stopped by the previous year, but Elkanah knew him quite well.

"How are things at the Tabernacle?" Elkanah asked, friend to friend.

Hod looked down and bit his lip before answering. "I haven't told anyone this, but because Eli oversees your son's care, I think you should know." The seriousness of his tone and the look of sadness in his eyes froze my heart. Maybe I tightened my arms unintentionally or the baby sensed my anxiety, because Jeroham began to cry. I moved him to my shoulder, patting and whispering comforting sounds in his ear, willing him to be silent so I could hear Hod.

"Two new moons ago I was cleaning the storage room next to Eli's room," Hod said. It must have been the one on the east side of Eli's room, I decided, the bigger room that Eli said was too full to clean out quickly. "I decided not to stop for the noon meal since I'd worked myself into a corner away from the door. A little later, I heard Eli go into his room. He lays down for an afternoon rest, so I tried to be very quiet so I wouldn't disturb him. Then I heard a voice calling at his door, and Eli shuffled across the room and invited someone in. I didn't recognize the other man's voice, but Eli seemed to know him.

"'Welcome!' Eli sounded surprised and happy. 'How do I merit this honor of having a prophet of God come so far to see me?'

"'It isn't good news I bear, Eli.' The prophet's voice cut through the wall, firm and very official.

"'Sit down,' Eli said, the cheer gone.

"As I heard the shuffling, I tried to figure out how I could leave, not wanting to invade their privacy. But I saw I couldn't leave without creating a great commotion. So, I made the decision to sit very still. Later, when I heard what the prophet said, I wished I'd been somewhere else."

Hod shifted and cleared his throat as if repeating the words would demand great effort. I kept patting Jeroham, hoping the thumping of my heart wouldn't alarm him. "The prophet told Eli that the Lord was going to punish him because he knew about his sons' sins, and he did nothing to stop them. Instead, Eli honored his sons more than the Lord by joining them in getting fat on the meat they stole." Hod paused again to chew his lip and rub his knuckles. "He said . . . he said that the Lord will take the priesthood from Eli's family . . . and to prove what the prophet said is true, both his sons, Hophni and Phinehas, will die . . . on the same day."

I felt blood drain from my cheeks. Jeroham began to wail, almost as if he'd understood the words of judgment. This time there was no quieting him. I willed my legs to stop trembling as I rose and carried my son inside. The Lord's judgment, not only on Eli's evil sons, but on Eli himself, and his whole family? My mind spun as I sat down in my room and began nursing my baby. How I wished I could be comforted so quickly!

Anxiety continued to come in waves. What had I been thinking? How could I be foolish enough to leave my son in a place polluted with wickedness? Yet, wasn't that why I'd asked for him? So he could stand firm for the Lord, challenge the evil? But he was still a little boy. What would happen to him? He was so far beyond our reach!

Those last weeks before our trip to Shiloh, Hod's words followed me day after day, tormenting me with many troubled thoughts. When I confessed my anxiety to Elkanah, he only said, "Hannah, when the Lord allows you to know of some troublesome circumstance, perhaps He's calling you to pray for the situation. Worrying accomplishes nothing good and does much harm. So pray. Pray for Samuel. Pray for Eli. Pray for his sons . . . and their families. Pray for Israel." So I did, many, many times each day. But knowing this situation intensified my longing to see my son with my own eyes. Somehow it felt that if I could see him, I would find a level of comfort.

I was also eager to go Shiloh to show Samuel his new brother. No baby could have been sweeter or more loved. How can I explain it? I loved Samuel in an extraordinary way because he wasn't mine to keep, and I loved Jeroham in a different way—because I knew I *could* keep him, as God's gift to me. As we neared Shiloh that year, I handed Jeroham to Elkanah, "So I can give all my attention to Samuel at first," I said. Elkanah smiled.

After the hugs, kisses, loving words, and tears, I nodded to Elkanah. "Now, Samuel, I want you to meet your new brother, Jeroham."

Elkanah placed him in my arms, and Samuel bent close, peering into the baby's eyes, gently touching his hand. "He's so small," he said. "But he'll grow."

I smiled and nodded, enjoying Samuel's delight.

"Now I'm a big brother, too, like Elihu, Giddel, and

Tohu." He looked up at Elkanah. "The baby's name is Jeroham? The same as your father?"

Elkanah nodded.

"Grandpa must be very happy!"

"He is," Elkanah agreed.

That year, as with our first trip to visit Samuel, our days in Shiloh whirled past, leaving me wondering where they'd gone. This time I had to divide my time between Samuel and his little brother. I noticed Samuel no longer drew unusual attention but had become a normal part of the Tabernacle scene. Only one aspect of that observation bothered me.

"Remember last year when so many people told us how Samuel's devotion to the Lord challenged them or their children to draw closer to God?" I asked Elkanah one night near the end of our stay, as we returned from taking Samuel back to the House of the Lord.

Elkanah nodded.

"Well, hardly anyone is saying anything like that this year. Why? Do you think Samuel has changed, or is it something else?"

Elkanah looked up at the stars twinkling in the company of a nearly round moon. "Novelty always grabs attention, Hannah. While on duty at the Tabernacle this year, I've seen Samuel worship many times. His devotion to the Lord seems even stronger and more mature than last year. I think people have come to accept him."

"Accept him? I'm not sure if that's good or bad. Do they believe he has a relationship with God different than what they need to have? Do they say, 'That's just Samuel' without being challenged to reach out to God as he does? Oh Elkanah, I didn't ask for a son to serve in the Tabernacle to have him admired as an oddity! That night when I prayed, I saw in my heart very clearly a man of great *influence* in Israel. What if that never happens?"

In the darkness, Elkanah stopped in the road and drew me into his embrace. But even the sound of his heart, the warmth of his body, the familiar smell of his clothes failed to comfort me.

"Hannah, some things we must leave in God's hands. Samuel is only six now, and we certainly hope his life has just begun. Trust God. Be patient while you wait on the Lord to do what only He can do—in and through Samuel. And in Israel, too. Just keep on praying and believing in what God showed you."

"But, Elkanah, it's so hard. I thought it would be easier, especially after all the good things we heard at the beginning. I guess I hoped things would continue to build from there. Yet, in some ways, it puzzles me that I'm so distraught. Look. Here I am with a baby of my own to keep, and Samuel so well and happy. Why am I concerned?"

Elkanah continued to hold me, but said nothing.

"Maybe it's what Hod told us," I continued. "I can't help wondering if Samuel heard the prophet's warning, too. Samuel often spends time in his room while Eli's resting. But Samuel hasn't said anything to me about it. Has he to you?"

Elkanah released me, and taking my hand, headed on down the path. "No, he hasn't. But even if he heard something, I doubt he'd tell us."

"But think how hard it must be for a child so young to hold a secret like that. Do you think he's afraid?"

"Afraid of what? God or the fulfillment of the prophecy?"

"I hadn't thought of him being afraid of God. But I guess he could be."

"I don't think he is," Elkanah said. "I've seen him

worship, and a person who's harboring any unhealthy fear of God wouldn't have the freedom, passion, and intimacy Samuel has. As far as being fearful of the fulfillment–anyone who believes the Lord will do what He says would have some apprehension." I heard him take a deep breath. "All we can do, Hannah, is pray for Samuel. Ask the Lord to be his strength."

Sometimes I got tired of Elkanah telling me to pray and trust God. He made it sound easy, but living out those words demanded more of me than I'd imagined. It wasn't that I lacked plenty to keep my mind and hands busy. That year and the year after, Eli again prayed a blessing over me before we left Shiloh. Both times, I became pregnant soon after returning home. By the time we were ready to go to Shiloh the Passover just after Samuel turned eight, Elkanah, Peninnah, and the older boys took turns carrying Samuel's two little brothers: Jeroham and Aaron—named after my father (and the first High Priest of Israel). I held tiny Eve, by now just over two months old.

"I'm glad for you, Mama," Samuel said when I put his baby sister in his arms. "It's right that God should give you more babies to love, because you are the best mother of all."

Every year he said those words. Each year, as I anticipated that moment, I thought that, this time, if he said it again, I would be able to hold back the tears. But I never did.

But that wasn't the only reason I cried at Shiloh.

"Then a man of God came to Eli and said to him,
'Thus says the LORD: . . .
"Why do you . . . honor your sons more than Me,
to make yourselves fat
with the best of all the offerings of Israel My people? . . .
I said indeed that your house and the house of your father
would walk before Me forever."
But now the LORD says:
"Far be it from Me;
for those who honor Me I will honor,
and those who despise Me shall be lightly esteemed.
Behold, . . . all the descendants of your house
shall die in the flower of their age.
Now this shall be a sign to you
that will come upon your two sons,
on Hophni and Phinehas:
in one day they shall die, both of them. . . . """
1 Samuel 2:27-36 NKJV

"The LORD visited Hannah;
and she conceived
and gave birth to three sons and two daughters.
And the boy Samuel grew before the LORD."
1 Samuel 2:21-22 NASU

CHAPTER

30

The Call

Soon after we arrived the year Zuph was an infant, I sensed something different about Samuel. But I didn't know what it was.

Elkanah smiled. "He just growing up."

"No." I shook my head. "It's different. He seems more pensive, thoughtful, almost solemn at times. It can't be from overhearing the prophet's warning to Eli. That was too long ago." Elkanah remained unconcerned, but I kept watching Samuel.

One day after completing a family trek across the western hillside, we headed back to Peninnah's parents' house. At the fork in the path, Samuel took his older brothers the longer way so they could stop by to briefly visit his friend, Ahitub, before returning for the evening meal. The rest of us took the shorter route leading past the House of the Lord. As we were passing by, Eli called to Elkanah and me. The old priest, I'd noticed, was very good at identifying voices.

Elkanah sent Peninnah on with the little ones, and Eli ushered us to his private room. As we settled, my eyes swept around remembering the first day I entered Eli's room, the day we gave Samuel to him. How Samuel had grown and matured since then!

"As you know things are not as they should be in Israel." Eli sighed as he stroked his beard. "The people believe it's permissible to worship the Lord *and* give honor to pagan gods as well. Some believe that's why the Lord rarely speaks any more to prophets and hardly ever gives visions to seers."

I frowned, puzzled. Why was Eli telling us this? Not that Elkanah and I didn't agree, but I'd assumed he'd speak to us about Samuel. I glanced over at Elkanah, but his eyes stayed respectfully focused on the old man.

I looked back at Eli. His nearly blind eyes, covered with a cloudy haze, gazed upward, as they often did, and he stroked the long white beard that draped itself over the round belly covered by his High Priestly garb. I shifted, hoping he wouldn't take too long. Zuph's feeding time had passed, and my milk was ready. Both the baby and Peninnah's mother, who'd agreed to watch him, would also be impatient.

"But perhaps things are finally changing. Perhaps a new day is dawning for Israel," Eli said.

A new day? I leaned forward.

"Just over two months ago Samuel came running into my room as I was falling asleep.

"'Here I am. You called me,' he said.

"'I didn't call you,' I told him. 'Go back and lie down.'

"Moments later he appeared again. 'Here I am. You called me,' he repeated.

"'My son,' I said, 'I didn't call you. Go back and lay down.'

An old man's story; nothing more. I rocked my foot, suppressing a sigh. I was trapped. I turned to Elkanah, but he remained attentive.

"This time," Eli continued, "Samuel took a long time leaving, as though he might be studying me, but he said nothing. If others had still been in the building with us, it wouldn't have been so strange. But everyone else had left much earlier. Then, almost immediately, Samuel returned.

"'Here I am. You *did* call me,' he said with firm, unyielding assurance."

In spite of my impatience, Jerusha, I smiled as I heard old Eli tell the story, because in my head, I heard the exact sound in my son's voice.

"This sort of thing had never happened before," Eli continued, "and it puzzled me. I wondered, *How can Samuel be hearing a voice calling him, if there's no one in the Tabernacle other than me?* I knew I'd been silent the whole time—except for answering him."

My eyes widened. I glanced at Elkanah; this time our eyes met. Were we thinking the same thing? Could it be? My heart quickened.

"Finally, I realized what had happened," Eli said. His voice shook.

I bit my lip, watching breathlessly as the old priest clench his hands. His mouth disappeared behind his beard as he pressed his trembling lips together.

Finally he spoke. "I told Samuel. 'Go back and lie down. If the Voice calls you again, say, "Speak, Lord. Your servant is listening."'"

I stopped breathing, my eyes riveted on the priest.

He took a deep breath and stroked his beard, slowly. "Samuel didn't come back that night. I couldn't sleep. Was it possible, I wondered, that the Lord would choose to speak to a boy when he refused to communicate with those with position and authority? As I lay there in the still of night, I thought I felt a special Presence. Perhaps it was only my excitement, for I heard nothing—not until many hours later when Samuel opened the doors of the House of the Lord. In a few moments he appeared in my room, as always, and I asked him the question that had pressed on my mind all night long. Yes indeed . . ." The tears in Eli's eyes overflowed and ran down his wrinkled cheeks to hide in his thick beard. "He'd heard the voice of the Lord."

A lump rose in my throat, and time stopped moving forward, as if nothing else but that moment mattered. Like that time when I made my agreement with God, when the Lord Himself stood near me. I lost my awareness of anything else.

I'm sure Elkanah led me out of the House of the Lord, but I can't recall anything until we were nearly halfway to Peninnah's parents' house. Even then we remained silent. What could we say? Some experiences transcend the use of words. I couldn't help but wonder about Samuel. He hadn't said anything to us about this experience, and we'd already been in Shiloh two days. Would he tell us? Should we ask him about it? Later as we discussed it, Elkanah decided the story remained Samuel's to reveal in his own time.

As the days went by, Elkanah overheard whisperings among the Levites. Somehow they, too, had heard Eli's story. "How can a child speak for God?" they asked. But none of them discussed it with Elkanah.

While I dressed on our last morning in Shiloh, I wondered if it might be easier for the Lord to communicate with a child than an adult. Children's lives are much less cluttered, their minds open to new thoughts, and their hearts tender and more prone to awe. No, I wasn't surprised that the Lord had spoken to my son. But I longed to share Samuel's experience with him. However, since he'd said nothing for thirteen days, I concluded this encounter had been too precious for him to put into words, and we wouldn't hear his version this time in Shiloh. But I was wrong.

As Elkanah, Samuel, and I romped the hills outside Shiloh that last day before returning home, my mind and heart stood back, observing, preserving those last precious hours of our final day with our son. Elkanah, as usual, engaged in light-hearted play—his way of ending our time together by filling it with laughter and joyful smiles. I found myself joining in—between times of storing away treasures in my heart: the sound of Samuel's voice, the bounce of his curls as he ran, the way his eyes reached out and grasped my heart, his smile, his laughter, his serious silences.

One silence came when we mounted that last rise after a laughter-filled run. Samuel beat us to the crest where he waited for us, delight shining in his eyes. But as we stopped on either side of him, the twinkle faded. His eyes like water on a cloudy day. We turned, following his gaze. His eyes rested on Shiloh spread out behind us—the little homes clustered around a large building that dominated the scene.

"Yaweh spoke to me," Samuel said.

The shock of his revelation held us silent, except for the sound of our labored breathing.

"At first I didn't know His voice, . . . but now I do."

My heart stood still, as if being careful not to frighten away a rabbit or bird.

"The Lord is going to punish Eli because Eli hasn't stopped his sons from stealing the Lord's sacrifices. They will die, both of them on the same day," he said, and his voice sounded much older than when he played with his father on the hillside just moments before.

The wind whipped at my skirt, and I shivered.

"How do you feel about that?" Elkanah asked Samuel.

"I feel sad. I love Eli very much. But it's right that the Lord judges them." The tender sweetness of Samuel's boy voice contrasted with heaviness of his words. "What Eli's sons have done is very wrong, and everyone knows about it. If they go unpunished, why shouldn't others do whatever they want–even when it hurts God, or someone else?"

I studied my son, looking for the baby I held to my heart. Already his head reached the bottom of my chin. By next year, or surely the year after, he'd look me straight in the eyes. Sadness mixed with joy. Samuel's face displayed the same intensity of devotion I'd seen in him as a young child, but the strength of manhood whispered in the straightness of his shoulders, the diminishing softness of the lines of his nose and cheekbones. My stomach tightened, and I blinked back the tears welling up in my eyes.

Samuel turned toward his father. "Eli said I must not hide from him anything the Lord said to me or the Lord would punish me."

Elkanah nodded.

Samuel gazed down at the House of God. "When the Lord gives a message, I'm not allowed to change it, not at all."

As we traveled home the next day, I pondered the situation in Shiloh. I'd hoped that Israel, including Eli's sons, would be corrected by a shining example of true devotion to the Lord. I'd hoped that my son's love of God would be enough to call them back. But it hadn't been sufficient. Would it be the same for Israel? Would judgment be necessary? I feared so.

My eyes rested on the spring flowers waving to me in the sunlit hills, but my heart refused to reflect their joy. As a mother, I couldn't help but wonder how the Lord's judgment on Eli's family would impact my son. When would the devastation come? How would it happen? How would old Eli be affected? What would happen to Samuel if some great disaster occurred? Who would watch over him?

My feet grew heavy. Already Shiloh felt so far away.

But, amid my motherly concerns, as we journeyed homeward, the Lord took me backwards in time. He pointed out how He had stood by my son through the challenges he faced, instructing Samuel in His ways. He showed me how He had given a warning through a more mature prophet *before* requiring Samuel to deliver the message to Eli. The Lord Himself had been behind Eli's command to Samuel to tell him everything, holding nothing back. The Lord Himself made sure, from the very first experience of speaking for Yaweh, that Samuel learned to fear God more than anyone else. Seeing the faithfulness of the Lord in guiding my son in the past encouraged me to believe He would be just as diligent in protecting and training Samuel in the future.

By the time we reached Ramah, I could rejoice with the flowers.

"Now the boy Samuel ministered to the LORD before Eli.
And the word of the LORD was rare in those days;
there was no widespread revelation.
And it came to pass at that time,
while Eli was lying down in his place,
and when his eyes had begun to grow so dim
that he could not see,
and before the lamp of God went out
in the Tabernacle of the LORD where the ark of God was,
and while Samuel was lying down,
that the LORD called Samuel.
And he answered, 'Here I am!'
So he ran to Eli and said,
'Here I am, for you called me.'
And he said, 'I did not call; lie down again.'
And he went and lay down.
Then the LORD called yet again, 'Samuel!'

So Samuel arose and went to Eli,
and said, 'Here I am, for you called me.'
He answered, 'I did not call, my son; lie down again.'
(Now Samuel did not yet know the LORD,
nor was the word of the LORD yet revealed to him.)
And the LORD called Samuel again the third time.
So he arose and went to Eli,
and said, 'Here I am, for you did call me.'
Then Eli perceived that the LORD had called the boy.
Therefore Eli said to Samuel,
'Go, lie down;
and it shall be, if He calls you, that you must say,
"Speak, LORD, for Your servant hears."'
So Samuel went and lay down in his place.
Now the LORD came and stood and called as at other times,
'Samuel! Samuel!'
And Samuel answered, 'Speak, for Your servant hears.'
Then the LORD said to Samuel:
'Behold, I will do something in Israel
at which both ears of everyone who hears it will tingle.
In that day I will perform against Eli
all that I have spoken concerning his house,
from beginning to end.
For I have told him that I will judge his house forever
for the iniquity which he knows,
because his sons made themselves vile,
and he did not restrain them.
And therefore I have sworn to the house of Eli
that the iniquity of Eli's house shall not be atoned for
by sacrifice or offering forever.'
So Samuel lay down until morning,
and opened the doors of the house of the LORD.
And Samuel was afraid to tell Eli the vision.

Then Eli called Samuel and said, 'Samuel, my son!'
He answered, 'Here I am.'
And he said, 'What is the word that the LORD spoke to you?
Please do not hide it from me.
God do so to you, and more also,
if you hide anything from me
of all the things that He said to you.'
Then Samuel told him everything, and hid nothing from him.
And he said, 'It is the LORD.
Let Him do what seems good to Him.'
1 Samuel 3:1-18 NKJV

CHAPTER

31

The Blessing

The next year, once again, I introduced a new sibling to Samuel. Finally, in addition to Samuel, I had three sons and two daughters. Each year Eli continued to call Elkanah and me in order to report on our son—although Eli had stopped asking God to give me more children.

One year in particular stands out. Our youngest had just been weaned, and Samuel was twelve. I remember thinking that the next time I saw Samuel, he would officially be a man.

"The hand of the Lord is on Samuel," Eli said that year at our meeting with him. I thought I heard his voice tremble. He paused and stroked his beard. "Samuel takes the words of the Lord very seriously, carefully remembering all His words. "Perhaps that's why the Lord speaks to him more and more with each passing year. People from Dan in the far north, to Beersheba in the far south, already accept him as a prophet of God."

I reached out for Elkanah's hand.

"This isn't a light thing I'm talking about," Eli continued. He turned his face from Elkanah to me and back again. "Do you realize how few people have heard the voice of the Lord?

Do you? Not just in recent years, but in all our history as a people?"

Later that night Elkanah and I counted those we remembered who'd heard God speak. "Of course there were the Patriarchs: Abraham, Isaac, and Jacob. Each of them heard the Lord at times," Elkanah said.

"And Moses and Aaron. How else could they have brought such a multitude of people from Egypt to the Land of Promise?"

Elkanah nodded. "And Joshua." Of course Elkanah would name his hero.

"And Deborah." I'd always admired the prophetess judge who lived quite near Ramah many years ago.

"There must be others we didn't know," Elkanah said, "like that prophet Hod overheard. But still, that's not many. Not many at all."

"Eli's right," I said, "Speaking for God is a great privilege."

"And responsibility."

That night I had difficulty falling asleep. Could it be that the fulfillment of the second part of my vision had finally come? Was this the beginning of people returning to God, putting Him first in their allegiance? I hoped so.

Each time we returned to Shiloh over the next years, as I saw my son maturing as a man, I searched for signs of a change in the atmosphere at the Tabernacle. I often heard reports of how the Lord used my son to speak for Him, but I saw no increase in the number of people coming to meet with God, to inquire of Him. Nor did those I observed at the Tabernacle display any greater passion for God. Or voice concern that others to be more devoted to the Lord. Neither did I hear news of the people of God rejecting the ways of the pagans, ways they'd practiced along with the worship of the

Almighty. No sign of repentance. I hoped, how I hoped, I was wrong! That maybe I'd missed something. So each year I asked Elkanah if he'd noticed improvements, any sign of renewed life. But, year after year, he failed to recognize significant spiritual growth in anyone but Samuel.

That, by itself, would never be enough. I knew that now. Not enough to complete the fulfillment of my vision. As happy as I was about the Lord answering my request for a son, and giving him a heart for God, the pain I shared with God for His wayward people had not diminished. In fact, now that I had no more babies to nurse, God's pain became greater. Every day, in quiet moments—at the mill, when working at weaving or spinning, or kneading bread—the desire I felt long ago sprang up again. Not sharp, but deep. Not on the surface, but in the core, the center of my being. The ache of trapped tears. Great, heavy sorrow.

Thinking of Samuel and how he'd lived up to all I'd imagined–and even more–only made it worse. I hadn't asked for a son who would shine like a light in a black, starless sky. No, my heart had longed for something much different. A man of influence. I searched for a picture to describe the longing of my heart. A wind moving the grass and trees? No. A shepherd leading sheep? No. A seed growing and producing fruit? Not that either. The picture in my heart did not focus on one individual being greater than the rest. I saw a group of people joining together with great joy to exalt the Lord, led and encouraged, but not dominated by their leader.

Suddenly I remembered. That feeling! I'd felt it that night when the others were in Shiloh. That night Samuel and I spent with Dan and the cousins under the open sky. Then, it seemed, heaven and earth had touched, even if only for a short time. I closed my eyes and allowed myself to be pulled into the memory. The memory of all of us being absorbed in the glory of the Almighty Lord, lifting our adoration and praise with joyful hearts. I wondered if Samuel remembered that night, if it had made as much of an impression on him as it had on me. *That's* what we needed as a nation, I thought.

Then, a few years later, I heard about the cloud.

I remember the year it was—the year of Elihu's wedding. It must have been the second or third day of the celebration when I sat down for a short rest and a chance to visit with guests. Timara breezed into the courtyard, spotted me, and took her place at my side. Eagerness danced in her eyes. "Has anyone told you what's happening in Shiloh?" she whispered breathlessly.

"No. What?" I asked sweeping my gaze around the courtyard, taking quick account of each of my children, all old enough now to be pretty much on their own. Today Peninnah would be of no help in supervising since she was fully absorbed in the wedding feast. Satisfied that none of them appeared to be headed for trouble, I turned my attention to Timara.

"My brother stopped by the Tabernacle on his way through Shiloh. He says that when Samuel prays. . . " Timara took a deep breath and her eyes gleamed. "Well, people see a bright cloud overshadowing him. They say it's the Glory, the Presence of the Lord!"

I blinked! My breath stuck in my chest. I pressed my fingers to my throat. Timara whispered on, but one thought captured my mind. The Shekinah glory! The holy light of God! Could it be? Like what happened with Moses and Aaron?

I had difficulty focusing on any conversation for the rest of the day. My mind spun with questions. Could what Timara said be true? I could hardly imagine it. I understood what it was like to *feel* the Presence of the Almighty One. My experience had been awesome enough. But a cloud? I remembered my father's stories of Moses and how the cloud came down when Moses met with God.

I could hardly wait to return to Shiloh to see for myself. Just as I expected, this new occurrence had caused a wave of excitement, renewed interest in the House of God. But, as I feared, that's all it was—a wave and nothing more.

By the next year, its novelty gone, the cloud no long captured Israel's attention. *Why, oh why, are the hearts of the people so hard, so deaf to the call of God to come close to Him?* I couldn't understand it. Why weren't they more impressed? Hundreds of years had passed since Moses' time, since God revealed his Presence in a cloud. I'll admit, what I saw with Samuel seemed small compared to my visualization of the huge pillar my father described that led the Israelites through the wilderness. But still. It *was* a light, a supernatural manifestation of God's Presence. Why couldn't the Israelites see this as confirmation that *all* the miracles we'd heard about from the past were indeed true?

With this great disappointment, my hope for God's people began to waver. It would take more than I'd imagined to turn the tide of apathy, much more. I'd become pretty certain that my son, no matter how dedicated to the Lord, would never have the influence necessary to do it. I began to lose hope, Jerusha, not in God but in His people. *Will* anything *ever bring them back to the Lord?* I wondered.

Then one night I awoke from a dream, the sound of those familiar words still ringing in my ears. "The Lord is my strength and my song. . . . Who among the gods is like you, O Lord?" I sat upright in the darkness, my heart pounding as I tried to recapture my dream. Many voices, layered, one on top of the other, calling out the same words. Elkanah saying his morning prayer. Little Samuel on that day when he stood with his hands raised to God, that day we gave him to Eli—and to the Lord. And many other voices, like a multitude of people. "Who is like You," they cried out to God, "majestic in holiness, awesome in glory, working wonders?"

As I listen, my heart understood. What I'd hoped for, what I'd seen in the vision that night I make my vow, the revelation of God's people returning to Him, that was not my son's responsibility. Yes, Samuel had a part to play, but the change in the hearts of people–that was up to God.

In the dark stillness of the night, I took a deep, slow breath. It seemed like a wind blew into the depths of my being, pushing out the heaviness, the weight that had held me down. The great turning was God's work, not Samuel's. Not mine. It was mine to worship; and God's to work the wonders.

So Samuel grew, and the LORD was with him
and let none of his words fall to the ground.
And all Israel from Dan to Beersheba
knew that Samuel had been established
as a prophet of the LORD.
Then the LORD appeared again in Shiloh.
For the LORD revealed Himself to Samuel in Shiloh
by the word of the LORD.
And the word of Samuel came to all Israel."
1 Samuel 3:1-4:1 NKJV

"Moses and Aaron were among his priests,
Samuel was among those who called on his name;
they called on the LORD and he answered them.
He spoke to them from the pillar of cloud;
they kept his statutes and the decrees he gave them."
Psalm 99:6-7 NIV

CHAPTER

32

Suspended

When Hannah ended her story that night, both she and Jerusha expected to pick it up the next day as they always did. But neither of them had known about the delegation coming from Beersheba. Their visit disrupted everything.

The men came requesting Samuel to send someone to live with them in the far south, to be his representative there. The people of Beersheba were tired of traveling so far to confer with a judge, they said.

Jerusha listened with interest until one man suggested that Samuel send his two sons. Her heart froze. No! How could she live so far from Hannah? Jerusha's eyes flew to Joel. His gaze locked with Abijah's, and their eyes sparkled with excitement and desire–both of them. Quickly, she turned to Samuel. He gazed upward, uneasiness in his dark eyes. She held her breath. Surely, he would say no. But he didn't. Instead, he requested time to ask God what he should do.

A strange silence surrounded Joel and Jerusha that night. How could they voice their hopes to one another when, even without one word, each knew the other's opposing desire? At least Jerusha managed to refrain from crying. She was glad of that. And so was Joel.

The next day the silence ended. The courtyard buzzed as everyone voiced opinions as to what should and would happen. Several times Jerusha rushed away to keep from crying out. It wasn't just her fears that upset her. She hated the division in the family as well.

"Of course, you must go," Joel's mother, Noga, said to her sons. "It's the chance of a lifetime. You deserve to benefit in some way from being your father's sons."

"So what if it's a desert?" Mazel had countered one of the cousin's comments. "At least there we'll be able to breathe without 'someone' watching our every move."

This was far from the first time Jerusha had heard Mazel speak of Samuel with disrespect. She despised his "overgrown image," his abhorrence of luxury. "Nothing against you, Abijah, my husband," Jerusha had heard Mazel say right at the wedding feast, "but I certainly thought when I moved into the home of the great judge of Israel, I'd be taking a step *up*, not down!"

With Mazel's arrival, Noga, Samuel's wife, became more vocal in her disapproval of her husband. When anyone reproved either Mazel or Noga, it only increased their attacks. So, most often the others tried to ignore their criticism. But with the proposal from Beershebah, the polluting undercurrent of discontent burst into flame.

Jerusha's gaze constantly shifted from Hannah to Mazel and back again. What would it be like to be separated from Hannah? Or to live with three people who resented Samuel? Hannah, too. Jerusha hoped–how she hoped–she would never find out.

"Don't worry," Joel said, a bitterness edging his voice. "Our father doesn't trust us. He'd never put us in such a high position, especially so far away from his supervision."

But Joel was wrong.

"Don't cry," Joel said that night after his father announced his decision, a decision no one could change.

Jerusha ignored Joel's plea. She didn't care if Joel and Abijah, Noga and Mazel, Samuel–and everyone in the world–felt differently. She didn't care what they thought. Never had she mourned like this! Not in regard to her father and brother; even her mother. That had been grief over relationships she'd wished for, but never had. This was different. She *knew* what she was losing; that hurt much more.

"You can come back sometime and see Hannah," Joel said that night as he drew her close, stroking her hair and kissing her forehead.

Jerusha feared they might be empty words, words to divert her as one would a disappointed child. Beersheba was so far away. So far!

Hannah wept, too, but no one saw her, no one but Samuel. He found her early the following morning huddled in her corner under the almond tree with its small green fruits many weeks from harvest. He sat down beside her, silent.

Finally, Hannah looked up. "Are you sure, Samuel?" Pain pinched her voice. "Are you *sure* He said to send them away?" It surprised her how much it hurt, even more than leaving her baby at the Tabernacle. She'd been prepared for that. This, however, this had shocked her.

Samuel reached over and took her thin hand in his. A lump rose in his throat. It hurt him to see her grieve, and Jerusha, too. He loved that girl. "Yes, Mother. I'm sure."

His voice rumbled with that authority she'd come to recognize, and she knew she could question him no more.

Samuel rubbed his forehead, wishing he could chase away the ache of fear. He knew he should trust the Lord, but it wasn't easy. Not this time. "I don't want to send them,

Mother." He licked his lips. "If I did, perhaps it wouldn't be so easy to know for *sure* that it's the Lord speaking."

Hannah saw the turmoil moving in his eyes. She pressed her mouth shut. Neither would say it. Samuel knew his sons, their lack of devotion to God. How would they use the authority he'd handed them? To profit themselves?

But in spite of all the arguments of his mind, the conviction in Samuel's heart remained the same. The Lord had spoken. He must send them, release them to God.

The quietness of the morning ended as one family member after another swarmed into the courtyard, and soon the clatter of activity took over. People everywhere doing what they could to get Joel and Abijah and their wives ready for their great adventure.

It all happened so quickly. Just six days from the time the delegation came, the huge family walked them outside the gate to bid them good-bye. Jerusha blinked as her eyes swept over the crowd, searching for Hannah's face, but she saw only a watery smear of color.

"It'll be okay," Joel whispered encouragingly as he gently grasped her hand and drew her firmly down the road away from Ramah. "We'll come back someday. I promise."

At the sound of love in his voice, she swallowed salty tears and stumbled along with him, tucking his words away in her heart. Before they'd taken a hundred steps, the bundle on her back slid down on her right shoulder, and she reached over to straighten it.

"Here, let me help," Joel said.

As he shifted the weight in her pack, Jerusha turned for one last look. Her eyes clung to Ramah's familiar gate, and her chin trembled. How much she'd changed since she first entered that gate just about two years ago! How different would she be when she returned? . . . If she ever did.

"I . . . I never got to hear the end of Hannah's story," Jerusha whispered. Her voice quavered.

"Hurry up!" Abijah called. "We have a long trip ahead of us."

Joel gave the strap one last tug and turned Jerusha toward him. "Then, my dear," he said tenderly as he looked down into her eyes, "you'll have to make your own story–the story of Joel's wife."

Surprisingly, not very long afterward, Hannah had that same revelation.

Along with the others, Hannah watched the little group making their way down the road to the unknown south. The end of the world. She stood beside Samuel, unable to hold back the tears that silently spilled down her cheeks. It felt as if her whole body, like a large jar, had been filled to the brim, overflowing with sadness.

"Come, Mother," Samuel said, when the travelers fell out of view behind the far hill and the others quietly turned and began the sad walk home.

Hannah shook her head. "I'm fine. I just need some time alone. Go on now." Her fingers fluffed him away. "I'll come shortly."

So he'd followed the others. Hannah never knew that Samuel sent one of his nephews to hide in the bushes to keep watch over her. The young man waited in silence, unable to hear the conversation in Hannah's heart—her conversation with Yaweh.

"I never got to tell her the best part of Samuel's life," she complained to the Lord. "About Mizpah and how the people of Israel finally turned to You. It doesn't seem right to leave her without the climax of the story."

She'd been right. It did take more than Samuel to bring about true repentance and turning to God. It took years of suffering under the hand of their great enemy, the Philistines. But finally the people had enough. They disposed of their idols, crying out to God. They fasted and confessed.

Jerusha had certainly heard about Mizpah. No one in Israel could have missed hearing about that. But Hannah had wanted to tell Jerusha *her* version, slowly, bit by bit. How it felt for her to see her son that day standing before the people, beseeching God on their behalf. Her exuberant joy! Then, the terror when the news came of the Philistines, sneaking up on them while Israel repented. Of her great joy, her delight, when, instead of running or fighting, the Israelites, in their despair, had lifted their voices louder and louder to God.

That time Hannah had heard the cries with her ears. First cries for mercy and deliverance. Then cries of thanksgiving and joy. Like in her dream. The people praising God together. "The Lord is our strength and our song! Who among the gods is like you, O Lord?" they cried, tears streaming down their faces. She hadn't finished her story. She'd wanted to tell Jerusha about that.

But she knew that wasn't what hurt the most; it was losing Jerusha and the special relationship that had grown between them. For one moment tears rose again, then abruptly, stopped.

The young man behind the bushes saw Hannah suck in a sharp breath and raise her hand quickly to her chest. His heart jumped into his throat, and he pressed back the branches, leaning forward to see more clearly. But nothing more happened. He watched her standing very still staring intently toward the south where the brothers and their wives had disappeared. He squinted, peering in the direction of her gaze, but he didn't see what she saw.

Hannah watched the south hills melt away. In their place appeared Jerusha's face. A face with a gentle, warm smile, . . . and no tears. Clustered about her, like numerous petals about a flower's center, were many, many faces. Young and old, surrounding her. Right beside her, Joel–but a different Joel than Hannah had ever seen. A Joel reminding her of Samuel. Not so much on the outside; but something from within. She blinked to see more clearly, but he only smiled at her. Then they all vanished, leaving only a lovely sense of peace covering her like a fuzzy blanket of light. She took a slow breath. Samuel had been right. She'd completed her assignment. It was time to let them go, to trust God to do what He needed to do in their lives. She rested content.

As she walked home, a new assurance came over her. Perhaps the ripples of her vow had not ended at Mizpah after all. No, she felt sure of it. Her story was not yet finished. Somehow, the effects of her promise would continue even farther–in life of Jerusha, Joel's wife.

Maybe even beyond.

"And Samuel said to the whole house of Israel,
'If you are returning to the LORD with all your hearts,
then rid yourselves of the foreign gods and the Ashtoreths
and commit yourselves to the LORD and serve him only,
and he will deliver you out of the hand of the Philistines.'
So the Israelites put away their Baals and Ashtoreths,
and served the LORD only.
Then Samuel said, 'Assemble all Israel at Mizpah
and I will intercede with the LORD for you.'
When they had assembled at Mizpah ,
they drew water and poured it out before the LORD.
On that day they fasted and there they confessed,
'We have sinned against the LORD.'
And Samuel was leader of Israel at Mizpah .
When the Philistines heard

that Israel had assembled at Mizpah,
the rulers of the Philistines came up to attack them.
And when the Israelites heard of it,
they were afraid because of the Philistines.
They said to Samuel,
'Do not stop crying out to the LORD our God for us,
that he may rescue us from the hand of the Philistines.'
Then Samuel took a suckling lamb
and offered it up as a whole burnt offering to the LORD.
He cried out to the LORD on Israel's behalf,
and the LORD answered him.
While Samuel was sacrificing the burnt offering,
the Philistines drew near to engage Israel in battle.
But that day the LORD thundered with loud thunder
against the Philistines and threw them into such a panic
that they were routed before the Israelites.
The men of Israel rushed out of Mizpah
and pursued the Philistines,
slaughtering them along the way to a point below Beth Car.
Then Samuel took a stone
and set it up between Mizpah and Shen.
He named it Ebenezer, saying,
'Thus far has the LORD helped us.'
So the Philistines were subdued
and did not invade Israelite territory again."
1 Samuel 7:3-13NIV

"When Samuel grew old,
he appointed his sons as judges for Israel.
The name of his firstborn was Joel
and the name of his second was Abijah,
and they served at Beersheba."
1 Samuel 8:1-2 NIV

For more of the story

read the sequel. . .

HANNAH'S PROMISE: JOEL'S WIFE

Readers Comments about Transformed in Bethany . . .

Delightful, skillfully crafted characters quickly become friends. Witnessing their transformation as their friendship with Jesus grows, makes one long for the same daily familiarity: Jesus just dropping by for a meal, to help paint a room, or prune the roses. Great character and context development! Great storytelling!
– *Donna Guerrero, Salvation Army*

Definitely an excellent read! Well worth the time and price. It shows Jesus as a real person–fully God and fully man–all the time.
– *Norman Hookway, Florida*

Ussery has a gift for revealing the inner workings of a soul being transformed by the process of salvation.
– *Victoria Richards, California*

Remarkable book! Very readable, good Christian literature. Excellent story line, research on the times and customs, and humanizing of these Bible characters. I found nothing that in anyway conflicted with the Biblical account. I found it easy to identify with the stress expressed by the characters. Excellent use of words to show emotions. I was deeply moved.
– *Forest Yoder, Colorado*

I recommend it to anyone, young or old, ones who know the Bible very well and those who have never read it, believer or non-believer.
– *Berly Watson, England, UK*

The book, *Transformed in Bethany*, touched my life. I can truly say that I have come to better understand Jesus' love and how I can trust him completely no matter what my need is. My desire is for Jesus to transform my own life, as he individually did the lives of Mary, Martha and Lazarus. I want Him to show me any destructive lies and replace them with His truth, so that I can also be all that God wants me to be.
– *Barbara Pinkley, WGM, Kenya, AFRICA*

Are you looking for uplifting entertainment for yourself and those you love?

Don't miss other books by Arlene Pinkley Ussery! Having studied in Israel, the author brings the rich atmosphere of that ancient land to life with unusual clarity. With passionate sensitivity she paints characters pulsing with personality and deep emotion. From her life-long intimacy with God, the author gently and subtly uncovers clues for those yearning to draw closer and those with questions about God. While in this strikingly different environment, readers feel safe looking at life's important, but often neglected issues, gleaning timeless insights to carry back into the modern world.

In her TIMELESS TREASURES COLLECTION Arlene Pinkley Ussery will be presenting about twenty Biblical historical novels based on the lives of characters in both the Old and New Testaments. The stories intertwine like a jigsaw puzzle, with main characters of one book sometimes appearing again in other books. Each book, however, stands well on its own, allowing readers to enjoy them in any order. While new readers enjoy the story, those who have read other books will delight in meeting old friends once again, seeing them from a different perspective.

Look for these soon to be published titles:

Hannah's Promise: Joel Wife

The continuation of Jerusha's story

Transformed in Bethany (a reprint edition)

The story of Mary, Martha, and Lazarus

Would you like to grow in your relationship with God?

If you wish to integrate the truths of TIMELESS TREASURES novels into your own life experience, the author has provided assistance in **Devotional/Study Guides.** These workbooks are excellent for personal devotional time and serve as the basis for exciting group interaction and discussion. Each chapter has its own theme. The sample below coordinates with the first chapter of Hannah's Promise.

HANNAH'S PROMISE

Chapter One – Dealing with Suffering

1. In addition to the problem of barrenness, what other kinds of suffering did Hannah experience?

2. What have been your major sources of suffering?

3. List responses Hannah had to her suffering.
   Which of those can you identify with?

4. Examine the responses of Hannah's two friends.
   How did their actions either help her or make her suffering worse?

5. Paul gave this instruction in Galatians 6:2 TLB. *Share each other's troubles and problems, and so obey our Lord's command.*

What is "our Lord's command"? Read it below.

Jesus replied, "'You must love the Lord your God with all your heart, all your soul, and all your mind.' This is the first and greatest commandment. A second is equally important: 'Love your neighbor as yourself.' All the other commandments and all the demands of the prophets are based on these two commandments."
Matthew 22:37-40 NLT?

Looking at these two verses and remembering Hannah's experience, how do you think "sharing each other's troubles and problems" relates to "obeying our Lord's command?"

Do you know someone who is suffering?
Ask Jesus to show you how you could apply the second command of Christ to that particular situation.

6. Hannah ends up feeling God is very far away.
Have you ever felt that in your suffering?

Listen to what Isaiah reports of the feelings of God's people in Zion in Isaiah 49:14 NIV. *But Zion said, "The LORD has forsaken me, the Lord has forgotten me."*

But if you chose to read the context in Isaiah 49:8-21, you will see an amazingly different picture that Isaiah paints of God.

What does Isaiah reveal in this passage about how God relates to us in our suffering?

Prayer: O Lord of Compassion, You alone understand my suffering. Help me to believe that You care, whether I can feel Your presence or not. Help me to forgive those who have made my pain worse by their responses. Thank you for those who have held me up. Help me to be a good friend to others in their time of need. Amen.

If you want **others** to be blessed by

HANNAH'S PROMISE

You can have a part in this ministry by. . .

- Praying for Arlene as she writes more novels
- Praying for the right people to get hold of her books
- Asking God to minister to the hearts of readers
- Purchasing books as gifts for family and friends
- Recommending the **Timeless Treasures Collection** by word of mouth as well as through your email, blogs, Facebook, Twitter, and other contacts
- Writing reviews of the books you read
- Scheduling Arlene Pinkley Ussery to speak on topics related to developing a deeper intimacy with God
- Checking the website to keep up with new information on this ministry

Timeless Treasures
P. O. Box 4966
El Monte, CA 91734

www.aussery.com